The Trouble in Willow Falls

Willow Falls Series Book Two

By
Pat Nichols

Sandi Thank you for your friendship

Pat Nichols

THE TROUBLE IN WILLOW FALLS BY PAT NICHOLS
Published by Lighthouse Publishing of the Carolinas
2333 Barton Oaks Dr., Raleigh, NC 27614

ISBN: 978-1-64526-271-8
Copyright © 2019 by Pat Nichols
Cover design by Hannah Linder
Interior design byAtriTex Technologies P Ltd.

Available in print from your local bookstore, online, or from the publisher at ShopLPC.
com.

For more information on this book and the author, visitpatnicholsauthor.blog.

Brought to you by the creative team at Lighthouse Publishing of the Carolinas
(LPCBooks.com): Eddie Jones, Denise Loock, Shonda Savage, Jennifer Leo, and Lucie
Windborne

Library of Congress Cataloging-in-Publication Data
Nichols, Pat
The Trouble in Willow Falls / Pat Nichols 1st ed.

Printed in the United States of America

Praise for *The Trouble in Willow Falls*

Pat Nichols doesn't disappoint with her sophomore novel, *The Trouble in Willow Falls*. It's filled with your favorite characters from the first book as the saga continues. I love this small town!

~ Ane Mulligan
Award-winning author of the bestselling Chapel Springs series

Small towns can be the scene of big dreams, high drama, and unforgettable romance. This is certainly the case in Willow Falls, Georgia. In Book 2 of her Willow Falls series, author Pat Nichols takes us deeper into the lives of twin sisters Emily and Rachel—into their individual journeys as they seek the fulfillment of their dreams and tackle the hurdles they must overcome along with way. Filled with colorful characters and unexpected turns, *The Trouble in Willow Falls* is a story you won't want to miss.

~ Ann Tatlock
Novelist, editor, and children's book author

The Trouble in Willow Falls is a delight. Nichols has created such a winsome small town that I actually thought about taking a side trip to this northern Georgia pearl the next time I was in Atlanta. I'd stay at the inn and take in a show. Nichols lifts "It takes a village" to a higher level in this sequel with a motley group of newcomers along with old favorites, which proves that with a shared goal, even disparate members of a community can rise above their differences.

~ Sherri Stewart
Author of *In Her Footsteps*

Pat Nichols weaves a story with characters who dig deep into your soul. *The Trouble in Willow Falls* catches on the wind and brushes through your heart.

~ Cindy K. Sproles
Author of *Mercy's Rain* and *Liar's Winter*

Pat Nichols' gift for writing shines in *The Trouble in Willow Falls*. As you read, you'll love watching a town and its residents in financial trouble come together to stay alive as only a small Southern town will. The characters are well defined, and you'll fall in love with them as they fight to save a home they love and want to preserve for future generations. No matter how often they are thwarted in their efforts—with setback after setback—their spirits rise and they refuse to give up. You will pull for Willow Falls and all its folks. You'll close the book with a big smile and a sigh over a very good read.

~ **Merilyn Howton Marriott**
Author of *The Children of Main Street*
and *God Bless the Child*

Acknowledgments

My journey as a writer has been made so much sweeter and more rewarding by those who read my debut novel, *The Secret of Willow Inn*. Every comment, every review touches my heart and helps me become a better writer. To the book clubs that chose my book, thank you for making my heart dance.

To my beta readers, Pat Davis, Bev Feldkamp, and Kathy Warner, I am deeply grateful for your insight and feedback. You are precious partners in my writing journey. Denise Loock, thank you for editing *The Trouble in Willow Falls* with expertise and grace, for taking the story to new heights. Thank you, Eddie Jones, for believing in me. I will be forever grateful for all you have taught me. I am blessed to be part of the Lighthouse Publishing of the Carolinas family.

To my friends in American Christian Fiction Writers of North Georgia and Word Weavers International, Greater Atlanta Chapter, your friendship and encouragement have made me a better writer. To all my writer friends and the writing community, thank you for sharing your talent and knowledge. It is an honor to know you.

A special thanks to my husband and best friend, Tim. Your love and support give my dreams flight. I cherish you and our life together.

Above all, I thank God for planting the desire to write in my heart, then giving me the courage to pursue it and the wisdom to prove it's never too late to follow your dreams.

To my beautiful daughter, Shelley Jordan,
whose courage, faith, and love inspire me
to face every obstacle with determination and confidence.
I love you.

Chapter 1

Rachel Streetman stood on the sidewalk in downtown Atlanta and imagined living on the street. Sleeping in a doorway or on a bench in Centennial Park. Penniless. Alone. Men and women stepping around her as if she were nothing more than an obstacle blocking their paths. Children staring at her.

She tilted her head back and gazed at the top of the seventy-three-story circular Peachtree Plaza Hotel. Until a dizzy sensation threw her off balance and forced her focus back to ground level. She pressed her hand against a light pole. A week away from the most important audition in her life, she couldn't risk passing out and breaking her arm or a tooth.

When the spinning stopped, she glanced at her watch. Fifteen minutes before lunch with her former assistant. She walked across the street and spotted a young man crouched on the sidewalk. His dog sprawled beside him. Brown hair brushed against his shirt collar. A scruffy beard covered the lower portion of his face. Was he the guy she'd befriended last year before she resigned as vice president for her father's company?

She moved closer and pushed her sunglasses to the top of her head. "Dennis Locke?"

His eyes widened. "Ms. Streetman?" He stood and wiped his hands on his jeans.

"It is you."

He nodded.

"I'm sorry I haven't been around in a while."

"No need to apologize. I didn't expect a fine lady like you to keep coming back."

She swiped a layer of sweat from her lip. Should she give him money and walk away? Or do some audition pre-work for the role—Penelope, a homeless woman who finds a winning lottery ticket. She stepped beside

1

Dennis, relieved he smelled of soap and shampoo. "Are you still staying at the homeless shelter?"

"Yes ma'am."

She leaned back against the wall. A man wearing expensive shoes and a three-piece suit tossed a handful of change toward the ball cap serving as Dennis's collection plate. A quarter and three pennies missed the target and landed on the pavement. He moved past without making eye contact or uttering a word.

Heat crept up Rachel's neck. "I guess he didn't want those pesky coins rattling around in his pocket."

"Don't give him a hard time."

"He could have said hello or at least nodded."

Dennis shrugged. "Why would he?"

Rachel turned her attention to men and women rushing past without acknowledging their existence. "It's like we're invisible."

"Easier for them." He slid back to the pavement.

She sat beside him and imagined this was her spot, her cap poised for contributions. How would it feel to be hopeless and invisible, then suddenly have enough money to turn your life around? Frightening? Challenging? What if she had no place to go? No one to love?

She swallowed the lump in her throat as images of Charlie, Mama Sadie, Emily, and Willow Falls played in her mind. Her refuge. She glanced sideways at Dennis. Maybe he needed something … or someone to motivate him off the street. A bizarre idea bubbled up. "July Fourth is in a few days."

He swatted a fly from his face and wiped sweat from his forehead.

Words tumbled off her tongue before she had time to think. "Why don't you spend the holiday in Willow Falls with me and my family? Emily, my twin sister, owns a lovely inn. You can stay there."

Silence.

What are you doing, Rachel? You don't need responsibility for a homeless man days before your audition. She pulled her knees up and wrapped her arms around her shins. Should she withdraw the invitation? Treat him like everyone who passed him by? She couldn't do that.

"Look, I know I've caught you off guard. Frankly, I'm a bit surprised myself. The invitation still stands. I'll come by the shelter on the third and pick you up." She opened her wallet, removed all the bills, and dropped them in his cap.

"Thank you, Ms. Streetman. My buddies back at the shelter can use the money."

"I know you'll put it to good use like you did last year. By the way, you can call me Rachel." She lowered her sunglasses, then stood and brushed off her slacks. "Until the third, stay safe."

She walked away, hoping she hadn't made an offer she'd live to regret. As she turned the corner, she saw Nancy standing on the sidewalk fronting Pittypat's Porch. She rushed to greet her former assistant. "Hope I didn't keep you waiting long."

"Just walked up. I thought you'd fallen off the face of the earth."

Rachel pushed her sunglasses to the top of her head. "Sorry it took so long to call. You picked a fun spot for a reunion."

"Did you know this restaurant is named for Scarlett O'Hara's aunt in *Gone with the Wind*? One reason I like it. The other is the scrumptious Southern cooking."

"All those years I worked at Streetman Enterprise I never ate here."

"About time you took the plunge." Nancy touched her arm. "You're in for a treat."

They entered the restaurant and followed the hostess down a wooden staircase. She led them to a table beside a movie poster of Rhett Butler embracing Scarlett.

Rachel sat across from Nancy. "You look great. I assume life is treating you well."

"Thanks. Everything's good. Although I imagine yours is way more exciting."

"I wouldn't bet on it." Rachel opened her menu. "What do you suggest?"

"The salad bar is awesome. I know it's only noon, but I'm in the mood for Scarlett's Passion." Nancy leaned forward. "A yummy strawberry daiquiri. Want to join me?"

"Hmm, I don't have a job or rehearsals to go back to, so why not."

"Now you're talking. I told my boss I had an important female appointment. I think he was afraid to ask questions, so you and I have lots of time to catch up."

Rachel laughed. "I always knew you had more brains than anyone else in the office. Maybe my father should promote you to vice president."

"Not a chance. I could never live up to his insane demands."

"Believe me, I know what you mean."

They ordered drinks, loaded their plates at the salad bar, and returned to the table.

Nancy sipped her daquiri and licked her lips. "Just like dessert, except with a kick." She set her drink on the table. "What's happening with your dream to star in a Broadway show?"

"Making a living in the entertainment world with a thin résumé is a lot tougher than I expected." She dipped her fork in the chicken salad. "Don't get me wrong. I've landed a few parts here and there."

"It's good your father has plenty of money for you to fall to back on."

Rachel froze her fork halfway to her mouth. "No way I'm taking one dime from him."

Nancy's eyes widened. "Uh-oh, I touched a sore spot."

"Sorry, I didn't mean to snap at you." She set her fork down. "I walked away from a lucrative job and a secure future, so it's up to me to make it on my own. The good news is I have an important audition coming up. Have you heard about the new theater in midtown?"

Nancy shook her head.

"A director with loads of clout transformed a storefront. He's producing a new comedy about a homeless woman. I'm trying out for the lead."

"Interesting role for a former business executive."

"No kidding. Anyway, I'm counting on the part to jump-start my career."

"I know I'll see your name in lights one day soon." Nancy swiped her mouth with a napkin. "I hope you don't think I'm being nosey, but I'm dying to know what's going on with you and Charlie Bricker."

"It seems he's found his calling as a country boy and a vintner. Everyone in Willow Falls is crazy about him."

"What about you?"

"He's a great guy. The thing is … we're on different paths. Willow Falls doesn't have a functioning movie theater, much less a venue for live performances."

"And Atlanta has a slew of theaters."

Rachel nodded. "If … I mean when I land the homeless woman role, I'll aim for a part in an Alliance production."

"The city's most exclusive theater."

"I've been in the audience countless times, dreaming about being on that stage." She paused. "Enough about me. What's going on at Streetman Enterprise?"

"From what I hear, your father's staff meetings are as boring as ever."

"Thank goodness I no longer have to sit through them and pretend to pay attention. Other than conducting mind-numbing meetings, how's he doing?"

"He still works harder than anyone else. Some employees swear he lives at the office."

"The consummate workaholic. Sounds like nothing's changed."

"How long has it been since you've seen him?"

"A while." Rachel fingered her diamond-and-emerald tennis bracelet, the last gift she and her father gave to her mother before she died. "We've talked a few times."

"You should pop in and surprise him."

"I'm not sure he'd welcome a visit from the daughter who abandoned him."

"If he were the only father I'd ever known … I'm just saying you might want to reconsider."

"I'll think about it."

"Don't wait too long."

Following more light-hearted conversation and a shared dessert, Nancy's phone pinged. "I think my female appointment time has run out."

"A text from your boss?"

"The one and only." She glanced at her watch. "Guess he figures two hours is long enough for any kind of engagement."

The women left the restaurant. Outside, Rachel embraced Nancy. "I enjoyed catching up."

"Don't forget my promise to start a fan club when you make it big."

"I'm counting on it," Rachel said, confident she was a few days away from seeing her name on a theater marquee.

Chapter 2

"Sixteen weeks and five days. Not a peep from anyone. You'd think someone would jump at the chance to publish a novel about Willow Falls. What other town on the planet has a history like ours? I'd even welcome a rejection. At least then I'd know my proposal wasn't deleted like yesterday's junk mail." Emily Hayes logged out of her email, then splayed her fingers on her right hand and stared at her mother's diamond engagement ring. "Everyone's counting on my book to bring attention to our town."

Scott stopped separating bills into pay-now and pay-later piles and glanced at his wife across the kitchen table. "You did make a big deal about the story fulfilling your parents' legacy."

"Don't forget, Hayes General Store is a big part of the novel."

"Yeah." Scott scoffed. "And I'm the first man in my family forced to close it four days a week and take a part-time job hammering nails."

"It's not your fault business is slow. Besides, Jacob needed your help."

"Don't know how much good it'll do. We'll be lucky to finish the hotel in time for the fall foliage."

"What's with the pessimism?"

"I'm being realistic. The building sat empty for thirty years. Who knows how many unexpected problems we'll run into?"

Emily leaned back and tilted her head. "Do you remember when we were kids, we believed ghosts roamed the halls?"

"Those were good times."

"Too bad so many of our childhood friends moved away." Emily scooted from the table.

"Who can blame them. The store's the only thing that keeps us from bailing."

She removed two sippy cups from the refrigerator and carried them to the playpen for her ten-month-old twin girls. "I love you sweet babies."

She patted their cheeks, then returned to the table. "We never talked about leaving Willow Falls."

"That doesn't mean I haven't considered it."

"Despite all the town's problems, our life is here. All the memories. The friends who stayed. Saving your family's business and turning my parents' vision into reality."

"We have a long way to go to make this town a tourist destination."

"One more reason my book has to be published."

The doorbell chimed, followed by footsteps striking the living room floor. "Anybody home?"

Scott shook his head. "We need to start locking the front door."

Mirabelle Paine, the town's number-one purveyor of mail and gossip, rounded the corner and dropped all but one envelope on the table.

"Are you adding personal delivery service to your job description?"

She dismissed Scott's comment with a hand flick and eyed Emily. "You got a letter from a publisher."

Emily popped up. "Are you serious?"

"See for yourself." She handed it over.

"The only one in existence that still requests proposals by snail mail. Maybe they want my entire manuscript. Unless …" Her chest tightened as she stared at the envelope.

Mirabelle propped her hands on her ample hips. "Are you gonna open it or what?"

Emily rolled her eyes, then ripped the envelope open. She read the letter, folded it, and slipped it in her pocket.

"Well, what did it say?"

Emily cringed under her pointed stare. "The story's not what they're looking for."

"Probably highfalutin big-city types who don't know squat about nice Southern towns." A thud on the oak floor drew Mirabelle's attention. She moved to the playpen, picked up a toy, and handed it to the baby peering over the edge. "Is this one Jane or Clair?"

"Check her anklet," Scott said.

"Do you think their eyes will turn the color of lima beans like yours, Emily? At least they inherited your curly red hair."

Emily sat across from Scott. "And their father's adorable smile dimple."

"They're cuties, that's for sure. This will be their first July Fourth celebration."

"The way everything's going it might be the town's last big event." Scott chortled. "With Charlie Bricker providing fireworks, at least we'll go out with a bang."

"Good play on words, honey."

"Our town's vintner is a good guy." Mirabelle moved away from the playpen. "Is your sister coming up for the holiday?"

Emily nodded. "Tomorrow."

"I hope she cut her hair so everyone can tell you two apart. It's been nice chatting, but I have a ton of mail to deliver."

Scott gave her a droll look. "Next time you have a personal delivery, try ringing the doorbell."

"Hmph." Mirabelle headed toward the exit, then stopped and glanced back. "Everyone's counting on your book to tell the world about Willow Falls." She waved over her shoulder. "See you two later."

Emily waited to hear the front door close. "That makes thirty-seven."

"What?"

"Number of times I've heard that comment this week."

"Now that she's gone, tell me what the letter really said."

"An acquisition editor sent it." Emily removed it from her pocket. "She read the chapters I submitted and had plenty to say."

"Like what?"

"It's illogical for anyone to create a town for a vaudeville singer."

"Of course, it's illogical."

"Exactly. Which is what makes Willow Falls unique. There's more. She says I did too much telling."

Scott's brows shot up. "Isn't that what a book's for, to tell a story?"

"According to her, it needs more showing. Plus, she says some of the dialogue is too on-the-nose."

"What does she want you to do, draw pictures? And what in the heck does on-the-nose mean?"

She released a heavy sigh. "If I knew I wouldn't have done it."

"Your first rejection letter came from a nitpicky editor."

"What do you mean first?"

"You said you'd welcome a rejection."

"Until I got one." Her eyes brimmed with tears. "What if she's right? What if my novel needs a ton more work?"

Scott reached across the table and touched her arm. "That's not a bad thing."

She swiped a stray curl away from her cheek. "It is when you have twins to take care of, a newspaper to deal with, and who knows what else."

Emily's cell phone pinged an incoming text. She plucked her phone from the table. "And there it is, the next big *what else*. Residents stormed the *Willow Post* headquarters in an uproar over some kind of bad news on the internet." She stood. "I have to put on my editor hat and rescue my reporter."

"That job doesn't pay enough to deal with this town's craziness."

"If I quit, the paper is likely to fold. Besides, we need every dollar until business picks up."

"I know."

"Will you take Jane and Clair to the inn? Mama Sadie agreed to babysit for a couple of hours. The diaper bag's packed and ready to go."

Scott pulled his keys from his pocket and tossed them to her. "Let me know if *you* need rescuing."

Emily stashed her laptop in her computer bag, dashed to the garage, and climbed into Scott's truck. As she pushed her key into the ignition, she caught sight of her father's tool belt hanging on a hook. "I can't let one rejection letter break my spirit." She glanced at the ceiling. "I promise I won't let you and Mom, or Willow Falls, down."

She backed into the street and turned toward town, determined to quash the latest drama before the town spiraled into chaos.

Chapter 3

Emily parked three doors from the *Willow Post* headquarters, shouldered her computer bag, and rushed past two empty storefronts. Inside, she pushed through the angry crowd and found Mary Dixon sitting at the worktable with her laptop open. She set her bag on the table and turned toward the angry faces. "What's going on, and why are you giving my reporter a hard time?"

A woman wearing a pink Guts, Grits, and Lipstick T-shirt pointed to the computer screen. "You need to write a response to that good-for-nothing Travel Titan."

Emily stared at a picture of a female strolling along Main Street, her back to the camera. "Who?"

"She's an undercover podcaster who never shows her face." Pink Shirt crossed her arms and tapped her biceps. "She secretly visits towns all over the country and writes reviews. Kind of like a food critic showing up unannounced at a restaurant."

"Okay, so she showed on our streets. What did she say about Willow Falls?"

"She called our town a real snore."

"And Scott's store a failure because the doors were closed four days a week," said another woman, unleashing a barrage of comments.

"Can you believe she called our fifty-foot waterfall mediocre?"

"What did she expect, Niagara Falls?"

"Why didn't she mention the winery Charlie and his dad are gonna build or that a famous artist used to live here?"

"What I want to know is who gave her all that information?"

"Not me."

"Me neither."

"Well, she darn tootin' talked to someone." Pink Shirt thumped Emily's arm. "You're gonna love this. She said some unknown wannabe writer intended to publish a book about a town that made watching paint dry exciting."

Emily shook her head. *And I worried about publishers.*

"You want to know how she ended her tirade?"

"Enlighten me."

"She said unless tourists are looking for mind-numbing boredom, they should pick someplace else to spend their precious time and hard-earned money."

"That's way beyond harsh." Emily puffed her cheeks and blew air. "Maybe her rants won't do too much damage."

"You don't understand." Pink Shirt tapped the computer screen. "This woman has thousands, make that tens of thousands of followers."

Gertie, one of the town's beloved senior citizens, faced her neighbors. "This—what'd you call her—Titan lady? Anyway, she's right about our town."

"What does she know? She's an old lady," said a young man wearing a red ball cap.

Gertie waggled her finger at him. "I don't know squat about this podcast thingy, sonny, but I for sure know boring when I see it."

Her comment set off another verbal ambush, until a shrill whistle disrupted the assault. Pastor Nathan, the town's mayor and Mary's husband, circled the crowd and stood behind his wife.

Red Ball Cap's eyes widened. "How long you been standing back there?"

"Long enough to know you owe Miss Gertie an apology."

"Sorry. I didn't mean no disrespect, ma'am."

"That's better. Now about our situation. If this podcaster is as influential as everyone seems to think, we need to do some serious damage control. Which is why I'll schedule a town hall meeting next week."

Gertie snapped her fingers. "An old-fashioned soda fountain, that's what we need. If we had one, the Titan lady would've had something positive to say about Willow Falls."

"Yeah, right." Red Ball Cap rolled his eyes.

"Don't knock it, sonny. Back in my day, we'd walk a country mile for a scoop of ice cream, chocolate syrup, and carbonated water topped with whipped cream. Why, I'd even make grumpy old codgers pop off their duff and do a happy dance."

"This is the twenty-first century, not the Stone Age."

"If you ask me, we can use some old-fashioned good times."

"Okay, folks," Nathan said. "Save the comments and ideas for the meeting. In the meantime, it's best if you go on about your business."

Grumbles and headshakes abounded as the crowd headed out.

"I'm not convinced we can fix this problem at a town hall meeting." Emily slumped onto a chair.

"I'll meet with the council members tomorrow morning. We might have to spend some money—"

"Is there any? Money?"

"A little." Nathan glanced at his watch. "Time to open my store." He kissed Mary's cheek. "See you tonight, honey."

Emily watched him leave and hasten past the window toward the corner. "What do you suppose the council will do?"

"Whatever they decide, it might not be enough." Mary's fingers raced across her keyboard. "This Travel Titan is an internet sensation. She's all over social media."

"That's just great. An entire town is taken down by a stealthy secret agent hanging out in cyber world."

"I wonder how she found out about Willow Falls."

"Who knows. What I do know is no matter what that editor said about my book—"

"Someone responded?"

"Yeah, with a big, fat rejection."

"I'm sorry. Maybe that means good news is coming."

"I can hope." Emily removed her ringing phone from her bag. "I need to take this." She pressed it to her ear and moved to the window. "Yes, sir, what can I do for you?" Her chest tightened as she listened to his explanation. *This can't be happening.* "I know, but—" She gazed across the street at the impatiens Mary had planted in front of the church. Did Titan lady see those flowers? "Is there anything we can do to change your mind?" She spotted a smudge on the glass and rubbed it off with her finger. "I understand. I'm sorry it didn't work out … thanks, you too."

She returned to the worktable and dropped onto a chair across from Mary. "It's not right for one person to wield so much power over an entire community. Our hotel manager just resigned."

Mary looked up from her laptop. "The one you hired three days ago?"

"Turns out his wife is a big Travel Titan fan. She told him there's no way they're uprooting their family and moving to a town on the brink of failure." Emily tossed her phone in her bag. "I ran a not-so-cheap ad in the Atlanta paper for three long months and received one response. From the guy who quit."

"Too bad."

"Not to mention a colossal waste of time and money."

"This is some test our town's going through."

Emily sighed. "One we could fail miserably. I need to talk to Scott."

"You go ahead. I'll take care of things here."

"Thanks, Mary. You're worth way more than your job pays."

"Believe me, every quarter helps."

"I know what you mean." Emily stepped outside, passed the empty storefronts, and turned left at the corner. She slowed and imagined viewing the century-old storefronts from an outsider's perspective. The scene wasn't as picturesque as residents claimed. While every façade stood out as unique, faded awnings and chipped paint spoke volumes. Across Main the streetlights along the sidewalk fronting the lakeside park looked old and washed-out.

She stepped up her pace, passed Pepper's Café and Patsy's Pastries and Pretties—the only restaurant and gift shop in town. She stopped at the corner of Falls and Main. Her eyes drifted to the marquee over the abandoned cinema. The *n* in the For Rent had been missing for years. Why hadn't someone bothered to fix it?

She crossed catty-corner and hastened to the sidewalk leading to the four-story brick hotel partially covered with ivy vines. She grasped the glass-inlay double front door handle, then glanced at the brass Redding Arms letters above the door. A stab of guilt pierced her soul. Her parents gave everything to save their town. "No way I'm letting some internet phenom tear us apart."

She pushed the door open and entered the two-story lobby. The gold veins in the white marble floor shimmered under the massive chandelier. To the right, Scott was on his knees framing a twenty-foot-long check-in desk. She caught his eye and motioned him over.

"You look like you were bit by a rattlesnake. Did you get another rejection?"

"We need to talk." She led him out to the rear veranda, which ran the full length of the hotel. They sat on the steps leading to the lawn and the lake beyond.

"More bad news?"

She relayed the Titan and resignation details.

"Phew." Scott ran his fingers through his thick brown hair. "Talk about a major setback."

"After Mom and Dad died, I accepted the responsibility to follow through with their plan to refurbish this hotel and get it up and running. That hasn't changed, which means I have to go with plan B."

"You mean ask the woman who brought you into this world to take the manager's job?"

"At least until I can recruit someone else."

"How do you know she'll accept?"

"I don't." Emily plucked a dried leaf off the steps, crumbled it, and let the pieces fall between her fingers. "The problem is, I'm out of options."

Chapter 4

Emily hastened through the hotel lobby, then cut across the lawn and driveway to the Willow Inn. Supported by white columns extending from a railing, the porch spanned the entire front. She climbed the stairs and spotted Charlie Bricker sitting in one of the white rocking chairs in front of the parlor's bay window. "Are you reading the *Willow Post* or a more important paper?"

"Nothing's more important than local news." He grinned and laid it on the marble-topped, wrought-iron table with the "In Memory of Nora and Roger Redding" plaque. "Do you have a sec?"

She dropped onto the other rocker. "What's on your mind?"

"My lease in Atlanta ends in a couple of days, so I'm free to move to Willow Falls permanently."

"Apparently you haven't heard the news."

"About the terrible Titan?"

"You have heard. I'm surprised you aren't packing your bags and heading back to Atlanta."

"Dad invested a lot of time and money in the vineyard. No way I'm bailing on him or this town." He scooted to the edge of his rocker. "You know I'm planning to build a house on the property."

"Yeah, after the hotel is finished."

"And the winery. I can't keep living at the inn. Will you consider renting me your parents' house for the time being? It would help both of us."

"That's the first good news I've heard all day. When can you move in?"

"Next week. How much is first and last month's rent?"

"I'll talk to Scott and let you know."

"Deal. Did Sadie tell you my dad's coming up for the Fourth?"

Emily shook her head. "I hope the bad news doesn't scare him off."

"Unless a black cat crosses his path or he finds thirteen pennies lying on the ground, he won't think much about it." He pushed off the rocking chair. "I need to head to the vineyard."

She followed him to the center of the porch. He headed down the stairs. She opened the front door and stepped into the two-story foyer where an antique crystal chandelier illuminated the space.

Giggles drew her attention. She turned right, entered the parlor, and found Clair and Jane sitting beside their grandma on the chocolate-colored settee with gold inlaid wood. Sadie closed a book and set it on the neoclassical coffee table with a smoke-glass top. "I didn't expect you to pick up my grandbabies so soon."

"Actually, I'm here to talk to you." Emily sat on a wingback chair facing the settee.

"About the cancellations?"

"No. What?"

"I'm surprised you haven't heard." The twins climbed off Sadie's lap and crawled to the box of toys on the oriental rug. "Three guests called to cancel their reservations. We didn't have that many to begin with."

Emily eyed the painting hanging over the fireplace—a silver-footed compote filled with pears, apples, and grapes, sitting on a marble table with a rose, a white lace napkin, and a fancy paring knife. "Is there no end to bad news?"

"There's sugar somewhere in all this vinegar."

"Which brings me to the reason I'm here." Emily shared the news about the hotel manager's resignation.

"That's too bad."

"It puts me in a real bind. I've been thinking." She shared plan B.

Sadie hesitated, then moved to the bay window. "Helping you finish the inn, then taking on the innkeeper job made it possible for me to transition from prison back to the real world."

Emily stepped beside her. "You've done a great job running this place."

"Managing a sixty-room hotel is way more complicated than running a six-room inn." She stared straight ahead. "I'm flattered you think I'm up to the job."

"The basics can't be that much different." A black limousine pulled to the curb in front of the inn and caught Emily's attention. "I hope that's not a news crew looking to do a follow-up story on Travel Titan's rant."

The driver removed a suitcase and a duffle bag from the trunk, then opened the back door. A man wearing a gray blazer, white shirt, and a red ascot stepped out and headed up the sidewalk.

"Looks like someone wanting to check in."

"You'd better grab him before he discovers the internet tirade."

Sadie dashed to the foyer and opened the door. "Welcome to Willow Inn."

The man stepped inside.

His driver followed, set the luggage down, then tipped his cap to his passenger. "Been a pleasure, Mr. Hamilton, and thanks for the generous tip."

"Cheers, mate." He moved into the foyer, fingered his neatly trimmed, dark beard, and glanced around.

Sadie closed the door behind the limo driver and turned toward the new arrival. "What brings you to Willow Falls?"

"I need a quiet place to write my book."

"You're a writer? So's my daughter. She also owns this lovely inn."

Emily moved Jane and Clair to their stroller and pushed it into the foyer. "Pleasure to meet you, sir."

He grasped her extended hand. "Likewise. I'd like to see the place."

"My mother is the innkeeper." Emily withdrew her hand. "She'll show you around."

Sadie escorted him through the parlor, dining room, and Carly Suite before leading him upstairs. When they returned, her guest eyed the crystal chandelier. "In Britain we'd call this a posh establishment."

"Until last year it was a private home."

He fingered his beard. "I didn't see anything on the internet about the hotel next door."

"That's because it won't open until October."

"Strange. The building looks old."

Sadie nodded. "Robert Liles started building it more than thirty years ago. Nobody finished it 'til now."

"Interesting. I prefer the downstairs suite. If it's available."

"It is. How long do you plan to stay?"

"I'm thinking five months."

Sadie's eyes widened. "You mean weeks?"

"I meant months."

"Okay, then. Follow me, Mr. Hamilton. I'll check you in." She stepped behind the antique desk that belonged to Emily's grandfather, opened the registration journal, and turned it toward him.

"I'd like to pay for the entire stay in advance." He removed a roll of bills from the duffle's side pocket and peeled off a stack of hundred-dollar bills. "Do you live on the property?"

"My apartment's out back, over the garage."

"I see. If you don't mind, I'm ready to settle in."

"Yes, of course." Sadie lifted a key from a pegboard and handed him a small black gift bag. "A welcome gift."

"Thanks." As he shouldered the duffle, he leaned slightly to the left.

Sadie released his suitcase's handle and pulled it to the end of the foyer.

The moment they stepped into the Carly Suite, Emily ran her finger down the registration log. *Winston Hamilton.* She picked up the cash.

"Let me know if you need anything, sir." Sadie closed the suite's door and returned to the desk. "Do you want to count the money?"

"Already did. I need to deposit it before he changes his mind."

"He won't." Sadie removed an empty envelope from a drawer and handed it to Emily.

"How do you know?"

"Like he said, he wants a quiet place to write."

"Guess we should adopt the motto, 'Come to Willow Falls if you're looking for mind-numbing boredom.'" Emily slipped the money in the envelope.

"Or a peaceful stay in a lovely inn." Sadie moved to the curved staircase and fingered the intricately carved newel post. "About the hotel, I need a couple of days to think it over."

"Fair enough." Emily watched her mother push the stroller back to the parlor and settle on the rug with her grandbabies. *At least she didn't say no.* She sighed, then slipped out the front door and walked straight to the bank.

Chapter 5

Rachel popped a dark-roast pod in her Keurig and turned on the morning news in the middle of Alicia Adams' report on a local student winning the national spelling bee. It had been four months since she last met with her friend's improv group. She vowed to reconnect soon.

After stirring honey and creamer into her coffee, Rachel stepped out to her deck. Once her Sunday-morning refuge, the second-story structure now served as her daily decision-making venue. She spotted the resident hawk perched on a high branch in the heavily wooded space behind the row of townhouses. "Hello, feathered friend." It pointed its beak toward her, then took flight. "Guess you're not ready for conversation."

She savored her coffee and relished the sun's warmth on her face. The forecast called for another hot day. Dennis and his dog came to mind. She hoped they'd find plenty of shade. Nancy's comment about visiting her father edged into her conscience. Yesterday she'd reached out to a homeless friend. Shouldn't she do the same with the man who raised her?

Before she changed her mind, she returned to the kitchen, called her father's office, and scheduled a one o'clock appointment.

 ★ ★ ★

Dressed in white jeans, an emerald green shirt, and gold sandals, Rachel stepped from the elevator on the thirty-eighth floor and entered Streetman Enterprise's downtown Atlanta office. A ten-foot ficus in a blue ceramic pot softened the hard edges in the sun-filled, ultra-modern lobby.

The receptionist looked up from her work and smiled. "Welcome back, Miss Streetman. I love your new style."

"Thanks. I call it casual unemployment."

"We all miss your upbeat attitude. After all, every company needs a redhead. Although Nancy is trying to fill your positive-motivation shoes."

"Good for her." Rachel strolled past cubicles, chatted with associates, then stopped at Nancy's desk. "I decided to take your advice."

"I'm not surprised. My boss is out to lunch with a client. Do you want to peek into your old office?"

"I have a couple of minutes to spare, so I might as well."

Rachel followed Nancy inside, then turned in a slow circle. "Brent changed a few things."

"He claimed the decor looked way too feminine for him."

"He obviously prefers a more masculine look." She moved to the window and gazed down at the twenty-story Skyview Ferris Wheel and beyond at Centennial Park.

Nancy stepped beside her. "Do you ever miss working here?"

"The people yes, especially you, and this view. The job, not one bit."

"Who would believe entertaining a theater full of admirers would be more fun than working in an office ten hours a day?" Nancy snickered. "Anyone with a lick of talent, that's who. Although you were the best boss I ever had."

"We were a good team."

"Yes, we were."

"Is your new boss treating you well?"

"He's getting better."

"Good to hear." Rachel glanced at her watch. "Time for my appointment."

"You don't want to keep the boss waiting, even if he is your father." She moved toward the door. "Oh, don't forget your promise."

"Which one?"

"To let me be a bridesmaid if you and Charlie ever decide to marry."

"Cross my heart." Rachel embraced her friend, then made her way to the corner office. Inside, her father sat in his executive chair, turned toward the credenza set against the wall. She settled in a plush armchair facing his desk. "Hi … Dad."

He pointed to the painting hanging above the credenza. "I bought that abstract as an investment. Truth is, I never much cared for it." He swiveled his chair around. The lines on his forehead were more pronounced than she remembered. His mustache more salt than pepper.

"What in the devil is going on in Willow Falls?" His brown eyes grew lightning fierce.

"Excuse me?"

"I agreed to fund the hotel refurb because I owed you and Emily. I also expected to turn a decent profit."

"I don't understand. What's the problem?"

"Some dame calling herself the Travel Titan did a hit job on the town." He punched his phone's keypad, then slid it across the desk.

Rachel's jaw dropped as she watched and listened to the scathing review.

"If something isn't done to counter this fiasco, I'll pull the funding and cut my losses."

She pushed the phone back to him. "Without the additional money, work on the hotel will stop."

"You were part of my company long enough to know Streetman Enterprise doesn't contract losing projects."

"Yes, but … this is personal."

"Business is never personal." His gaze probed then softened. "You look good, Strawberry Girl."

"Thanks, so do you." She forced her shoulders to relax.

"Any big breaks in your acting career?"

"I'm expecting one next week." She relayed details about the audition.

"If it doesn't work out, I can secure interviews with a dozen companies."

"I appreciate your offer. But the corporate life isn't what I'm aiming for."

Her focus shifted to a photo on the credenza of her posing with him at a ceremony honoring him with a lifetime achievement award. Whether he liked it or not, she counted him as part of the Willow Falls family.

"Have you seen a recent photo of Emily's babies?" She pulled her phone from her purse and scrolled to the twins' photo. "They're ten months old now."

He glanced at the picture. "They look a lot like you did at that age."

His assistant entered the office. "Excuse me, Mr. Streetman, your next appointment is here."

Is ten minutes all I get? Rachel retrieved her phone. "Guess it's time for me to leave."

"Wait." He pulled a package, half the size of a shoebox, wrapped in white paper and pink ribbon, from his desk drawer. "Give this to Emily for me."

"What is it?"

"A gift for her daughters."

"Why don't you go up for the Fourth and give it to her yourself?"

"Can't. I'm flying to New York to close a deal on a real-estate development company that will expand our reach into the Northeast. Maybe I'll make it up for Christmas, if the town still exists."

His tone sent a shiver up her spine. "Don't give up on it yet."

"I'll give you until next Friday to find a reason I shouldn't abandon the project."

She stood and reached for the gift. "I'm glad you squeezed me into your calendar. Maybe we can do lunch sometime."

"Thanks for coming by, Strawberry Girl."

She left his office and said goodbye to Nancy and her friends. At the elevator bank, she eyed the gift box and tried to imagine what a wealthy, hard-nosed businessman would give to ten-month-old babies. And how could he possibly consider pulling the plug on Willow Falls' key to survival? *Because he has the emotional intelligence of a gnat.*

A ping announced the elevator's arrival. The doors opened. Rachel stepped in and pressed the first-floor button. Too many people she loved lived in Willow Falls to let it go down without a fight. She couldn't let her father follow through on his threat.

Chapter 6

The wooden floorboards in Hayes General Store creaked as Emily pushed the stroller past cabinets and barrels filled with scented soaps, candles, and unique household items. She set her phone on the counter, then lifted the twins into the fenced-off play area. "What happened at this morning's council meeting?"

"Nathan has a crazy idea about hiring some outsiders to fix the town's image. I'll fill you in later. Your purse is ringing. Your sister's tone."

"Will you grab it for me?"

He pulled her phone out and handed it over.

She pressed it to her ear. "Hey, what's up?" As she listened, a dull ache formed in her temples. She closed her eyes and squeezed the bridge of her nose. "I can't believe the bad news made it all the way to Atlanta." Sweat popped out on her upper lip as she listened to Rachel relay her conversation with her father. "Do you think he'll actually do it?"

Scott caught her eye. "What's wrong?"

She held her hand over the phone. "Greer's threatening to pull the hotel funding." She removed her hand, finished the conversation with Rachel, then released a heavy sigh. "Just when I thought things couldn't get worse."

Scott shook his head. "Seems the whole town's been snakebit."

Emily dropped her phone in her purse. "Rachel wants to come by tonight after dinner with Charlie, to deliver a gift from her father."

"Let me get this straight. He wants to stop paying for the hotel, but he's sending us a gift?"

"Not us. Jane and Clair."

"What, two silver spoons?"

"She didn't say."

The bell over the front door jangled. Mirabelle dashed in carrying a package. She locked eyes with Emily. "Did your mother put the Brit upstairs in my room?"

"And hello to you."

"Well, did she?"

"He requested the downstairs suite."

"Wouldn't you know." She plunked the package on the counter. "Other than his wad of cash, what do you know about him?"

Scott opened his pocketknife and sliced through the tape. "How is it you haven't already discovered everything about the guy?"

"Give her time, honey. He's only been in town one day."

Mirabelle scowled. "You two are a bucket of chuckles."

"All I know is he's writing a book," Emily said.

"About what?"

"I don't know."

"Some reporter you are."

"That's the point. I'm a reporter, not an investigator."

"Then I guess it's up to me to find out."

"Like you wouldn't anyway." Scott pulled the flaps back and removed bags of old-fashioned candy.

Mirabelle licked her lips. "Scoop me some jellybeans. With all the bad news going on around here I need a pick-me-up."

He lifted the lid off a jar, filled a white paper bag, then pushed it to her. "There you go, your morning sugar high."

She slapped two dollars on the counter. "Why did Winston show up in a limo instead of a car?"

"One more mystery for you to solve," Emily said.

"Without me, nobody around here would know anything." She grabbed the bag and dashed outside.

Emily waited for the door to close behind Mirabelle. "How long do you think it will take her to wheedle information out of him?"

"One lunch at Pepper's."

"I wouldn't be surprised if she learns his life story before she digs her fork in her dessert."

He placed the lid on the candy jar. "She was today's first customer."

How much longer could he keep the store open? Her heart ached for him. "Maybe I should cancel my appointment."

"Didn't you say Pearl has a two-for-one special?"

Emily nodded. "Pay for a manicure, get a free pedicure."

"You deserve a break."

"Are you sure?"

"Positive. I'll watch our girls."

She splayed her fingers. "These nails haven't seen a stroke of polish in more than a year." Emily leaned across the counter and kissed Scott's cheek. "You're a sweetheart. I'll see you in an hour."

Outside, she crossed Main Street and walked the block and a half to Pearl's Hair and Nail Salon. Inside, she hung her purse on a hook by the door.

Pearl—dressed in a short black skirt, gold tank top, and cropped denim jacket—aimed a blow-dryer and pulled a brush through a teenager's long blonde hair. "Hey, girl, it's about time you came in for some TLC." She motioned Emily closer. "You won't believe who's sitting under the dryer. Go ahead, take a look."

A woman reading a *Good Housekeeping* magazine lowered it to turn the page.

Emily gaped. "Mama Sadie?"

"The one and only. She wanted a color and a cut. You'll love the auburn shade, claims it's her natural color. She's also getting a facial and wants me to teach her how to do her eyes."

"Doesn't look like the bad news is hurting your bottom line."

"Beauty and booze thrive in tough times. Besides, if customers stop making appointments, I'll offer WWCC."

"Uh huh, and what is that?"

"Wine with cut 'n' color. From Charlie's vineyard, of course. If it ever produces anything." She switched the blow-dryer off, swiveled the chair, and handed her customer a mirror. "There you go, sweetie."

The teenager held the mirror and viewed the back of her silky hair. "You made it so pretty. Thank you, Ms. Pearl."

"You tell your momma about my two-for-one mani-pedi special."

"Yes ma'am." She returned the handheld, took a last look in the big mirror, then sashayed out of the salon.

"Willow Falls has to thrive so sweet girls like her won't go off to college and never come back." Pearl swept hair into a dustpan, then pointed toward the back. "My nail tech will be ready for you in a jiffy."

"Thanks." Emily moved to the dryer beside Sadie and tapped her mother's knee.

She lifted the hood. "Hey, honey."

"It's about time you treated yourself to the works."

"Pepper and me are going to see an old friend tomorrow morning. I don't want to look like I just got out of jail. Don't worry about Mr. Hamilton's breakfast. Patsy's gonna take him coffee cake. Folks around here help each other out, even in the toughest times. One more reason I love living in this town."

"Can't wait to see your new look."

The manicurist tapped Emily's arm. "I'm ready."

Sadie pulled the dryer hood down and turned to the next page in her magazine. Emily glanced sideways at her. *She'd tell me if she planned to turn the manager's job down ... wouldn't she?*

Chapter 7

Rachel stared at the concrete wall in the underground parking garage and fought the urge to return to her father's office and demand he withdraw his threat. She gripped the steering wheel, knowing it'd be foolish to approach him again until she could present a compelling reason for him to stick with Willow Falls. The problem was coming up with one. She filled her lungs, slowly released the air, then backed out of the parking space.

Three minutes later, she eased onto the interstate highway and forced her mind to shift to her date with Charlie.

His ringtone sounded. She pressed her Bluetooth. "Hey, I've been thinking about you."

"Good thoughts, I hope. How far away are you?"

"I'm still in Atlanta. If traffic isn't too terrible, it should take the usual two hours." She paused. "Uh-oh, I spoke too soon. Nothing but brake lights ahead."

"One more good thing about small towns. No traffic jams."

She'd take traffic over boredom any day. Rachel punched her brakes as a car cut in front of her. Or would she.

"I'll let you go. Drive safely."

"Will do."

A four-car pileup on Interstate 85 added an hour to her trip, putting her in Willow Falls a few minutes after six. She turned onto the driveway between the inn and hotel and pulled into the narrow parking space beside Charlie's truck. She checked her image in the rearview mirror, then grabbed her suitcase and walked into Willow Inn. The chandelier cast a dim mellow glow. Soft jazz filled the air. Tomato and garlic aromas drifted into the foyer and conjured images of her favorite Italian restaurant.

Charlie sauntered in from the dining room. "Hey, pretty lady."

"Has Mama Sadie added dinner to the bed and breakfast concept?"

"Nope." He moved her bag beside the staircase. "I hope you're in the mood for Charlie's spaghetti and meatballs."

"You fixed dinner?"

"Most of it."

"If it tastes as good as it smells, I'm in for a real treat."

He slipped his arm around her waist and led her to the twelve-foot-long dining room table, set for two on one end. Two flickering candles and an antique brass chandelier with etched glass globes lit the space. She settled in the chair Charlie pulled out for her. He kissed the back of her neck, igniting a delicious tingling sensation.

"What's the special occasion?"

"I haven't seen you since last month. I want you all to myself tonight." He opened a bottle of red wine and poured two glasses. "Be back in a sec." He disappeared into the kitchen, then returned carrying two Caesar salads and a ceramic serving bowl filled with spaghetti. "I call this Charlie's Italian specialty." He served the pasta, then sat across from her and grinned. "You look beautiful in candlelight."

"Maybe I should take a candle to next week's audition." She tasted the salad. "The dressing's yummy."

"Pepper made it. The spaghetti sauce is all mine."

"Not out of a jar?"

"Well, not completely. I added Parmesan, olive oil, and fresh rosemary."

Rachel twirled noodles around her fork, then sniffed the piney scent and relished the taste. "Delish. And I thought your cooking skills were limited to ordering pizza."

"The nearest pizzeria is an hour away, so I had to improvise."

"A necessity in a town miles from anywhere." She sipped her wine. "Any changes in your plan to stick around?"

"You mean because some internet sensation punched Willow Falls in the eye?"

"I figured it would at least give you pause."

"Why?"

"I don't know, because your future's at stake?"

"When everyone recovers from the shock, they'll pull together and turn things around. Did Emily tell you I'm renting her parents' house until I build?"

Rachel shook her head.

"Good news is, it has two guest rooms, so you can stay with me when you're in town."

"And become juicy fodder for Mirabelle and her grapevine? I don't think so. Are you keeping the apartment in Atlanta?"

"Nope."

Rachel stared at her plate. "Does that mean … your move here is permanent?"

"I haven't learned to strum a guitar, yet, but I did say yeehaw once."

She made eye contact. "Is that your way of saying yes?"

"What's with the gloom and doom expression?"

"Sorry. It's just … I'm counting on getting cast in a new play next week. It could run for the rest of the year, maybe longer. Which means this is likely my last trip to Willow Falls for a while." She twirled her fork in the spaghetti. "I'll have performances six nights a week, with an afternoon matinee every weekend."

He laid down his fork. "What are you trying to say?"

"I'll be super busy."

He stared at her for a long moment. "In that in case, I'd better give this to you now." He moved to her side, pulled the chair away from the table, and removed a small, black velvet box from his pocket.

Rachel's heart pounded. *No. Not now. I'm nowhere near ready for a proposal.*

"While you're away chasing your dreams, I want you to wear this." He opened the box, revealing a gold heart-shaped pendant encircled with diamonds, on a delicate chain. "It belonged to my great grandmother. After my mother ran off with another man, Grandma gave it to me and asked me to save it for the woman who won my heart."

Rachel's breathing accelerated.

"You look like you're about to pass out."

"I'm honored you're offering it to me." She pressed her hand to her chest. "I … can't."

"You can't what?"

"Accept it. I'm not ready."

"Not ready for what?"

"Right now, my career is super important to me."

"And mine's important to me. That doesn't mean I wouldn't accept a gift from you."

"Please, Charlie, I need more time."

"How much time? Six more months? Another year? Or maybe you're waiting for a better offer to come along?"

"That's not fair."

"Then tell me what's really going on."

She closed her eyes, searching for the right words. Images of shackles inching toward her ankles burst into her head.

"Well?"

She lifted her lids. "You have to understand, as far back as I can remember, I lived the life my father wanted—"

"Hold it right there." His eyes narrowed. "You think I'm trying to control your life?"

"I ... need space."

He snapped the box shut, stuffed it in his pocket, then headed to the exit.

"Where are you going?"

"You want space? You've got it."

The front door opened, then slammed shut.

Rachel's body tensed, shocked he'd walk out on her like an immature, jilted teenager and leave a half-eaten mess. She stacked the dirty dishes, carried them to the kitchen, then returned to the dining room and grabbed the bottle of wine. She fled to the foyer and plucked the key to the Patsy Peacock Suite off the pegboard. Her body tensed as she dashed up to the second floor.

At the top of the stairs, she set her bag down and released the handle. She took a step, then halted, caught off guard by a man wearing a blue ascot and a long-sleeve shirt, sitting on the couch in the common area. He swirled golden liquid in a short-stemmed glass.

"Good evening, Ms. Hayes."

"Obviously you've met my twin. I'm Rachel Streetman, and you are?"

"Winston Hamilton. I'm returning from the café. Charming place, good food."

"Pepper's an excellent chef, always trying new recipes." She moved closer. "Are you a guest here?"

"I checked into the Carly Suite yesterday. Would you care to join me for a brandy? My nightly indulgence."

"Thanks, but I'm a bit tired."

"Perhaps another time."

"Have a pleasant evening." Rachel moved to the right-rear corner and unlocked the suite. Inside, she set the bottle on the dresser and heaved her suitcase onto one of the twin beds. Her eyes drifted to the framed print of one of Monet's water lily scenes. The colors fit perfectly with the peacock theme. She opened her bag, removed the script for her audition, then sat in the upholstered armchair beside the window.

Halfway through the first page, Charlie crept into her head. She'd seen his temper flare at bad drivers, but never at her.

She dropped the script on the floor, poured wine into a water glass, and turned on the television, hoping to find a distraction. After flipping through a dozen channels, she landed on a rerun of the *Andy Griffith Show*. She'd last watched the program a year ago before coming to Willow Falls for the first time. Little did she know then that Charlie would abandon the city for a Mayberry-like town. She sighed. Could she ever live where nothing more exciting than eating at Pepper's Café, gabbing with neighbors, and watching cable TV existed? At least the town had a decent gift shop.

"Oh my gosh, I almost forgot." She set her glass down, dug her father's gift from her suitcase, then texted Emily. "On my way to your house."

She texted back. "Door's open. We're on the patio."

Chapter 8

Rachel locked her suite door, relieved to discover the inn's newest guest had left the common area. She rushed downstairs, out the front door, and found Charlie's parking space empty. How far could he go in a town the size of Willow Falls?

During the short drive to her sister's house, her body tensed as regret consumed her. Why didn't she accept his gift? Fear of commitment? Did she drive him away?

When she pulled into the driveway, she breathed deep hoping to soothe her frazzled nerves. She checked her image in the rearview mirror. At least she didn't look like a jilted woman. She stepped out, walked to the front porch, and opened the door. Did anyone in Willow Falls ever bother with locks? If the town managed to become a tourist destination, residents would be forced to change their habits.

She moved through the kitchen, to the patio, laid her father's gift on the glass table, then sat beside her sister.

"I'm surprised you're here this early." Emily held a wine glass in both hands. "How'd dinner go?"

Cody, the Hayes' golden retriever, padded over and plopped his head on Rachel's lap. His tail thumped the concrete in a please-pet-me tempo. "Dogs make great companions. They love unconditionally and expect nothing in return other than food, a ball toss, and a head-scratching or belly rub."

Emily elbowed her. "There's a double meaning in there somewhere."

"It ended early."

"And what are you not telling me?"

"Nothing."

"You can't fool me. That's not a nothing expression."

Rachel stroked Cody's ears. "Charlie and I had ... a disagreement."

"A lover's spat?"

35

"Something like that." She pointed to the half-empty wine bottle. "Are you two celebrating?"

Scott tipped his glass toward her. "More like licking our wounds. Grab a glass and join us."

"I've had enough wine for one night. How are residents taking the bad news?"

"Pretty much like you'd expect." Emily ran her finger along the rim of her glass. "Today's front-page headline could've read 'Travel Titan Tosses Town over Willow Falls.'"

"Interesting play on words."

"That's what I do. Play with words. But according to one editor not good enough for publication."

Rachel pushed her father's gift to Emily. "Maybe this will cheer you up."

"Do you know what it is?"

"Not a clue."

"What does a business tycoon give to baby girls?"

"Same thing I wondered."

"Only one way to find out." Emily untied the ribbon, peeled back the white paper, and opened the package.

Rachel glared at two identical slender black boxes. "Typical."

"What?"

"Go ahead, open one."

Emily lifted the lid. "A pen? For a baby?"

"Not simply a pen." Rachel reached for the box and removed a gold-trimmed white ballpoint. "An engraved Montblanc writing instrument, my father's favorite outrageously expensive success symbol. He gave me the same gift the day he promoted me to vice president." She pointed to two envelopes. "There's more."

Emily opened the first envelope and unfolded a sheet of paper. She gasped, then pressed it to her chest. "Oh my ... I mean ..."

Scott tapped his fingers on the table. "How long are you gonna keep us in suspense?"

She handed it to him.

His mouth fell open. "I don't believe it."

"Enough with the mystery. What the heck is it?"

"A forty-thousand-dollar education fund."

"Are you serious?"

"Oh yeah."

Rachel's heart pounded as Emily opened the second envelope.

"A letter." She paused. "Dear Emily. Although it seems like years away, time passes quickly. One day your daughters will be ready to move on with their lives. This fund will grow and provide the means for them to attend whatever university they choose. When they're old enough to appreciate the pens' significance, present the gifts to them and tell them to follow their dreams."

She choked back the fist-sized lump in her throat. "I think this is his way of apologizing to us."

Emily dabbed her eyes. "Whatever the motivation, the gift is perfect. At least if the town ... and the store fails, our babies' future is secure."

Scott nodded. "You need to call and thank him."

"I don't know his number."

Rachel called it out.

Emily pressed her phone to her ear. "It's going to voicemail." She paused. "Mr. Streetman, this is Emily Hayes. We opened your gift. I ... uh ... a simple thank you over the phone hardly seems like enough. We hope you come up to Willow Falls soon"—her voice cracked—"so Scott and I can tell you in person how much this means to us. Until then, take care."

Emily set the phone down and reached for Greer's letter. "His words seem so heartfelt. Do you really think he'll cut the hotel funding?"

"He's the consummate businessman. If the town doesn't come up with a convincing bottom-line solution?" Rachel fingered her mother's tennis bracelet. "In a heartbeat."

Emily refilled her wineglass and stared at the dark-red liquid. "For the first time in my life, I'm thinking Scott's right. Our friends who fled this town were smart."

"You two can't give up."

"That's a strange comment from my twin who won't stay around more than a couple of days at a time."

"Okay, I admit I prefer the city. Not only is Willow Falls your home, it's Mama Sadie's ... and now Charlie's, which makes it worth saving. Fact is I won't be around much after next week, but if there's anything I can do to help, I will."

"You'd better mean it, sis. Because I intend to hold you to your promise."

"Maybe I will take another glass of wine." She poured, then stared into the glass, questioning if she'd regret that offer.

Chapter 9

Emily parked beside the garage apartment behind Willow Inn as the sun reached its peak and found Rachel standing at the foot of the steps. "Mama Sadie called you too?"

"She and Pepper returned a half hour ago. She has some news."

Emily crossed her fingers. "I hope she's taking the manager's job."

Sadie opened the door before she and Rachel reached the top of the stairs. "Thanks for coming."

Emily stared wide-eyed at her mother's new appearance. "Wow, you look amazing. If people didn't know better, they'd swear you were our sister."

"Pearl knows her stuff." She stepped aside. "Thanks for coming up."

A plate of fresh-baked cookies sat on a round, glass-top coffee table. Emily breathed in the rich chocolate scent. "From Patsy's?"

"Only the best for my daughters."

Rachel reached for a cookie. "Hmm, are they to help celebrate good news or soften bad?"

Sadie sat on one of the slipper chairs. "That depends."

"You've aroused our curiosity." Emily tilted her head. "What's this meeting all about?"

"The manager's job."

"Are you saying yes?"

Sadie folded her hands in her lap. "I … have to turn you down."

Emily scooted to the edge of the love seat. "Why?"

"Because, I'm not qualified—"

"You're the most qualified person in town—"

"Heavens to Betsy, honey." She unfolded her hands. "Give me a chance to finish. I'm not qualified, but I know someone who has all the experience you need."

"What? I mean who?"

"Her name's Kat Williams. I met her in prison—"

"A criminal?"

"Yeah … like me."

Heat inched up Emily's neck. "It's not the same."

"I don't know why not. She's done her time, and she's ready to move on."

"Why was she in jail?"

"Embezzlement—"

"Are you kidding? You want me to hire a thief?"

"Give it a rest, Emily." Rachel nudged her arm. "I don't think Mama Sadie would recommend someone who couldn't handle the job."

"Okay, lay it on me." Emily leaned back and crossed her arms. "Why do you think this Kat person is qualified to manage a hotel?"

"To begin, she has a master's degree in business and twenty years' experience with a big international company."

"Before she chose a life of crime."

Sadie propped a hand on her hip. "Are you going to keep complaining or let me finish?"

"Sorry."

"Kat last worked as a vice president in charge of opening and staffing new branches for a giant corporation. Before you ditch the idea, I want you and Rachel to talk to her. If you think she's a good fit, then one of your problems is solved. But if you don't, I'll accept your decision."

Emily sighed. "Okay, when?"

"In ten minutes."

"She's here?" She raised her brows. "Oh, now I understand. She's the friend you and Pepper visited this morning."

"You don't think I'd suggest her if I didn't already know she'd accept, do you?" Sadie grabbed her cell phone from the glass-topped table and pressed a number. "Bring them on over."

Rachel's brow cocked. "Them?"

"Did I forget to mention? She kind of has a daughter."

"How … never mind." Emily bit into a cookie. "Why do I have the feeling you're bribing us with the best cookies in Georgia?"

"Everything goes better with sugar and chocolate."

"The guy who quit on me … I hired him based on his résumé. Which means I don't know how to interview corporate types."

"That's why I invited your sister to come up as well."

"Good. We can share the blame for turning her down."

Sadie shook her head. "Or the glory for making a smart decision."

Moments later, Sadie stood. "They're coming up now." She opened the door.

A tall, middle-aged woman with short, black, curly hair breezed in, carrying a manila folder. A twenty-something blue-eyed blonde followed her into the apartment.

Emily leaned close to Rachel. "This is getting stranger by the second." She stood and accepted the tall woman's outstretched hand.

"Your mother and I hit it off the first day we met. I'm Kat Williams." Her smile revealed perfect white teeth.

"I'm Emily."

"The newspaper editor and author." She turned to Rachel. "Which makes you the corporate twin turned actress. I'd like you both to meet my unofficial daughter, Missy Gibson."

The young woman lowered her chin, avoiding eye contact. "Pleased to meet you."

"She's shy, but making progress," Kat said.

"Ladies, have a seat." Sadie pointed to the slipper chairs, then sat on the love seat beside Emily.

"Thanks for giving me an opportunity to interview." Kat handed Emily the folder. "Here's what you need to know about my qualifications."

Emily skimmed the document, then gave it to Rachel. "Impressive."

"Sorry, I didn't include recommendations. I didn't think endorsements from a warden and a couple of prison guards would help seal the deal."

"How long have you …"

"Been out of jail?"

Emily nodded.

"No need to beat around the bush, I know where I've been. To answer your question, I was paroled two months ago. I met Missy in prison. She's been out for six weeks. We've been living at a woman's shelter ever since."

"Do you have a job?"

"I fill in at a burger joint when one of the employees fails to show up."

Rachel looked up from the résumé. "Talk about being underemployed."

"Employers don't take too kindly to people with felony records."

No kidding, thought Emily. "Did Sadie tell you what's going on around here?"

"You mean that the hotel manager quit over the internet hit job? Your town's troubles don't bother me. Being cast aside as an unworthy member of society, that scares the snot out of me."

Emily detected a hint of fear in her eyes.

Kat leaned forward. "I understand your reluctance to trust me with an important job. But the fact is, I'm a highly educated, accomplished woman who plunged from grace and paid the price. If you decide to hire me, I'll use my skills and work my tail off to earn my place back in society. I'll also make your hotel—"

"You mean the Redding Arms—"

"Uh-huh. The best small-town hotel this side of the Mississippi, maybe the whole country. Do you have any questions?"

Emily stared at Kat for a long moment. At least the woman had spunk. "I don't." She eyed her sister.

"I think we have enough information."

"Good." Kat stood. "Missy and I will let you ladies talk things over. You can find us in the park when you've made your decision."

Sadie escorted her friends to the door, then returned to a slipper chair. "You can't tell me you're not impressed."

Rachel laid the résumé on the coffee table. "If she hadn't gone to prison, Kat would easily command a hefty six-figure salary."

"The problem is, she did go to jail," Emily said. "And there's no way we can pay her anything close to what she's accustomed to."

"Are you kidding?" Rachel nudged her sister. "The woman's been flipping burgers. I don't think she'd quibble about salary."

"Okay, I see your point. But what about people living around here?" Emily locked eyes with Sadie. "You remember the uproar when you came back to town. Can you imagine how everyone will react to a stranger who's been behind bars?"

"No one other than the three of us and Scott needs to know."

"You mean deceive everyone?"

"Mama Sadie's right," Rachel said. "What matters is Kat's experience and qualifications. Her personal life isn't anyone's business."

"The truth will eventually come out."

"I don't know how." Sadie's gaze zeroed in on Emily. "No one other than the three of us know Kat is her middle name, short for Katina. I understand your hesitation. But the cold, hard fact is you need her. And she for doggone sure needs this job."

Emily closed her eyes and pinched the bridge of her nose as she weighed her options. Hire a convicted felon or go without a hotel manager. She took a deep breath and opened her eyes. "I have one final question. Do you trust her?"

"With my life."

"Okay, then. That's all I need to know." Emily sprang to her feet. "Are you two ready to welcome Redding Arms' newest residents?"

Rachel stood. "At least now I can tell my father you have a highly qualified executive to manage his investment."

Emily nodded. "I hope there's enough to convince him to stick with us."

They left Sadie's apartment and found Sadie's friends sitting on the foot-high, stone retaining wall at the lake's edge. Missy dangled her bare feet in the water. Kat faced the park. She shaded her eyes with her hand and stood when the trio approached. "Based on your expressions, I'm guessing you decided I'm worth the risk."

"I reckon you're right." Sadie embraced her friend. "Welcome to Willow Falls."

"I'll do everything I can to win this town over." She nodded toward the street. "Beginning with her."

Mirabelle stood beside her mail truck, facing the park.

"She came out of that café a couple of minutes ago. There's no one else in the park, so I'm guessing she has her eye on us."

Sadie chuckled. "Our mail lady can spot a stranger two blocks away."

Kat shook her head. "She's gonna be mighty busy when we have the hotel up and running."

Mirabelle crossed Main Street and headed in their direction.

"You're about to meet the town's one-woman telegraph service." Emily motioned to Mirabelle. "Come welcome our hotel's new manager."

Mirabelle stopped and eyed Kat from head to toe. "The other manager just quit. How'd the news spread so fast?"

"Pleasure to make your acquaintance." Kat extended her hand. "My name is Kat Williams."

"Mirabelle Paine."

"To answer your question, a friend knew I wanted to move to a lovely small town. Turns out my experience is exactly what Ms. Hayes needs."

"I see. Who's the pretty blonde?"

"My daughter."

Mirabelle's eyes widened.

Kat grinned. "Adopted, of course."

Her face flushed. "Where are you staying?"

"At the inn," Sadie said. "Until they can find a more permanent place. In fact, I'm about to check them in."

"I hope you put one of them in my suite."

"I promise."

"Good. One more thing. I know everyone in town, so if it's okay with you, I'll introduce you two around during our big July Fourth shindig."

"Why, it'd be an honor, Ms. Paine," Kat said.

Mirabelle's chest puffed. "Alright, then. I'll see you Saturday."

Emily waited for the self-appointed one-woman welcoming committee to move out of earshot. "You've met Willow Falls' modern version of a town crier."

"In that case, Missy and I will make her our number-one ally."

"That's a smart move," Sadie said. "Time to settle you into your new home."

They made their way through the park, past the hotel, to Willow Inn's front yard. Sadie led them up the steps.

The moment they stepped into the foyer, Missy's mouth fell open. "I've never been in a house this fancy." She stood under the chandelier and turned in a slow circle. "It's so pretty ... and big."

Sadie removed two keys from the pegboard. "Missy, you're in the Mirabelle Suite. Every room is named for someone important to the town."

"Interesting concept." Kat chuckled. "I assume there's more to Mirabelle's story than her role as the town's mouthpiece."

Sadie nodded. "She worked here as a housekeeper before Mama married Robert Liles."

"Now, that's a story I'm dying to hear. I want all the details."

"I promise. You're in the Nora Redding Suite. We named it after Emily's mother." Sadie handed Kat a key. "We have a no-smoking policy. Did you ditch your habit?"

"Not exactly. Don't worry. I won't light up inside."

The front door swung open, emitting a blast of warm air and Winston Hamilton. "Good afternoon, ladies."

Sadie spun toward him. "I hope you enjoyed lunch. We have two new guests who'll be joining you for breakfast." She introduced her friends.

Winston eyed Missy, then Kat. "How long are you staying?"

"Until we find a place to live."

Emily moved closer. "Kat's our new hotel manager."

"Interesting. You can learn a lot from Sadie. She's an excellent innkeeper."

"So I've heard."

"If you'll excuse me, I must work on my book." He nodded, then moved on to his suite.

Kat shook her head. "Long sleeves and a scarf in this heat? He's like a character straight out of a British comedy."

"One that pays for five months in advance," Sadie said.

"Did he win the lottery?"

"All we know is he's an author and a gentleman." Sadie plucked two keys off the pegboard. "Right now, I'll show you to your rooms."

Emily watched her mother escort her friends to the second floor. "This town is turning into a refuge for strange characters."

Rachel thumped her arm. "Fodder for future novels."

"If I ever fix the first one."

Chapter 10

Rachel tossed her script on the floor and glanced at her watch. Dennis Locke expected her to show up today. She shouldn't go alone. *Why did you walk out on me, Charlie?* She dressed in jeans, a light blue V-neck tee, and white sneakers, tucked her purse under her arm, then walked out of her suite.

"I've been wondering if you were coming out."

Charlie's voice caught her by surprise. He sat on the sofa, his ankle propped on his knee.

Rachel sat on a chair facing him. "How long have you been sitting here?"

"Long enough to meet Kat and Missy. My Dad checked in a half hour ago. Said Sadie looked like a million bucks."

"Same thing you told to me the day we met."

"So much for originality."

"You were sweet, considering I had a nasty cold and nearly sneezed all over you. I hear you're providing fireworks for tomorrow's celebration."

"Ten minutes' worth. About last night." He uncrossed his leg and leaned forward. "I'm sorry I acted like a jerk."

"You were upset."

"I should have stayed."

"You're here now."

"I'm not leaving you again." A smile lit his face. "How about I treat you to lunch."

"The thing is … I promised to bring a friend up from Atlanta. I meant to ask you to go with me …"

"Your ride or mine?"

"Yours."

He stood and reached for her hand.

They left the inn and headed to his Ford F-150. He held the passenger door open. She climbed in and set her purse on the floor.

He rounded the front and slid into the driver's seat.

She leaned across the console and kissed his cheek. "Thank you for coming back."

"I never really left." He backed onto Main Street and drove past four more Southern-style, two-story houses and one Newport-style mansion. He turned on the radio and tapped the steering wheel to the beat of the country-pop tune. "Are we headed to the city or the suburbs?"

"Downtown. I'll direct you when we exit the highway."

"Fair enough." Two miles from Willow Falls, he pulled off the road. "See those stakes over there? They mark the entrance to the winery. It'll sit up on that ridge and overlook the vineyard. A crew's coming in next week to cut a road."

Rachel's gaze shifted to acres of grapevine trellises and rootstock stretching across gentle rolling hills. "It looks a lot different without all the trees and brush. When do you expect your first harvest?"

"In a couple of years. Until then, we'll purchase grapes and create some varietals—"

"Some what?"

"Cabs, merlot, chardonnays, maybe a blend. That'll help us publicize the vineyard."

She pointed to a structure resembling a miniature barn. "What is that?"

"A temporary office and dog shelter."

"When did you buy a dog?"

"I didn't. The trainer's bringing two next week. They're working animals, trained to keep wildlife away from the vines."

"Huh, there's a lot more to this wine business than one might think."

"One more reason I needed to move here." He pulled back onto the road. Enthusiasm punctuated his comments as he launched into a dialogue about grape varieties and the production processes for red and white wines.

"You've become quite an expert."

"The wine business is way more fascinating than I expected."

"I can tell."

They talked about the winery, then shifted to neutral topics. When the Atlanta skyline came into view, Rachel glanced at Charlie. "There's something I need to tell you about the guy we're picking up."

"Let me guess. He's your former boyfriend."

"Hardly. He's a young veteran."

"One of the good guys.

"There's more. He um … lives in a homeless shelter."

"You're joking. Right?"

"Seems he's down on his luck."

"Wait a minute." He stared wide-eyed at her, then faced the windshield. "Are you telling me you were planning to pick him up on your own? And how is it you know him in the first place?"

"I met him last year not long before you and I met. Something about him caught my attention. He took the money I dropped into his hat to the shelter—"

"And you knew that how?"

"I called the shelter. The manager confirmed his story. Anyway, I ran into him again a couple of days ago. That's when I invited him to stay at Willow Inn for the Fourth."

Charlie shook his head.

"I don't even know if he'll come with us. Regardless, I have to show up because I told him I would."

"Does Sadie know he's homeless?"

"I told her this morning. She said he'd fit right in with three ex-cons."

"Three?"

"Oops. I wasn't supposed to say anything." She stared at his profile. "You have to swear not to breathe a word to anyone."

"Scout's honor."

Rachel brought him up to speed.

"A Brit, three parolees, and a homeless vet. Good theme for a country song or a crazy sitcom. Where is this homeless shelter?"

"Take the first exit past Georgia Tech. If he's hanging out on the sidewalk, I'll assume he rejected my offer."

They drove down Spring Street, past the Peachtree Plaza Hotel. "I don't see him anywhere."

"Are you sure you want to go through with this?"

"Positive."

Charlie found a parking spot, then escorted Rachel across the street.

Inside the shelter, a gentleman greeted them. "I'm guessing you folks are here for Dennis."

Rachel nodded. "We are."

"These guys are used to people letting them down. I'm glad you showed up. I'll bring him out."

He returned escorting a clean-shaven man dressed in khaki slacks, a polo shirt, and sneakers. His hair had been trimmed; his eyes were clear and sharp. The scent of soap and Old Spice drifted around him. He carried a duffle bag and a bag of dog food. His dog walked beside him. "Can I bring Sarge?"

Rachel hesitated.

"I'm Charlie Bricker. The inn doesn't allow pets, but the house I'm renting has a fenced backyard. Your dog's welcome to stay there."

"Thanks, she's never been alone."

"Then it's settled," Rachel said. "It looks like we're ready to go."

"Yes ma'am."

They left the shelter and headed to the truck. Dennis tossed his duffle in the bed and climbed into the back seat. Sarge jumped in beside him. He tapped Rachel's shoulder and handed her a small stack of bills. "This will help pay for the room."

She opened her mouth to decline until she noticed Charlie's slight headshake. "Oh, okay, thank you."

Charlie winked, then cranked the engine and pulled into the street.

She counted the money. Fifty-seven dollars. How many days of panhandling did it represent?

Silence filled the cab until they merged onto the interstate. Charlie glanced in the rearview mirror. "I hear you're a veteran. What branch?"

"Army."

"Where were you deployed?"

"Middle East."

"Did you see much action?"

"Too much."

More silence.

Rachel glanced over her shoulder. "What did you do before the army?"

"Construction work with my dad."

"Have you considered working with him again?"

"Can't. He's dead."

"I'm so sorry." The character in her upcoming audition came to mind. A tragedy drove her to the streets. Maybe something tragic happened to Dennis. "Why'd you name your dog Sarge?"

"To honor the Army's canine units."

"She looks a little like my sister's dog, Cody."

"I rescued her after a stray dropped a litter in that park across from the hotel."

"She seems like a sweet dog."

"She wouldn't hurt a fly."

Country music and idle conversation filled the cab during the two-hour drive. When they arrived in Willow Falls, Charlie drove to Emily's parents' home. "We'll drop Sarge off, then check you into the inn." He climbed from the truck and opened the gate to the backyard.

Dennis removed two bowls and a rawhide bone from his duffle, then led Sarge inside the gate. The dog bounded around the wooded space, sniffing. "She likes it here." He found a spigot, filled one bowl with water, and placed it on the stoop by the back door to the garage. "Do you mind if I prop this open for her?"

"Not at all."

Dennis wedged a small branch under the door, then whistled, bringing his dog springing to his side. He squatted and scratched behind her ears. "I'll check on you later." He peeled the wrapper off the bone. "This will keep you busy for a while."

Sarge wagged her tail, then carried her treat to a shady spot and stretched out to gnaw.

"Maybe I should stay here with her. She eats first thing in the morning."

"No need," said Charlie. "I'd planned to stay here tomorrow. One day sooner won't make a difference."

Rachel touched his arm. "Are you sure?"

"Positive. Besides, my sleeping bag's already inside. After we get Dennis checked into Willow Inn, the three of us can grab dinner at Pepper's."

She kissed his cheek. "What would I do without you, Charlie Bricker?"

Chapter 11

Emily carried her laptop to the living room, set it on the coffee table, and sat cross-legged on the floor. Her babies crawled behind her. Cody padded in and sprawled in the center of the room, enticing Jane to climb on his back. "You didn't know you doubled as a horse, did you fella? At least we don't have to strap a saddle on you."

Cody's tail thumped the floor in a lazy rhythm.

Clair grasped the table edge, pulled up, and inched toward Emily.

"Hey, pretty girl, do you want to sit with me?" She placed the baby in her lap and opened her manuscript. "Mommy has a lot of work to do to make her book ready for prime time." She stared at the screen, wondering how to begin. "Should I start with chapter one or try to figure out how to correct everything the editor pointed out? Or delete the whole thing and start over?"

Clair sneezed.

"You're right, that's too extreme."

The back door banged closed, followed by footsteps striking the kitchen floor. "Where are my girls?"

"In the living room, honey."

Scott strolled in and dropped on the floor beside Emily, compelling Jane to abandon her furry friend and crawl onto her daddy's lap. He kissed her cheek, then checked her anklet.

"Still having trouble telling them apart?"

"Just making sure."

"How'd everything go at the store today?"

"Couple of customers wandered in. Gertie bought two bars of lavender soap and said I needed to add a soda fountain."

"Her solution for fixing Willow Falls' woes."

"Too bad it's not that simple. I don't know how much longer I can keep the lights turned on." He tapped her computer screen. "Is that your novel?"

"Mm-hmm. The more I look at it, the more I realize it's full of novice mistakes. I was naïve to think my first attempt would be publication-ready."

"Good thing you found out."

"Problem is, I sent the first three chapters to a lot of publishers."

"Since only one bothered to respond, maybe no one read them."

Clair giggled and pressed a key, sending a string of *n*'s dancing across the page. "Are you trying to help Mommy make her book all better?" Emily deleted her daughter's contribution, then moved the laptop out of reach. "I've been thinking."

"Should I alert the media?" Scott snapped his fingers. "Oh wait, you are the media."

"I'm serious."

"Okay, lay it on me."

"You remember how half the town shunned Mama Sadie when she returned from prison."

"Your point is?"

"She could have left Willow Falls and avoided the ridicule. But she stayed and made a life for herself. Kat Williams is in her forties with a criminal record. She's taking a salary that's a fraction of what she's worth and starting her career from scratch, in a town on the brink of failure."

"What does all that have to do with your book?"

"When I decided to write it, I believed it would make a difference."

Clair pulled to her feet, plopped onto her diaper-padded fanny, then crawled to Cody. Jane followed her.

"The editor who sent me that letter didn't have to take the time to give me feedback. But she did. At first, I saw it as a slap in the face."

"And now?"

"I know she wanted to help me." Emily turned toward Scott. "I can't let my wounded pride keep me from taking her comments to heart."

"Does that mean you figured out what on-the-nose means?"

"Not yet, but I intend to. What's more, I've decided to clear my calendar of everything that isn't essential and devote the next two, maybe three months to fixing this story. Then I'll work like crazy to find a publisher. Go to conferences, knock on publishers' doors, whatever it takes."

"That's a big commitment."

"I know, but it's important to you, Mom and Dad, the whole town. Which means I can't let anything stand in my way."

"Have I told you lately how proud I am of you?"

"Does that mean you don't think I'm nuts?"

"Nah. I still think you're a crazy, but the good kind."

She touched Scott's smile dimple. "You know, I'll need your help."

"How about I start tonight."

"What do you have in mind?"

"Firing up the grill and cooking us some burgers." He stood and lifted Jane.

"Now you're talking." Emily scooped Clair into her arms, followed Scott to the kitchen, and placed her in the playpen beside Jane.

Scott moved behind her and slid his arms around her waist. "A gorgeous, talented wife and two beautiful daughters. I'm the luckiest man in the world."

Emily turned and melted into his arms. "No matter what happens, we will always have each other."

Chapter 12

Rachel's alarm awakened her from a deep sleep. Her body yearned to press snooze and pull the covers over her head until her mind nudged her to crawl out of bed. Today she'd experience her first small-town July Fourth celebration.

Twenty minutes after a hot shower, dressed in white shorts, a blue tank top, and white tennis shoes, her hair pulled into a ponytail, she tapped on the Roger Redding Suite. Dennis, wearing faded jeans and a tan T-shirt, opened the door.

"I hope you slept well."

He stepped out. "It took a while to get used to the quiet."

"I know what you mean."

The door to the Everett Hayes Suite opened. "Good morning," Charlie's dad said as he closed the door behind him.

"Nice to see you again, Brick. I'd like you to meet my friend, Dennis Locke."

He extended his hand. "Any friend of Rachel's is a friend of mine." A grin deepened the lines around his eyes and creases in his cheeks.

"It's a pleasure, sir."

"I hope you're hungry. Sadie serves hearty breakfasts."

As they headed to the first floor, the aroma of smoked bacon and coffee set off a rumbling sensation in Rachel's stomach. They joined Kat, Missy, and Winston around the dining room table. She introduced Dennis, then sat between him and Brick.

Kat slathered jam on a biscuit. "What brings you to Willow Falls, Dennis?"

"Rachel invited me up for the holiday."

"Small town's a good place to spend the Fourth."

Sadie entered carrying a large tray. "I hope everyone has a big appetite." She passed plates heaped with bacon, scrambled eggs, grits, and biscuits.

"A real Southern breakfast." Kat licked her lips. "It doesn't do much for the waistline, but it's fodder for the soul." She bit into her biscuit.

A smile lit Sadie's face. "How's everyone enjoying their stay?"

"Willow Falls is a nice town. I do have one complaint." Winston pointed his fork at Kat. "She smokes outside my window."

"Excuse me?" Kat's eyes narrowed. "Your window and blinds are closed."

"I like fresh air. I might want to open it sometime."

"In this heat?"

"Evenings cool down."

"Don't get your scarf in a wad—"

"It's called an ascot."

"For you and your ascot, I'll pick a different spot to light up."

"Good."

"Then it's settled." Sadie refreshed Winston's coffee.

Rachel glanced at Kat's smirk. *What's with her snarky attitude?* She made a mental note to ask Sadie, then tuned into the blend of clinking utensils and conversation about the vineyard, Kat's new job, and July Fourth. Only one of the guests sitting around the table qualified as a bona fide tourist, and according to Sadie, the inn didn't have a single new reservation. How could it survive without paying guests? Had anyone told Kat about the threat to yank the funding?

"… What's it about, Rachel?"

"Pardon me?"

"The role." Kat grinned. "We were talking about your audition?"

"Oh, sorry." As she described the part and explained the potential impact on her career, a twinge of guilt pricked her conscience. Truth was, she couldn't wait to leave the troubled town and return to the city.

When they finished eating, Sadie gave Rachel a Styrofoam to-go box and utensils wrapped in a napkin. "For Charlie."

"Thanks, I imagine he missed your breakfast."

She touched her daughter's cheek. "You've found yourself a great guy. Hang on to him."

What prompted her to say that? "I will."

"Good. Now scoot before his breakfast gets cold."

Rachel dismissed her mother's remark as coincidental as she and Dennis left the inn and drove to the home where Emily grew up. She followed her friend to the backyard. His shrill whistle brought Charlie, barefoot and shirtless, his hair tousled, to the patio door. Sarge bounded out behind him. "Your pup didn't take to being alone, so I let her sleep inside."

"Thanks, man, I owe you."

"No big deal. She's a good dog."

Rachel's pulse pounded as her eyes drifted to Charlie's chest and arms. At five foot ten, solid muscle made him look more like an athlete than a vintner.

He moved closer. "Is that a care package?"

She blinked. "Breakfast, from Mama Sadie."

"She's one great lady." He wrapped his arm around Rachel's shoulders, sending a quiver through her limbs. "Come on into my new digs."

"I, uh … Dennis, do you want to join us?"

"Think I'll stay out here with Sarge."

Charlie squeezed Rachel's shoulder. "Guess it's you and me." He led her through the kitchen, pulled a bottle of juice from the fridge, then moved to the den.

"This is the first time I've been in Emily's parents' home."

"It's a good house, plenty big for one guy." He sat on the floor and leaned his back against the wall.

"When does your furniture arrive?"

"Early Monday morning." He opened his breakfast. "You head back to Atlanta tomorrow, right?"

She nodded. "Auditions begin first thing the next morning."

"Dennis just arrived. Maybe he'd like to hang around for a few more days."

"Instead of going back with me?"

"If he wants to return to the city later, I'll take him."

She sat beside him. "Are you thinking of Dennis or me?"

"Both." He forked a mouthful of scrambled eggs.

Rachel wrapped her arms around her shins. "Mama Sadie's right. You are a good guy."

He swallowed. "Remember that when you're on stage kissing some handsome actor dude."

She tilted her head. "Are you admitting you're jealous?"

"Nah … well, maybe a little."

"You don't have anything to worry about."

"I hope not."

Rachel rested her chin on her knees and tried to imagine how she'd react during a love scene in front of an audience watching her every move. Could she pull it off, or would she come across as stiff and unnatural? She hadn't kissed anyone other than Charlie since she graduated from college.

"Hey, where'd you go?"

His voice snapped her back to the moment. "Sorry, my mind wandered off."

He grinned. "Not too far, I hope. This is my first July Fourth away from the big city."

"Hope you won't be disappointed."

"Are you kidding? I planned a killer fireworks show." He closed the container, pushed off the floor, then helped her to her feet. "Before we leave, I need to shower. While you're waiting, why don't you mention my offer to Dennis?"

"I will."

He kissed her cheek, then left.

Rachel found Dennis sitting on the grass, tossing a stick to Sarge. She sat beside him. "Your pup seems to like it here."

"First time she's been in a yard."

"Would you like to stay in town a while longer?"

Sarge dashed back to Dennis and dropped the stick at his feet. He picked it up and tossed it high. "I don't have any more money."

"The inn's kind of in a slump right now, so it's good to have guests, even if they don't pay. Besides, the cash you gave me covers breakfast for at least five days."

"I won't stay unless I can earn my keep."

"Maybe you could trade some work for room and board."

"Seems fair."

"Does that mean you'd like to stay a while?"

He shrugged. "Might as well. I don't have anything to go back to."

"Okay, then." Rachel plucked a weed from the lawn and watched two squirrels racing across a low-hanging branch.

Sarge dropped beside Dennis, panting, her tongue dangling from her mouth, dripping. He stroked her back. "Thanks for inviting me."

"You're welcome, Private First Class Locke."

"You remembered."

"Yeah, I did."

Chapter 13

Emily pushed the stroller up the alley beside Hayes General Store, then snaked her way around families gathered in the park. Cody padded beside her, panting, his tail slapping arms as he passed. Scott followed, carrying four lawn chairs and a quilt. He spread the blanket under a willow oak, close to the retaining wall, then set up the chairs. "Anything else you need from the car other than the coolers?"

She pointed to an assortment of boxes and coolers stashed underneath a row of tables covered with red, white, and blue cloths lined up on the blocked-off section of Main Street. "You can put the cookies over there with the rest of the food."

"After I steal one, maybe two or three."

"Exactly like you did every time you came to my house when we were teenagers."

"Who could resist your mom's oatmeal-raisin cookies?"

"Obviously not you or Dad." Emily lifted the twins—dressed in matching red-and-white-striped rompers—from the stroller. She removed a bag of toys from the back pocket, then sat beside her babies and focused on people arriving, turning the park into a patchwork of colorful blankets and outdoor seats. The scene warmed her heart. Kids and adults stood in line to take turns at three cornhole games. American flags attached to light poles fluttered in the breeze. Families cooled in the lake. Teenagers gathered on the floating platform anchored thirty yards from the wall.

Clair snuggling with Cody made her smile. "You love your doggie, don't you, sweet girl?" She paused. "When I was a little girl, my mom and dad often brought me to the park for a picnic. Sometimes your daddy's family came here at the same time."

As Emily tuned into the chatter going on around her, it didn't take long to discover the Travel Titan's podcast topped the list of topics. She sighed and refocused her attention on Jane and Clair, until Scott returned, pulling a wheeled cooler.

He settled on one of the chairs, removed his ball cap, and swiped his hand across his forehead. "I've never heard so many folks ready to call it quits."

"That Titan woman's punch in Willow Falls' collective gut forced everyone to take a hard look at our town. Including me." Emily moved off the ground and sat beside him. "We all need to do way more than look. I mean, how difficult would it have been to take that sign down?"

"What sign?"

"The cinema marquee. The missing *n* is tacky as all get-out."

"Guess nobody noticed." Scott opened the cooler and removed a bottle of water, two cans of lemonade, and two sippy cups.

"Or thought it mattered. Someone better start paying attention to the details."

"You sure are riled up." He handed out the drinks, then poured water into a container for Cody.

"For good reason." She pulled the tab on her lemonade. "I'm going to bust my behind making my book publication-ready. I don't want people who read about our past to come here and find our present dreary and disappointing."

He nodded toward the hotel. "Mirabelle making the rounds with our newest residents should give folks something positive to talk about."

"Our mail lady might be the biggest mouth in the South, but one thing's certain. She loves this town."

"So do a lot of people."

Emily sipped her drink and watched Kat and Missy's newest fan work the crowd, then spotted her sister. "It looks like Charlie, Rachel, her Atlanta rescue, and his dog are headed our way."

"Sadie and your sister are bringing some colorful characters to Willow Falls."

"Interesting choice of words."

"I meant metaphorically."

"I know."

When the trio plus one canine arrived, Rachel pushed her sunglasses to the top of her head. She introduced her guest and shared Dennis's plan to stick around.

"I imagine Mama Sadie will find plenty of work for you," Emily said as she eyed the young man.

Sarge's and Cody's tails wagged while they sniffed each other and forged a doggie friendship.

Dennis sat on the ground. Rachel and Charlie settled on chairs across from Emily and Scott. They talked about Charlie moving into his new home until Scott jumped off his seat. "First time I've seen that beauty around here."

Emily thumped his leg and chuckled. "Are you ogling another woman, honey?"

"Never. A fifties Caddy. Come on, Charlie, Dennis, let's check it out."

As the guys headed toward the street, Emily noticed a woman stepping from the antique red convertible with whitewall tires. "I think that's Naomi Jasper."

"The famous artist?"

"Rumor is she's coming back home to retire."

Rachel lowered her sunglasses. "Oh my gosh, look. In front of the red Cadillac. Mama Sadie and Brick. I think they're together."

"You mean like a couple?"

"Uh-huh."

"That's not possible."

"Why not?"

"For one thing, he's a lot older than her."

"Twelve years isn't all that much, and why wouldn't he be attracted to her? She looks fabulous."

Emily noted Sadie's white capri pants, red tank top under an open blue-and-white short-sleeved shirt. "Like a movie star."

"And Brick's handsome in his own way."

"Even if they're nothing more than friends, they're bound to crank up the local rumor mill."

Rachel shook her head. "This town definitely needs more entertainment."

"Fat chance of that happening."

Brick and Sadie stepped off the sidewalk and snaked their way through the crowd, stopping every few feet to chat with locals.

Twenty minutes passed before Scott and Charlie returned and relayed details about Naomi's ride.

"Okay, we understand. The car's incredible," Emily said. "We want to know what you learned about its owner."

"You mean besides the fact that she has the coolest car in town?" He opened the cooler and removed three bottles of beer.

"All that time and you didn't learn a thing?"

"You're cute when you're peeved." Scott handed Charlie and Dennis beers, then sat beside Emily and patted her knee. "The rumor's true."

"She is moving back?"

He grinned. "Yep."

"Finally, some good news."

"That's some vehicle," Brick said as he and Sadie stepped around one more family. The car conversation resumed as he pulled two canvas bags off his shoulder and set up a pair of sling lawn chairs.

The twins crawled toward Sadie the moment she settled beside Brick. She picked up one baby, Brick the other.

"I'm ready for a cold drink," Kat's voice boomed as she and Missy approached.

Emily opened the cooler. "Beer, water, or a soft drink?"

"I'd love a beer. But have to stick to soft drinks."

"Parole requirement," whispered Sadie.

Kat pulled the tab on a Coke can, took a drink, then settled on the quilt. "Almost as good as a brew."

"What about you, Missy?" Emily kept the cooler open.

"Coke's fine."

"Coming right up."

"I want to hear all about your introduction to the natives," Sadie said

Kat swiped her fingers across her upper lip. "Missy and I met lots of nice people, with a slew of negative attitudes about the town's future. One thing's certain, the inn's mysterious Brit has everyone's curiosity roused."

Emily scanned the crowd. "I don't see him anywhere."

"He's staying in his suite today." Sadie bounced Clair on her knee. "Says he's in the writing zone."

"I can relate." Emily laced her fingers behind her neck and watched Missy and Dennis glancing at each other. She assumed the pretty young blonde might be one big motivation for him to stick around. For the remainder of the afternoon, she relaxed, enjoyed laughing with her family and new friends, and played with her twins.

The adults shared stories about past July Fourth festivities, debated the benefits of life in small towns versus big cities, and discussed why guys were fascinated by old cars. At six, they joined residents in the buffet line and filled their plates, while Mama Sadie stayed with her grandbabies.

When the sun made its final dip below the horizon, Mayor Nathan's voice crackled over the ancient loudspeakers as he thanked everyone for coming out. "And now, sponsored by Willow Oak Vineyard and Winery, we present Willow Falls' Fourth of July spectacular."

Patriotic music began to play. Emily and Scott each cradled a baby in their arms. As bright colors exploded and danced across the sky, Emily's heart soared. Jane and Clair teetered between wide-eyed wonder and loud-bang-triggered lip quivers. When the show ended with a dazzling display, residents cheered and applauded.

Scott clasped Charlie's shoulder. "Best fireworks show our town has seen in a long time, maybe ever."

"I came up with the idea. Dad paid the bill."

Brick shrugged. "No big deal."

The world around her enveloped Emily like a warm bath. At least for the moment, all seemed right in Willow Falls.

Chapter 14

Rachel laid her fork on her plate and glanced across the table at Kat's tight jaw and narrowed eyes as Winston carried on about life back in England. What about him irritated her? His comments? Mannerisms?

Sadie stepped in from the kitchen carrying a coffee carafe. "How'd you like breakfast?"

"Best ever," Charlie said.

Kat held her cup out for a refill. "Been years since I've had such fancy fare."

Dennis nodded. "The egg dish—"

"Frittata."

"Was mighty fine, ma'am."

Brick tipped his orange-juice glass toward her. "Sadie Liles, you're a first-class innkeeper."

Her cheeks flushed as she refilled coffee cups, then returned to the kitchen.

Rachel touched Charlie's arm. "I want to talk to Mama Sadie before I leave."

"I'll wait on the porch."

She pushed away from the table and followed her mother. "Interesting mix of guests."

"Makes my job fun."

"I'm curious about Kat's harsh reaction to Winston."

"It's his accent."

"She doesn't like foreigners?'

"Back in prison, she spent a lot of time protecting Missy from a hard-core lifer who claimed she came from a well-to-do family in Manchester, England." Sadie wiped her hands on a towel. "The woman's swearing would make a sailor blush. Funny thing is, her British accent made her seem more like royalty than a foul-mouthed criminal."

"So, now Kat doesn't trust anyone whose accent sounds like hers?"

"It takes time to forget all the junk that happens behind bars. Once she's busy with hotel business, she'll move on."

"I suppose that makes sense." She stroked her mother's arm. "I'm going to miss you."

"Don't forget about us little people when you become a big star down there in Atlanta."

Rachel embraced her mother. "I love you so much."

"Next week you show that director what you've got, honey."

"I'll do my best."

She joined Charlie on the porch, leaned on the railing, and watched a colorful butterfly flit among the coral begonias Sadie had planted. "I enjoyed yesterday more than I expected."

"Holidays bring out the best of small-town life."

"Thanks for coming over for breakfast."

"I didn't want to miss seeing you before you took off." He flicked a spider off the rail. "Dad's staying in Willow Falls for a while. Maybe through Christmas."

"At least Sadie will have two paying guests." She spotted a squirrel clawing the ground. "Is Brick thinking about moving to Willow Falls?"

"What brought that up?"

"It seems logical since he owns the vineyard and winery."

"He's taking a bigger interest in the business side."

"There you go."

"But moving here? I doubt it. He's a big-city guy."

She glanced at Charlie's profile. "So were you."

"Good point. I guess it's possible the town will grow on him." He spun around and leaned back against the railing. "Are you nervous about tomorrow?"

"A little. Getting that part is a big deal. I've been thinking … two hours isn't that far away. You can stay at my townhouse when you come to Atlanta."

"After my dogs arrive, it'll be hard to leave."

Rachel turned and focused on their reflection in the parlor window. "While Brick's here, can't he take care of them?"

Charlie stroked her arm, awakening every nerve ending in her body. "I know that role means a lot to you."

She sensed the urge to leave before his touch compelled her to stay. "I … need to head out." She took a step toward the stairs.

"Wait."

She stopped, then turned and gazed into his eyes.

He gathered her in his arms. "I'll be here when you're ready to come back."

"You mean the world to me." She breathed in his musky scent, then pulled away and dashed down the stairs to her car. Seconds after pulling onto Main Street, she slammed on the brakes. *I have to go back.*

She pushed the driver's door open and stepped out.

A quick glance at the porch confirmed Charlie had already gone.

Her heart leapt to her throat. She slipped back in the driver's seat and drove out of town. When she reached the vineyard, she pulled off County Road. A miniature barn-like structure drew her attention. She stepped from her car and moved closer. A swinging pet door had been set in the bottom of the entrance. She tried turning the knob and found it locked, proving Charlie hadn't abandoned all his city habits. She peered in the window at a desk, straight-back chair, a file cabinet, and a pallet for the dogs. She turned toward the vines and tried to imagine waking up every morning to the view.

"You're getting way ahead of yourself, Rachel." She returned to her car, plugged her phone in, and headed south.

Two hours after leaving the vineyard, Rachel drove into the garage on the lower level of her three-story townhouse. After pressing the button to close the door, she stepped out and yanked her suitcase from the trunk. Eager to prepare for her audition, she climbed to the main floor and set her bag on the living room floor.

She ran her fingers along the soft, velvety fabric on the back of her diamond-patterned couch and glanced around the space she'd decorated in a blend of contemporary and traditional style. Memories of taking a job at her father's firm two weeks after graduating from the University of Georgia played in her mind. She'd bought her townhouse six months later and had called it home for eight years.

She plucked a life-sized, brown-and-white puppy off the floor and hugged it to her chest. The gift from her mother on her seventh birthday when her father refused to grant her wish for a real dog still gave her comfort. "You understand why acting is so important to me, don't you, Brownie?" She stared at the pup, then shook her head. "Why am I talking to a stuffed animal?"

She set the toy on the couch, then pulled her phone from her purse and pressed Charlie's number. The call went straight to voice mail. "Hey, I'm back in Atlanta. I'll let you know how everything goes tomorrow." She tossed the phone aside.

"Quit stalling and go to work, Rachel." She moved to the kitchen, pulled a bottle of water from the fridge, then returned to the living room, and removed her script from her suitcase. She spent the rest of the afternoon studying Penelope's lines and practicing scenes until Charlie's ringtone startled her. "Hey."

"Sorry I missed your call. I spent the afternoon walking the vineyard."

"That's okay. I've been crazy busy studying the script."

"I won't keep you. Just want you to know I'm rooting for you."

"Thanks, Charlie. Your support means a lot."

"Call me when it's over."

"I will." She ended the call and returned to the task at hand. At nine o'clock she changed into pajamas and climbed into bed, confident she'd done everything within her power to prepare for the audition she knew would change her life.

Chapter 15

Rachel's eyes popped open ten minutes before her alarm was set to wake her. She showered, dried her hair, and applied makeup, then headed downstairs. She fixed coffee and poured it into an insulated to-go cup. Too tense to eat, she dropped a granola bar in her purse and dashed to the garage. After backing into the street, she turned toward downtown and gripped the steering wheel, ready to fight Atlanta's Monday morning traffic jams.

Twenty minutes later, she found a parking spot, hastened two blocks to the theater, and stepped inside. The black-and-white marble floor and deep-red upholstered walls in the lobby screamed elegance. Inside the theater, the scent of fresh paint served as the only indication the venue once functioned as a retail space. As her eyes adjusted to the dim overhead lights and dark walls, she noticed more than a dozen actors.

She selected an empty seat, three rows from the front, beside a stunning brunette. The woman's face beamed as she extended her hand. "Hi, I'm Michelle."

"Nice to meet you. I'm Rachel. I saw you in a musical at the Alliance a couple of months back. You were really good."

"Thanks, I loved playing that character. What part are you auditioning for?"

"Penelope."

"The lead. Same here. The script is excellent. I hear it was the director's first attempt at writing."

Rachel eyed the other candidates. She recognized two women from plays she'd seen. Both were loaded with talent. "What else do you know about him?"

"He left Atlanta a decade ago to work off-Broadway. Rumor is he returned to bring New York vibes back to his hometown. Did you notice the posters in the lobby?"

"I didn't pay much attention."

"Take a look when you leave. They're all plays he directed." Michelle nodded toward the front. "There he is."

A handsome man with dark hair, a mustache, and a goatee walked onto the stage. "Good morning. My name is Gordon Wells. This morning I'll start auditioning for the five supporting roles. When I've narrowed that field, I'll move to the male lead and finish with the Penelope character. In addition to individual skills, I'm looking for players who connect well with each other. Which means I'll ask you to do some scenes with other actors." He pointed to the front row. "My assistant has your résumé and will call each of you to the stage."

A middle-aged woman with salt-and-pepper hair, holding a clipboard, stood and waved. "Welcome, everyone."

Gordon stepped off the stage and scanned the crowd. "This play is the result of my year-long effort to bring a taste of Broadway to regional theater. Atlanta is already a mecca for the film industry. I believe it's destined to become the South's leading live-theater venue. A lot is on the line. Therefore, I'm trusting each of you to bring your A-game. Any questions?"

He waited a few seconds. "Okay then, let's begin. I need the four front rows cleared."

The actors scrambled to change seats. Gordon and his assistant settled in the center of the second row and called their first candidate.

Rachel opted for the last row.

Michelle scooted beside her. "There's no fudging with this guy."

"No kidding." She tucked her purse under the seat. "Going last gives us time to figure out what he's looking for."

"He'll also expect a lot more from us."

"Good point." Throughout the morning, she watched his technique as he put each actor through the paces. At noon, he announced finalists for the supporting roles. Following a catered lunch, he began auditions for the male lead.

As the afternoon moved on, Rachel's stomach progressed from churning to full-throttle flip-flops. She drank two bottles of water and dashed to the restroom twice. At two thirty, Gordon thanked the male candidates and ordered the contenders for Penelope's role to line up on the stage.

"It's showtime," whispered Michelle.

Rachel joined her five competitors. Her back stiffened while Gordon walked the line and eyed each woman as if inspecting pieces of art. When finished, he took a step back and crossed his arms. "Everything hinges on Penelope. The audience must connect with her on a deep, emotional level. She's strong yet vulnerable. Deeply hurt yet eager to please."

An empty sensation settled in the pit of Rachel's stomach as he continued to describe his expectations. Although she'd prepared well, she knew her résumé and her experience were painfully thin. If she didn't outperform her competition, she'd be out on her ear.

When he finished his monologue, he ordered the women back to their seats, then conferred with his assistant.

Rachel leaned close to Michelle. "If he calls me last, I'll be so nervous I'll sweat like a racehorse."

"Don't you know Southern women don't sweat? They glisten."

"In that case, I'll glisten like a sweaty racehorse."

Michelle chuckled. "Much better."

When the director called his first candidate, Rachel released a sigh. At least she'd have the chance to watch one audition before her turn.

For the next two hours, he auditioned three more women.

Rachel uncapped a water bottle, considered her bladder, then recapped it. "One thing's clear. One of us will go last."

"Michelle, you're up," the assistant's voice boomed.

"Congratulations, you drew the last straw," Michelle whispered as she stood and moved to the aisle.

Rachel's heart raced as she watched her new friend perform with grace and ease. She connected well with the two male-lead candidates and responded to coaching like a pro. When the audition finished, Gordon thanked her for a primo performance.

When he called Rachel's name, she gulped a lungful of air and stepped into the aisle. She'd have to deliver the performance of a lifetime.

Michelle passed her. "Break a leg, kid."

"Thanks." She climbed the stairs and turned toward the front.

Gordon eyed her. "A red-headed Penelope. Interesting concept. Let's see if you can act. Take it from the top of page four."

Rachel opened the script, relieved she'd rehearsed the section more than once. She imagined standing on the Alliance Theatre stage. *And now, introducing Rachel Streetman, with her interpretation of Penelope.*

For nearly an hour, she poured her heart into playing the part alone and with other actors. She accepted direction and coaching with an appreciative attitude. Her muscles were relaxed and her confidence high until a romantic scene with a male candidate ended.

Gordon stood and approached the stage. "He's not playing the role of your brother, Rachel. You need to kiss him like a woman burning inside with unrequited love. Think you can do that?"

She hesitated. "Yes sir." She had to overcome her discomfort or throw away a chance to land the part. *Pretend he's Charlie.* She repeated her line, closed her eyes, and kissed the man with abandon.

Gordon applauded. "And, that, my friends, is what a proper stage kiss looks like. Thanks, honey, you two can take a seat." He climbed onto the stage. "Thank you all for your patience. Now that auditions are officially concluded, you can relax while we review our notes." He strolled off stage. His assistant followed him.

"I'm exhausted." Rachel dropped on the seat beside Michelle.

"Great audition. And that love scene, girl, you nailed it."

"Believe me, it didn't come easy."

"I know what you mean. I have to imagine kissing my boyfriend to make it through."

"Exactly what I did. Although, I'm not sure Charlie would understand."

"He'll get used to it." She pointed to the other performers gathered on the side. "Come on, let's join the others."

They mingled and exchanged praises to assuage fragile egos. The moment Gordon appeared center stage, all conversation stopped.

Rachel's pulse accelerated.

"First, thank you all for your patience and professionalism. Everyone here is talented; however, we had to choose those we believe are best suited for this play." He held up his clipboard and read the final selections for the supporting roles and the male lead. "That brings me to Penelope."

Rachel held her breath. *This is it. The moment of truth.*

Gordon paused for a long moment. "As I mentioned earlier, this is the most important role. We've managed to narrow the field to Rachel and Michelle. Fact is, I need more time to review my notes. I'll be in touch with both of you once I've made a final decision. We'll start rehearsals at nine Wednesday morning."

Michelle ran her finger along the back of the seat in front of her. "I have to admit I'm normally confident about my chances. Now, I'm sensing this might go your way."

"You have way more experience."

She touched Rachel's arm. "He didn't applaud my love scene. Whatever happens, I'm glad we met"

"So am I."

During the drive home, Rachel replayed Michelle's comment. Maybe she did fit Gordon's vision for Penelope more than Michelle. After all, he'd described the character as fiery.

Back at her townhouse, she grabbed a bottle of water from the fridge, carried it to the living room, and tuned the television to the local news. Her mind wandered to the audition until she heard the words "Willow Falls."

Chapter 16

Emily wiped her babies' faces, removed their bibs, then carried Clair from her highchair to the playpen. "I shouldn't be gone more than an hour."

Scott lifted Jane from her chair. "Why does Naomi want to meet you at the old cinema?"

"She didn't say. I'm guessing she wants me to write an article about her return."

"Why not show up tomorrow at *Willow Post* headquarters?"

"She's an artist. Creative people are sometimes quirky and unconventional."

"Like you and your sister?"

She patted Scott's cheek. "Are you calling us peculiar?" Emily's phone announced Rachel's ringtone. "Talk about timing." She pressed the Speaker icon. "Hey, how'd the audition go?"

"Is your television on?"

"No. Why?"

"A local reporter did a piece on Georgia towns likely to fail. You're not going to believe this. Willow Falls topped his list."

Scott slammed his fist on the counter. "Which station?"

Rachel relayed the information. "It won't help to tune in now."

"That's the last thing we need." His phone rang. "Nathan." He grabbed it and hastened to the patio.

Emily dropped onto a chair at the kitchen table. "So much for hiring a PR firm."

"Don't you know, negative news sells?"

"Not in the *Willow Post*. Back to your audition."

"It's not over yet. The director narrowed the lead to me and one other candidate."

"A fifty-fifty shot is promising."

"I think the odds are way more in my favor." Rachel shared the details.

"It sounds like the role is yours. Have you told Charlie?"

"I want to wait until it's official. Hold on a sec. Another call's coming in."

Scott walked back in. "Nathan caught the news."

Emily held her hand over her phone. "Was it as bad as Rachel said?"

"Unfortunately."

"Emily, are you still on the line?"

She moved her hand. "I'm here."

"Would you believe the director just called? He wants to meet me for dinner, at seven. Tonight."

"Oh my gosh, he's going to give you the good news in person. Call me later and tell me all about it."

"As soon as I know something definite." Rachel ended the call.

"Dinner with the director." Scott's eyes narrowed. "I hope he's one of the good guys."

"He's been living in New York. I imagine most people conduct business at restaurants. I can't keep our famous artist waiting." Emily slipped her phone in her purse and headed to the garage.

Five minutes later, she parked in front of the abandoned cinema and stepped onto the sidewalk. The faded *Jurassic Park III* poster taped to the inside of the ticket booth window caught her eye. Ironic that a movie about dinosaurs played the day the venue closed for good.

She approached the double glass doors and gripped the brass handle, tarnished with age. Inside, a musty odor permeated the narrow lobby. Dirt caked the faded, cracked linoleum floor. An orange-colored concession stand, with a lifetime of dents, lined the wall opposite the entrance. On each side of the stand, dark drapes covered openings. Emily sneezed as she pulled back one of the drapes, stepped up, and entered the two-story auditorium.

As her eyes adjusted to the dim light, she focused on rows of upholstered theater seats stretching from the back wall to ten feet from a raised platform. The elaborately carved copper ceiling and walls upholstered with heavy black-and-gold damask fabric hinted of a bygone era. Emily moved down one of the aisles dividing the rows into three sections.

A tall, attractive woman dressed in white slacks and a flowing, multi-colored blouse, appeared from behind the screen. "Back in the day, the entire town considered this a first-class theater." She descended the steps and extended her hand, jangling the array of bracelets adorning her arm. "I'm Naomi Jasper."

"I've heard a lot about you."

"And I you." She withdrew her hand and pointed to the balcony. "When I was a little girl, I spent a lot of weekends sitting up there, peering over the railing, watching stories unfold on the big screen. I especially liked *Lady and the Tramp*."

"My friends and I also spent a lot of Saturday afternoons here. I cried when Mom told me there wouldn't be any more movies in our town."

"What a shame the owners couldn't afford to keep it open."

"An unfortunate sign of the times."

"This place reminds me of Charleston's Dock Street Theatre, except it's a fraction of the size. I landed roles in a couple of plays in that historic venue."

"You're an artist and an actress?"

She brushed her fingers through her salt-and-pepper, stylishly cut hair. "They were small roles, but a nice break from my routine."

Emily locked eyes with Naomi. "I hear the rumors are true."

"You mean about me moving back to Willow Falls despite the flood of bad news? I'd always planned to retire here and turn the old homestead into an art museum."

"That'd be a huge plus for our town."

"Have you seen the studio behind the house?"

"Years ago, your parents gave me and some of my friends a tour."

"It's the perfect place to work."

"I take it you're not retiring from art."

"Honey, I'll keep on painting as long as these old fingers can hold a brush. Come with me. I have something to show you." Naomi sat in the front row, then removed a frayed, leather binder from beneath the seat. "I found this in an old trunk in my family's attic."

Emily sat beside her and fingered the cover. "This has been around a while."

"More than a hundred years. Go ahead, look inside."

She pulled back the cover. Her breath caught in her throat at the sight of a yellowed, typewritten cover page. "Willow Falls First Couple—A Three-Act Play."

"A partial script. My great grandfather, Eugene Butler, died before he finished writing."

"My novel is about Percy and Peaches."

"I know. Percy's Legacy. That's why I invited you here."

"I don't understand."

"Picture this theater restored to its glory days. The stage expanded to accommodate a play. Then imagine tourists pouring in, eager to watch a delightful story filled with laughs and tears about Willow Falls' beloved founders. A play co-written by one of the town's original inhabitants and a budding young novelist."

Emily's brows shot up. "You want me to finish writing it?"

"Write, cast, and direct it in time for the hotel's grand opening."

"All that in three months? First, I'm not qualified—"

"You're a writer and the only person in town who's capable of pulling it off."

"Writing a play isn't the same as writing a book, and I don't have a clue about casting or directing."

"Your sister's an actress. She could help you."

"Impossible. She's about to land a major role in a play back in Atlanta. Besides, this theater isn't set up for live performances."

"A situation I plan to remedy as soon as I can hire a construction crew."

"Look, I'm honored you're considering me. But the truth is I'm trying to make my novel ready for publication. No way I can squeeze one more item on my list."

"I realize I've sprung my request on you out of the blue. But I want you to think about it. People in our town need something positive to give them hope. Not to mention that I know a lot of influential people who support the arts and local theater. They'd be more than happy to spread the word."

"Why don't you recruit one of them to finish writing?"

"Because a big part of the appeal is a production created and performed by the town's descendants. In case you're wondering, I don't expect you to take the project without compensation. I'll pay you three thousand dollars and a percentage of the ticket sales."

Emily struggled to find the right words as she closed the script. "I … your offer is more than generous … it's …"

"Before you turn me down, will you at least give it serious consideration?"

She ran her fingernail along a scratch on the cover and pictured an old man pecking at an ancient typewriter. "Tomorrow night, Nathan's conducting a town hall meeting about Willow Falls' future. I'll let you know before it ends."

"Fair enough."

Emily handed the binder back and stood.

"Thank you for taking time away from your family to meet with me." Naomi pushed off her seat and tucked the binder under her arm. "I have a feeling something good is about to happen in our corner of Georgia."

Chapter 17

Emily left the theater and stopped on the sidewalk. She pictured the words "Percy's Legacy" on the marquee, replacing the For Rent sign with the missing *n*. She wiped a smudge off the ticket booth window and questioned how much strangers would pay to watch a play about the town she loved.

She stepped off the curb, climbed into her car, and drove the short distance home. She pulled into the garage, cut the engine, then leaned her head back and stared at her dad's toolbelt. The construction business he and her mom started from scratch had built, refurbished, or repaired dozens of homes in Willow Falls, including hers and Scott's. She shuddered at the possibility that everything her parents worked for could collapse and send dozens of people scrambling to unemployment lines.

We can't let biased internet and television stories destroy us. She stepped from the car, walked into the kitchen, and tossed her purse on the table. "I'm home."

"We're in the den."

She found Scott on the floor with the twins. The television was tuned to an Atlanta Braves game. "Folks around here are ticked. Had to turn the phone off to keep from throwing it in the trash. I hope you have better news."

"That depends."

He aimed the remote at the television and muted the sound. "Fill me in."

"One thing's for sure, Naomi's a dreamer." She sat beside him and shared details about the project and the offer.

His brows shot up. "Are you sure she said three thousand?"

"Positive."

"That's a lot of dough."

"I know. It's also a monumental task. Other than Naomi, I don't know a single person who has any acting experience. Even if I did, I don't have a clue how to audition people. And where on earth would I find a director? The high school's one and only drama teacher left town more than a year ago."

"Did you turn her down?"

"I promised to think it over. We need the cash. But what if I accept the project and the whole thing falls apart? Would I have to return the money?"

She pulled her knees up and wrapped her arms around her shins. "Then there's my book. Even if I do manage to attract a publisher, I don't have a clue how long it would take to make that much money. On the other hand, a lot more people could potentially read my book than schlep up here to watch a play."

"Your head must be spinning from your mental roller coaster ride."

"I must sound like a crazy lady."

"Mostly confused."

"There's a lot to think about." She watched a ballplayer smack the ball and race to second. The umpire signaled an out, sending him back to the dugout. "Just like Willow Falls. We never make it to third, much less home base."

"The town's due for a grand slam."

"In our dreams." Emily focused on the screen as another hitter stepped up to bat and struck out, ending the inning. "What do you think I should do?"

"I can't make the decision for you."

She scooped Clair into her arms and breathed in her sweet scent. "I love being a mom and spending time with our babies. Taking on Naomi's project would mean more time away from them. And yet ... with all this negative news I want to do all I can to help us and the town."

"You have to do what's best for you and your future."

She breathed deep and released a long sigh. "There's the problem. I don't know what that is."

"You'll figure it out."

"I told Naomi I'd have an answer by Tuesday night."

"You have some serious thinking ahead. I know what will help."

"Lots of prayer? And a giant crystal ball?"

"Sorry, sold out yesterday. Wait here." He pushed up and disappeared around the corner. Five minutes later, he returned carrying a tray with two bowls and four spoons.

"Hot fudge sundaes?"

"With whipped cream."

Clair crawled over and stuck her finger in the bowl. "Do you want a taste, sweet girl?" She wiped her baby's finger, then spooned a dab of ice cream into her mouth. Clair wrinkled her nose, then aimed straight toward the bowl. Emily moved it before her little fingers hit pay dirt. "Mommy will give you more."

Naomi's offer drifted back into her mind. She didn't know if a play could even begin to counter the negative publicity. Or if adding a wad of cash to their bank account could compensate for missing moments like this.

Chapter 18

Rachel flung her closet door open. Should she wear her slacks or change into a dress? "For goodness' sake, he invited you to a working dinner, not a date." On the other hand, if Gordon was still on the fence, a different outfit might project confidence and push him to make a decision. The real question, what would Penelope do?

She settled on a royal-blue dress, then refreshed her makeup and rushed from the third floor to ground level. As she backed her car out of the garage and headed to mid-town, her chest tightened. How should she react when he offered her the part? What if he rejected her? He wouldn't invite her to dinner to give her bad news. Maybe that's how people conducted business in New York.

She breathed deep to slow her heartbeat and tamp down her anxiety. By the time she turned her car over to a valet and entered the restaurant, she'd managed to assume an air of calm professionalism.

The hostess greeted her with a smile. "Good evening, do you have a reservation?"

"I'm meeting Gordon Wells."

"Yes ma'am. He's waiting for you." The woman led her to a plush, high-back booth shaped in a semicircle. Gordon stood and eyed her from head to toe. "You do have legs, and you look stunning in blue."

Heat flowed up to Rachel's cheeks. Maybe a dress wasn't such a good idea. She slid into the smooth leather booth and stopped across from the director. "I didn't expect to hear from you this soon."

He removed a bottle from a silver chiller and filled two glasses. "I ordered Sauvignon Blanc. Have you dined here before?"

"No, I haven't."

"My favorite mid-town restaurant. The food's exceptional and the location convenient. A block from my condo." He lifted his glass. "To a successful audition and future possibilities."

She tapped her glass to his, sensing he had already made up his mind.

The waiter approached with menus. "Good evening, Mr. Wells."

"How are you, Larry?"

"I'm good, sir. You'll be pleased to know Dover sole is on the menu tonight."

"Marvelous." Gordon eyed Rachel. "Chef Chad's specialty. Delicate white fish, sautéed in butter, with capers and a hint of lemon. I suggest the lobster bisque to start."

Did he expect her to accept his recommendation or make her own selection? She did like both dishes. Might as well play it safe. "Works for me."

"Excellent." He unfolded a napkin and laid it on his lap. "Your résumé is interesting. You went straight from college to performing."

"Not exactly. I spent seven years as an executive with a real-estate investment firm."

"What prompted you to shift from the business world to acting?"

How much should she reveal? She didn't want to cross a professional line. "I found corporate life too structured and predictable."

"Ah yes, the lure of the capricious creative culture."

"What about you? What inspired you to move from New York to Atlanta?"

"The desire to bring Broadway-style theater to my hometown. Have you been to the Big Apple?"

"Not yet."

"The city is amazing. The theater district is alive with anticipation. Nothing compares to the thrill of a new production receiving smash reviews and becoming an overnight sensation. I wrote my play to create that same vibe here."

"It must have cost a fortune to convert the storefront to a fancy theater."

"And worth every penny. A dynamic location and a superb script warrant high ticket prices."

The waiter arrived with the bisque, drizzled sherry in each bowl, and swirled it with a spoon. "Enjoy."

In between sips, Gordon detailed his experience writing *Penelope*. During the main course, he shared his vision to open a second theater on Peachtree Street. Rachel found his exuberance both enticing and troubling. He obviously loved his craft, but why hadn't he mentioned the lead? Maybe he wanted to paint an irresistible vision to ensure she'd accept the role? Or did he plan to wine and dine Michelle to assess both their reactions before coming to a conclusion?

With his last bite of fish, he laid his fork aside. "How'd you like the sole?"

"I understand why it's the chef's specialty."

He grinned. "There's a little place a couple of blocks from here that serves the best ice cream in the city. Are you up for a walk?"

Dinner and a walk? What did he have in mind? She mentally kicked herself for questioning his motive. After all, he'd spent years in New York, the city the song claimed didn't sleep. "Why not? I mean, sure."

He motioned to the waiter. "Put the meal on my tab, with my usual tip."

"Yes sir. And thank you."

The sun had begun its final descent when they stepped onto the sidewalk in front of the restaurant. Gordon talked about the future of theater in Atlanta until they'd walked a block. "Hold on a second." He plucked his phone off his belt and held it to the side. "An investor needs some information right away." He re-clipped the phone. "Do you mind if we make a quick stop at my condo?"

If she said she did mind, would he be insulted? On the other hand, if she said no …

"It will only take a couple of minutes."

Get a grip, Rachel. "Dessert can wait."

"Good." Two doors further, they entered a lobby, stepped into an elevator, rode to the top floor, and entered his apartment. "Make yourself comfortable. I'll be right back."

She glanced around ultra-modern space washed in a sea of black, white, and gray, then moved to the window. She always loved the view of the city at night.

"I have to say your tenacity impressed me." Gordon stepped to her side. "Most actresses with a résumé as thin as yours wouldn't compete for a lead without making it clear they'd settle for a minor role."

"I've paid my dues and believe I'm ready for a starring role."

"Providing a springboard for aspiring actors is my specialty. The last actress I cast landed the lead in a Broadway play."

"I imagine she learned a lot from you."

"Under me her talent soared to a whole new level." He paused. "Fact is, Michelle is my first choice. She has far more experience, and her acting is superior to yours."

A cold chill skittered up Rachel's spine.

"But there's a delicious vulnerability in your performance. Something raw and moldable. I sense you're ready to reach new heights. If you let me, I can take you there. Put your name in lights. Make you a star."

"What are you trying to say?"

He slipped his arm around her waist and pulled her close. "Tonight, we can begin a journey that will satisfy both our desires."

Her back stiffened. "Are you offering me the part ... if I sleep with you?"

"Affairs have paved the way for aspiring starlets for decades. The intensity brings out the best in them."

A wave of nausea swept through her. "Not this actress." She pushed away from him.

"I suggest you reconsider before you let this opportunity slip from your fingers." He moved close and stroked her cheek.

She slapped his hand away. "There's nothing to reconsider. My answer is no."

"What a shame."

She glared at him. "The real shame is that a talented director like you is nothing more than a disgusting pig." She held her head high and headed for the door.

Her heart plummeted as she rode the elevator to the first floor. Outside, she turned toward the restaurant and struggled to control her breathing. How did everything go so wrong? Had she done something to make him think she'd trade her body for a part in his play? Had the audition kiss given him the wrong idea, or her dress?

She climbed into her car, then pulled into traffic and turned toward Buckhead. During her drive home, her anger soared. He had baited her all evening, and like a fool, she fell for it. When she arrived at her townhouse, she slid from the driver's seat and slammed the door shut. Her muscles quivered. How dare he peg her as an easy target. She climbed the stairs to her living room and collapsed on the couch. She spotted the script lying open on the coffee table, to the love scene she'd nailed. A beautiful play written by a man with incredible talent and not one iota of scruples.

She grabbed the script and hurled it across the room. "I hope your play is a big fat failure." She climbed the stairs, changed into pajamas, and fell into bed. In the darkness, reality hit her like a sledgehammer. She buried her face in her pillow and sobbed until no tears were left.

Chapter 19

A splitting headache woke Rachel from a restless sleep. She pressed her fingers to the back of her neck and trudged to the bathroom to splash cool water on her face. After swallowing two aspirin, she picked up her phone off the nightstand, lumbered downstairs, and popped in a coffee pod.

When her mug filled, she held it in both hands and breathed in the rich scent. Last night's events burst into her head and rekindled her anger. Everyone expected her to land the role. How could she tell Emily, Mama Sadie … Charlie, that an experienced director considered her talent second-rate? She eyed her checkbook lying on the counter. One more failed attempt to make it in the entertainment world. She couldn't live on her savings forever. At some point, she had to land decent roles or toss her goal on the pile of broken dreams.

Her phone vibrated. Charlie. "Hey."

"I've been thinking about you all morning. How'd auditions go?"

She set her cup on the counter. "I … didn't get the part."

"The director must be brain-dead."

"Sometimes things don't work out."

"Come back to Willow Falls. I'll throw some burgers on the grill and treat you to lunch at my place. My furniture arrived yesterday, so we won't have to eat picnic style."

She longed to go back to bed, pull a blanket over her head, and let her wounds heal. On the other hand, if she turned Charlie down, he'd consider it a personal rejection. Maybe a few days away from the city would help her recover and figure what to do next. "How can I turn down a proper place to sit?"

"Good. By the way, I have something that will help make up for the director's bonehead decision. Don't worry. It isn't jewelry."

"Sounds intriguing. I'll be there by two."

"I'll leave the garage open for you."

Rachel showered, dressed, and packed for a weeklong stay.

By the time she pulled into Charlie's garage, her anger had moved through the five stages of grief. She'd settled on accepting that while her talent might be subpar, her values were still intact. She knocked on the kitchen door.

He opened it, wearing shorts, a tight T-shirt, and a "Mr.-Good-Lookin'-Is-Cookin'" apron. "Hey, gorgeous."

"Is this your new fashion statement?"

"I hear women like men who know their way around a kitchen." He closed the garage door.

"Muscles and aprons go together quite well."

"Are you hungry?"

"I'm more curious about the surprise you promised."

He wiped his hands on the apron. "In that case, close your eyes and be prepared to fall in love."

"What are you up to?"

"You'll see. Eyes closed."

Her imagination went into overdrive as she listened to his footsteps recede, then return. "You can open them now." His face beamed as he placed a writhing bundle of fur, the color of wheat, into her arms.

"Oh, Charlie."

"She's Cody's cousin. Her name's Brownie."

"Just like the stuffed puppy my father gave me."

"About time you had a living, breathing dog."

Rachel blinked tears away and locked eyes with him. "Have I told you lately how much I love you?"

"All it took was an adorable pup."

"And a man who knows my heart."

"She's from the local breeder. Already housebroken."

"Even better."

"While you become acquainted with the new love in your life, the grill master will go to work." He picked up a platter holding two burgers and buns and opened the glass door.

She followed him to the backyard, placed her puppy on the grass, then sat at the patio table. Watching Brownie romp in the grass and chase a butterfly made her heart swell. "I can't think of a better gift."

"She loves this big yard as much as Sarge."

"I can see that. By the way, where are Dennis and his dog?"

"Hiking up to the waterfall with Missy. He decided to stick around a while longer."

"I wouldn't be surprised if she had something to do with his decision."

"It won't be the first time a pretty woman helped a man make up his mind—or the last."

While Charlie played chef, Rachel steered their conversation to the July Fourth celebration and the vineyard.

When the burgers were ready, he carried them to the kitchen, added salads to the plates, then set them on the dining room table.

Rachel carried Brownie.

"Your pup is probably ready for a nap."

She pointed to a wooden crate in the corner. "I assume that's her bed."

"At least for now."

She placed Brownie in the crate on top of a fluffy blanket. The puppy yawned and curled up in the corner. "Does Emily know about her?"

"I told her yesterday. Does she know you're here?"

"Not yet, unless someone saw me drive into town."

They settled at the table and rambled on about dogs, wine, and Willow Falls. When he'd taken his last bite, Charlie pushed his plate aside and rested his forearms on the table. His eyes met hers. "We've talked about everything under the sun except the elephant in the room."

"You mean the audition?"

"Yep."

"It's complicated." Brownie's whimper prompted Rachel to scoot away from the table and lift her new pet from the crate.

"That's her my-bladder's-full whine." Charlie chuckled. "She also came with instructions."

"I guess we'd better head to the backyard." Outside, Rachel set her pup on the grass, then settled on a chair. She couldn't stall any longer. Charlie deserved to know the truth. "I haven't been completely honest about yesterday."

He moved a chair beside her. "Tell me what's going on."

She laced her fingers and spilled the details.

His jaw tensed. "The man's a revolting pig."

She sniffed back tears. "What hurts most is knowing I wasn't good enough to land the part without compromising my ethics."

"You can't let that man's stupidity tear you down."

"Hard not to. Even if I had the talent to make it as an actress, I have no idea when another play with the perfect blend of comedy and drama will come along."

"When it does, you'll be ready. In the meantime, you can stay in Willow Falls. At your sister's house, of course."

"She wants to focus on fixing her book, so she'd appreciate help with the twins." Brownie jumped on her leg and whimpered. Rachel picked her up and stroked her silky-soft fur.

"And this guy would love having you hang around for more than a few days." Charlie caressed her arm, sending a volt of electricity through her limbs. "Are you up for some fireworks tonight, the human kind?"

Her pulse pounded in her ears as her gaze zeroed in on his. "What?"

"The town hall meeting."

Heat rose from her neck to her cheeks. "Oh."

"What'd you think I meant?"

"I, uh …"

He grinned.

She breathed deep to regain her composure and mask her disappointment. "I'm game for some small-town drama."

Chapter 20

Emily entered the church and stood behind the last row of pews as residents filed into the crowded space. She rolled her head from side to side to ease the tension from the hours she'd spent agonizing over Naomi's offer. On the one hand, she and Scott desperately needed the money. On the other, devoting time to a play would delay her writing for months. Worse, the idea of accepting payment for a project with a high probability of failure turned her stomach.

She filled her lungs, slowly released the air, then slid into a seat two rows from the back. She pulled her phone from her purse and checked for messages. Still no word from Rachel. *Relax, she'll let you know when she has an answer. Unless she has bad news.* She dismissed the thought and turned her attention to the front.

Pastor Nathan, in his role as mayor, along with council members Scott and Pepper, sat behind an eight-foot-long table, facing the crowd. A microphone rested on a stand at the front of the center aisle. By six o'clock, residents filled every seat, forcing dozens of latecomers to stand along the back and side walls.

A series of gavel raps quieted the crowd.

Nathan lifted a hand-held microphone. "Thank you for coming out. By now everyone knows about the negative publicity recently heaped on our town. Last week our town stood at a crossroad; either topple in defeat or fight. As a result, the council made a decision."

He glanced at Scott, then Pepper. "We hired an Atlanta public relations firm to fix our town's image."

A man wearing a plaid shirt stood. "How much did that cost?"

Nathan hesitated. "Everything we had."

"Are you telling us there's nothing left to spruce the place up?"

"We need professional help."

"What we need is a new council."

The statement unleashed a barrage of angry remarks.

Nathan rapped his gavel until the crowd silenced. "If you have any complaints or suggestions, line up behind that mic."

More than a dozen people scrambled to the center aisle. Nathan nodded to the elderly woman at the head of the line. "What's on your mind?"

"Some of us think that lady did us a favor."

Jeers erupted.

Nathan pounded the gavel. "Everyone has a right to their opinion. Go ahead, ma'am."

"We like living in a town the way it is now, without a lot of strangers coming and going."

"Ain't nobody gonna be doing nothing 'cept going, if we don't take some action," yelled a man sitting two rows in front of Emily.

More shouts.

Another gavel bang.

A young man stepped up next. "I don't know what so-called public relations people can do. What I do know is Willow Falls needs to catch up with the rest of the world. Every town worth its salt has a website. We've got nothing."

"That's a crazy idea," said a man sitting in the crowd. "What are we gonna advertise, a run-down town that's flat broke?"

The young man glared at him. "Do you have a better idea?"

"Maybe I do."

"Please, folks, show some respect and courtesy," Nathan said. "Thanks for the internet suggestion. We're making note of all your ideas. Who's next?"

A woman moved to the mic. "Since the council is out of money, the rest of us need to come up with ways to make Willow Falls more inviting."

"Like any of us have a dollar to spare," said Plaid Shirt.

"It doesn't have to cost a lot. For example, a couple of months back while we were visiting our son in Dahlonega, we went to a country store that had a player piano. Cost a quarter to turn it on. Can you believe it racked up more than three dollars while we were roaming around? That's what we need over at Hayes General Store, but Scott should charge fifty cents."

"That's a good idea," Gertie said as she stepped up next. "Along with an old-fashioned soda fountain. With someone dressed in nineteenth-century clothes serving milkshakes, sodas, and root-beer floats. And while we're at it, the front window display needs some work. Scott can put old sewing machines and typewriters in there, like an antique museum. That'd draw a lot of attention."

Nathan nodded. "Thank you, Ms. Gertie."

Patsy Peacock followed Gertie. She lowered the microphone stand to accommodate her five-foot height. "I've been pondering about the hotel—"

"If the place ever gets finished," shouted a man two rows away.

"I swanee. Quit being an old curmudgeon." She shook her finger at him, then adjusted her straw hat sporting two peacock feathers. "As I was about to say, we need to give every room at the hotel a different theme."

Curmudgeon guffawed. "Who's gonna pay for that?"

Patsy shook her head. "There you go again, mouthing off before you let me finish. I'm thinking sixty families could each adopt a room and decorate it special. I'd do a peacock theme. Each room would be named after the adopting family, like the suites at Willow Inn are named after real people. If the hotel's new manager is okay with the plan, I'll work with her and head up the project."

Kat stood and signaled a thumbs-up.

"One more thing before I sit down. We have to spruce up the town with paint and new awnings. Maybe add some planters and hanging flower baskets."

"Where do you people think the cash to do all this stuff is gonna come from?"

When Emily glanced over her shoulder to see who asked the question, her mouth fell open. The woman stood along the back wall, two feet from Charlie and Rachel. She dashed to the back, gripped her sister's hand, and led her from the building to the front sidewalk. "What's going on? Why didn't you call me? Did you land the part?"

Rachel stooped and pinched a blossom off a begonia. "The director offered me the role"—she straightened and stared at the flower—"if I traded my body for fame." She relayed the details.

"You should sue the bum."

"To what end?"

"Revenge? Self-satisfaction?"

"He's a famous director. I'm a nobody. Who do you think would come out ahead in that lawsuit?"

"It's not fair."

"Fair has nothing to do with it. The director made an offer. I turned it down." Rachel let the blossom flutter to the ground. "The fact is, I wasn't talented enough to land the role on merit."

"You can't believe that."

"Why not? It's the truth."

A dull ache gripped Emily's chest as she detected defeat in her sister's eyes. "What are you going to do?"

"You mean about the future? I haven't figured that out. But right now, I'm going back inside before Charlie comes looking for us." She turned and hastened up the steps.

"Wait, I'm coming with you."

They stepped back inside as Naomi, the last person in line, moved to the microphone. "I've spent most of my life living in Charleston. A beautiful town, with great restaurants, a ton of history, and more than its share of art galleries. In other words, a lot to offer tourists. But my heart never left Willow Falls and the fine people who call this town home." She paused. "Which is why I've decided to move back and turn my family's house into an art museum."

Mirabelle stood and faced the crowd. "Someone should do the same with the house across the street from yours, the one Willow Falls' founder built for his wife. It's been on the market for years."

"For good reason," shouted Curmudgeon. "No one around here can afford to buy the old place or the other house on Main Street that's for sale."

Mirabelle propped her hands on her hips. "If enough cranky old guys like you get off their duff and do something to spruce up the town, maybe an outsider will step up with the money."

"Who're you calling old?"

"If the overalls fit."

Nathan rapped his gavel. "Okay, you two, Naomi still has the floor."

"Thank you, Mayor. I also want to announce that I'm donating two of my father's prized possessions to the town. The Cadillac I drove July Fourth and a car some of you will remember—his 1933 Rolls-Royce Phantom Two."

It seemed everyone in the building cheered and applauded, except Rachel. Emily glanced sideways at her downcast eyes and knew she needed something to heal her broken spirit and restore her dreams. She needed her sister.

Emily touched Rachel's arm and leaned close. "Do you trust me?"

"What?" Her brows pinched. "Why?"

"I don't have time to explain. I need an answer."

"Yes, of course, I trust you."

"Good." Emily moved to the aisle. Her breathing accelerated. *It's the right thing to do, for Rachel, the town, Scott.* She stepped beside Naomi and placed her hand over the microphone. "Is your offer still good?"

"Indeed, it is."

"Do you want to break the news?"

A smile lit the artist's face. "Let's do it together."

Chapter 21

While Nathan announced another town hall meeting, Emily mentally debated how to entice Rachel to partner with her. As the crowd moved toward the exit, she pulled her sister aside. "You need to come with me. I want to show you something."

"Now?"

"It's important."

"You two go ahead." Charlie kissed Rachel's cheek. "I'll drop your suitcase off at Emily's."

"You're a good man, Charlie Bricker." Emily escorted her sister out the front door and down to the sidewalk. "How much do you know about Willow Falls' past?"

"Bits and pieces."

"I'll fill you in on the way to our destination."

"Where are you taking me?"

"You'll see." They turned toward the park. "It all began in the mid-nineteenth century with Percy Buchanan, a wealthy East Coast landowner's son. He had a reputation as a free spirit who snubbed his nose at society and conventional behavior. Especially after he fell in love with Peaches, the beautiful young daughter of domestic servants, who made a living as a vaudeville singer."

"Bet that didn't go over with the upper crust."

"Like a skunk in a perfume factory. After a couple of months, he married her and joined her act. When she discovered she was pregnant, they abandoned show business and settled down. They had a daughter and two sons. All went along fine until she discovered an itch for a place in high society. It didn't take long for Percy to discover he'd cooked his goose."

"Let me guess. The rich and famous gave him the cold shoulder."

"Big time. However, he adored Peaches far more than he detested the wealthy class. So, he schlepped his family to Newport, Rhode Island, to spend the summer in his parents' vacation home."

"The seasonal playground for the wealthy."

"More like party central. More than anything, Peaches wanted to fit in, so she planned an elaborate event and invited all the important people. Unfortunately, she failed to seek approval from the town's self-appointed social maven. Not a single person showed up."

"So much for high society."

"When they returned home, she fell into a deep depression. Worried sick about her, Percy purchased hundreds of north Georgia acres and set out to create a haven where she could serve as queen bee. Inspired by the waterfall and abundance of willow oaks, he chose this location and named it Willow Falls."

"A town born from one man's unconditional love for a woman." Rachel brushed a lock of hair away from her cheek. "How did it expand from an idea to a community?"

"Percy found three more young heirs who shared his rebellious spirit. Together they laid out a plan for a row of storefronts, modest houses for workers, and four luxurious homes. After folks were settled, Peaches planned another elaborate party and invited the whole town. This time everyone came. She became the social darling for their little enclave."

Emily brushed a gnat away from her face. "A few years later Percy's parents died, leaving their three children a wealth of land. He sold a large portion of his inheritance and invested the money to expand the town. Over the next few years, two additional young families with tons of money built large homes."

Rachel nodded. "Completing six of the seven on Main Street."

"Correct."

"What about the seventh, and where does Hayes General Store fit in?"

"I'm getting to that." They walked past the park. "The Hayes family moved here as worker bees. They had three daughters and a son named Everett. Eventually, he fell in love with Lillian, Percy and Peaches' daughter. Percy wasn't about to allow his precious daughter to marry a man who hadn't shown himself worthy. So, he made a deal with Everett—build a business to prove he could take care of a family. Kind of like Jacob's arrangement with Laban."

Rachel's brows pinched. "Who?"

"A guy who lived thousands of years ago." They continued past the hotel. "Anyway, Everett accepted the challenge and developed a plan to build and run a general store. He finished the job in five years. The seventh house was a wedding gift from the bride's parents."

They passed Willow Inn. "For years the town thrived, until the Great Depression. Five of the seven wealthy families lost everything. Percy spent the last of his money to purchase their homes. To keep the town from falling into ruin, he allowed the former owners to remain. As their children became adults, some stayed to raise their families, others left. Over time, two families managed to recover financially. Naomi's grandparents were one."

"And the other?"

"Robert Liles' grandfather. Which means you and I have an indirect link to the town's heritage."

"I'm not sure that's something to brag about." Rachel smirked. "Did Everett and Lillian stay in Willow Falls?"

"They did. When he died, she moved in with her son, Scott's grandfather. The family's devotion to their business is why my husband sacrificed his own career goals after his father died. A lot of the original townsfolk's heirs stayed around. Including my mom and dad's, Patsy's, Pepper's, Jacob and Nathan's, even Mirabelle's clan."

They stopped in front of the last house on the right, the grandest of them all. "Rumor is Percy built this mansion to rival those in Newport, but on a smaller scale. Come on, I'll show you inside."

"Do you have a key? Don't tell me the door's unlocked."

"Are you surprised?"

"Doesn't anyone around here bother to lock their doors?"

"It's a small town." Emily opened the front door. They stepped into the twenty-foot-high entry hall, with a six-foot-wide staircase leading to a landing. A large tapestry hung on the wall. The ceiling featured a gold frieze and hand-painted cherubs.

Rachel followed Emily into the large living room, ornately paneled, with floor-to-ceiling windows. An elaborate oriental rug covered the floor. She stood beside the massive carved-stone fireplace. "This is amazing, but I don't understand why you brought me here." She blinked as if a light suddenly came on. "Wait a minute. You want me to help you with that play Naomi found, don't you?"

"Yes."

"You're the writer. Why do you need me?"

"Because I don't know beans about writing a play."

"And you think I do?"

Emily flicked an ant off the fireplace. "At least you've read a few."

"I've also read recipes. That doesn't mean I can cook."

"Naomi expects me to recruit a director and find people to fill all the roles—"

"How do you expect to find a decent cast in this burg?"

Emily thumped her arm. "Hey, you're talking about my town."

"Don't take it personally. I'm being realistic."

"So am I, which is why I need your help."

"Look, I understand you want to do everything possible to help Willow Falls survive. But finishing the script, finding players, rehearsing, and launching in three months is nuts."

"You're right, it is crazy, and maybe I shouldn't have taken the project on. But I did, and now the whole town knows. So, I'm stuck with it. The cold, hard fact is you're the only person besides me who has any relevant experience."

Rachel lifted her hair and rubbed the back of her neck. "You understand there's a good possibility the whole thing will fail."

"Or maybe we'll pull it off and create something spectacular."

"Why do I feel like I've been suckered like a big fat fish chasing a lure?"

"Are you capitulating?"

"You're my twin. There's no way I'm letting you take the fall by yourself."

"That's the most negative acceptance in the history of acceptances." Emily embraced her sister. "I'm betting something good will come of this."

"I hope you're right, for both our sakes."

Chapter 22

"We haven't written the first word, and there's already a problem. Why am I not surprised?" Rachel rinsed her glass and set it in the dishwasher.

"Naomi's expecting me to come up with a solution." Emily set pieces of melon and banana on the twins' high-chair trays.

"Here's an idea. We chalk the project up to lost causes and walk away."

"Easy for you to say. You can return to your townhouse in Atlanta and avoid residents' wrath."

"It's not your fault there's no one to do the work."

"Doesn't matter."

"And you wonder why I prefer living in a big city."

"You mean where predator directors dash dreams and break hearts?"

Rachel glared at her sister. "That's harsh."

"You're right. I shouldn't have said it."

"We've both had more than our share of frustration."

Emily picked a piece of melon off the floor and tossed it in the sink. "Is Charlie still coming for dinner tonight?"

"Yeah."

"If we're lucky, he and Scott will help us come up with a street-smart idea."

Her comment conjured a vision of a downtown Atlanta sidewalk. Rachel snapped her fingers. "I have the perfect solution." She shared it with Emily.

"Do you think it will work?"

"I don't know, but I intend to find out." She shouldered her purse, hastened to her car, and drove to town. She parked across from Pepper's Cafe, stepped from her car, and paused to take in the view. The sun glistened on the lake's surface like tiny diamonds. A cat stretched out on the retaining wall. Two ladies sat on a blanket watching three young children romp in the grass.

One of the ladies spotted her and waved. She smiled and returned the gesture, wondering if they were Emily's friends. Or did they wave to everyone?

She closed her eyes and tuned into the sounds around her. Unlike downtown Atlanta—where the roar of engines and impatient drivers' horns bounced off tall buildings—chirping birds and rustling leaves, punctuated by a barking dog and a car driving by, created a relaxing symphony.

Rachel opened her eyes, squared her shoulders, and rushed to the hotel. She found Jacob and one of his workers on scaffolding installing lights in the dining room ceiling. "Your construction crew is doing an amazing job."

He peered over the edge. "My guys are top-notch."

"Do you have a minute?"

"Sure." He climbed down and wiped his hands on his jeans. "Are you Emily or Rachel?"

"The Atlanta twin. I want to run an idea by you."

"I'm listening."

She outlined the details.

He shrugged. "It could work."

"Thanks. I'll let you know how it goes." She left the hotel and walked next door to Willow Inn, where she found Dennis in the side yard trimming bushes. "Looks like Sadie's keeping you busy."

"Her list isn't long enough to pay for many more days."

She plucked a twig off the ground. "I'm curious. What do you think about Willow Falls so far?"

"Nice enough. People are friendly."

"A lot of folks think it's a great place to live." She snapped the twig in two. "Did you go to the town hall meeting last night?"

"Stayed at the inn and watched TV."

"Residents came up with some creative ideas, including Naomi Jasper." She relayed the play project.

"Seems like a good plan."

"The problem is Jacob needs his entire construction crew to meet the hotel's October deadline. When that's finished, he's contracted to build the winery and Charlie's home. Which means he can't take on the cinema renovation project. However, he is willing to supervise it if he can find someone to do the physical work."

She paused, hoping Dennis would respond. He didn't.

"Didn't you tell Charlie and me that you and your dad worked construction before you enlisted?"

He nodded and continued clipping.

"How'd you like to go back in the business?"

"Hadn't thought about it."

"Jacob's willing to take you on for a special project at the old cinema."

A bee buzzed Dennis's ear. He swatted it away. "What's it need?"

"Lobby reno, enlarged stage, dressing rooms."

"That's more than a one-man job."

"Are you interested?"

He dropped the clippers on the ground, then removed his cap and wiped sweat from his forehead. "A couple of vets back at the shelter have been looking for work. Both good guys. I'll do it if my friends can come and help me." He pulled a piece of paper and a pencil stub from his pocket and jotted a note. "Here's their names."

"Jack Parker and Jonathan Thomas Brown."

"He goes by J. T."

"Why haven't they found jobs?"

"Consequences of war." He retrieved the clippers and went back to work.

"Fair enough. I'll talk to you tomorrow."

Rachel hastened back to her car, returned to Emily's, and brought her up to speed.

"Bringing two more guys to town we don't know anything about is risky."

She handed over the piece of paper. "If you're worried, ask someone to check them out."

"I'll call Pepper's husband. Mitch—"

"The sheriff?"

"Yeah, he'll know what to do."

After helping Emily settle the twins in their cribs, Rachel carried a dish of lasagna to the table. Emily followed with Caesar salads and bread.

Scott sniffed the air. "Smells like my favorite Italian meal." He said grace, then opened a bottle of wine.

Emily slid a serving onto his plate. "Rachel and I have something to tell you."

"Lasagna bribery?"

"Something like that. It involves Dennis." She detailed the plan. "Mitch says his friends checked out okay. So, what do you think?"

"Here's another idea." Scott locked eyes with her. "Postpone the play's opening until a real construction crew is available."

"He's right," Charlie said. "I don't know much about the entertainment business, but three months doesn't seem like enough time to get the job done."

"Emily and I understand we don't have a lot of time." Rachel spread her napkin on her lap. "And it's possible we won't pull it off. The fact is, we owe it to this town to give it our best shot."

Charlie's fork stopped in midair. "Where'd the real Rachel go?"

"I don't know why you're so surprised. My sister made a commitment, and I agreed to help."

"For a minute I thought you might feel a connection with Willow Falls."

"The people I care about most live here. Besides, if we pull it off, I'll stick around for a few months and have something to add to my résumé."

"I like that sticking around part." Charlie grinned.

"There is one problem." Emily dipped her bread in olive oil. "Assuming J. T. and Jack are willing to come up here and help Dennis, they'd need somewhere to live."

Charlie swallowed a bite and pointed his fork at her. "How about my place, actually your parents' house?"

"Are you sure? I mean you don't know anything about the two new guys."

"If Mitch and Dennis think they're okay, I'm game."

"Okay then, we have a plan."

Scott lifted his wine glass. "If you two gals manage to hit Naomi's target date, you'll deserve a toast and Academy Awards."

"Sorry," Rachel said. "Oscar's for the movies."

Emily's head tilted. "What about a Tony?"

"Broadway shows."

Scott set his glass down. "In that case, we'll have to create our own prize. Maybe call it the Willow Falls Wonder Woman Trophy."

Emily grinned. "Make it ostentatious and present it to us at a fancy ceremony in the Redding Arms' ballroom."

"Ladies and gentlemen"—Scott held his fist close to his mouth—"now appearing on the red carpet is the wacky duo who dreamed big and brought fame and fortune to a winsome village known as Willow Falls. Tell me about your dress, Ms. Hayes."

Emily pressed her hands to her cheeks and giggled. "Why, it's an original, created from two fabulous thrift-shop finds."

"What about yours, Ms. Streetman? Is it also secondhand?"

"Heavens, no. This purple creation is from the Scarlett O'Hara collection, inspired by your town's lovely hospital. For the life of me, I can't figure out how she kept these big ole ostrich feathers from tickling her nose." She faked a sneeze.

"And there you have it, folks, our town's heroes, Happy and Sneezy."

Emily thumped Scott's arm. "Maybe you should audition for a part in our play, honey."

"Not one chance in a million. How about you, Charlie?"

"More likely I'll be struck by lightning than set one foot on a stage."

Emily tilted her glass toward Rachel. "Looks like the only two people in this family who are out to win awards are you and me, sis."

Chapter 23

Emily turned off the engine and stared at the sidewalk leading to her parents' front porch. "I haven't been inside in months."

Rachel touched her arm. "Are you okay?"

"Yeah." She stepped out, opened the back door, and lifted Clair from her car seat. "I forgot to bring a key."

Rachel released Jane from her seat. "Charlie left the front door unlocked."

"He's sure enough turning into a small-town guy."

"He along with everyone else in Willow Falls better adopt some big-city habits before the town's overrun with tourists."

"Old habits are hard to break."

Rachel reached for Jane. "The first time someone's house is ransacked, maybe people will wake up and realize locking doors is common sense."

"What makes you think criminals will flock to town?"

"I'm just saying."

They walked up the sidewalk and opened the front door.

Nostalgia overwhelmed Emily the moment they entered the foyer. She stared at the living room, empty except for a painting sitting on the fireplace mantel. "It looks like Charlie doesn't have enough furniture to fill the house."

"He moved from a two-bedroom apartment."

She stepped into the room and put Clair on the floor. "So many memories live in this house. Family dinners. Girlfriends sprawled on the living room floor for my sixteenth birthday slumber party. Scott sneaking a kiss while we watched football games with my parents."

Rachel set Jane beside her twin, then walked into the dining room and circled back through the kitchen. "Sarge is in the backyard. I think Charlie took Brownie with him. Wait until you see her. She's so adorable you'll want to pick her up and cuddle her."

"Like Cody, before he grew up. Although in a lot of ways he's still a lovable puppy."

Rachel centered the painting sitting on the fireplace mantel. "I imagine growing up in this warm, cozy home gave you a sweet childhood filled with a lot of happy moments."

"More than I can count. What's your dad's house like?"

"Think Percy's mansion on steroids." She ran her finger along the edge of the mantel. "After my mother died, it felt more like a luxury hotel than a home."

"Given how different we were raised, it's amazing we're alike in so many ways."

"The miracle of genetics."

Emily's mind drifted back to her childhood pleas for a sister. "It would've been a blast growing up with you."

"At least we're together now."

A truck engine drew Emily's attention. "I think they're here." She moved to the window. Charlie lifted a puppy from the back seat while three men climbed out of his truck. Her eyes widened. "You're not going to believe this."

"What?"

"One of the guys is on crutches."

"Broken leg?"

"Not exactly."

Charlie led his new roommates up the sidewalk, through the foyer, into the living room. "Ladies, meet the newest members of the construction crew, J. T. Brown and Jack Parker."

Dennis clasped his hand on J. T.'s shoulder. "Don't let his missing limb fool you. He's stronger on his right leg than most guys are on two."

The muscular black man tapped Dennis's foot with his crutch. "This guy's the real hero. He did a lot to help me and Jack deal with all the crap we brought back from the war zone." He glanced at Jack. "Is it okay to say crap?"

Burn scars on the left side of Jack's face rendered his smile lopsided. "We've been working to convince J. T. to clean up his language."

"They convinced me an army vet shouldn't talk like some ignorant street rat."

"Especially when he's around ladies." Jack rubbed his scarred arm. "Don't you worry about J. T. and me not having any construction experience. We don't look like much, and it's a fact we've had a tough time adjusting to life after the war. But we're smart and ready to learn whatever we need to know."

Dennis shoved his hands in his pockets. "I told you they were good guys."

Brownie jumped from Charlie's arms. The puppy scrambled to Jane and tongue-bathed her face, triggering a nose wrinkle and a giggle. Clair grabbed a handful of fur, inviting her own face-licking.

Rachel scooped Brownie off the floor. "Naomi's eager to meet the new crew and show them the theater."

"Give us thirty minutes to haul the guys' gear inside."

"Good. I'll let her know." She handed the puppy to Charlie and picked up Jane.

Emily lifted Clair. "For now, we'll leave you guys alone."

They returned to the car and secured the twins in their car seats. Clair yawned and rubbed her eyes. "Are my girls sleepy?" Emily patted her cheek, then closed the door and slid into the driver's seat. "Meeting those two guys shocked the dickens out of me."

"How long before residents discover we plucked them from a homeless shelter?"

"Depending on who the guys talk to, maybe a week." Emily snickered. "One thing's for sure, they'll test the town's tolerance and ability to extend grace."

"Wait 'til Naomi discovers she's hired a one-legged man and his language coach."

Emily backed onto the street. "She'll either find a soft place in her heart for them—"

"Or fire them on the spot. Do you want to go with me?"

"I have to put the twins down for their nap. Fill me in when it's over."

Rachel parked in front of the abandoned cinema and climbed out. Someone needs to take the *Jurassic Park III* sign out of the window. She shook her head, passed the ticket booth, and headed to the door. Inside the theater, she strolled down the sloping aisle. The four guys stood in front of the first row, facing the stage. "I hear back in the day the whole town loved coming here."

Dennis turned toward her. "It has good bones."

"This will take a lot of work." J. T. leaned on his crutch. "Good thing my buddy knows his stuff."

Charlie nudged Rachel. "She's here."

Naomi, carrying a yard-long, rolled-up sheet of paper, breezed down the aisle. She stopped and stared at the guys. "Is this my crew?"

Rachel grimaced.

Dennis stepped forward. "Construction's in my genes, Ms. Jasper. Me and my dad were planning on starting our own business before I enlisted. And these two guys are quick learners. Won't take long to train them."

Naomi stepped in front of J. T. "War injury?"

He stood tall. "Yes ma'am."

"Why don't you have an artificial limb?"

He shrugged. "Bureaucratic screwup."

"Our government should do better by our country's heroes." She touched his bicep. "You're plenty strong."

"I work out."

"So did my husband, God rest his soul. He served as a Marine before we met. If we'd had sons, they most likely would've followed in his footsteps."

She moved to Jack and touched his scarred cheek. "Also from a war?"

He nodded.

"You're a handsome young man."

"Thank you, ma'am."

"Such lovely manners." Her head tilted. "Y'all act like fine Southern gentlemen."

"All three of us are Georgia-born," Dennis said.

"Well now, seems I've acquired one fine crew."

Rachel released a sigh, then watched Naomi unroll the paper and listened to her describe the changes she needed. At least they had the construction dilemma solved. Now she and Emily had to deliver on their commitment.

Chapter 24

Emily added bananas to the cereal puffs on her babies' trays. "In a few months, you sweet girls will learn how to use a spoon. Then you'll have bowls to tip over and more temptation to finger paint your trays and drop food over the side."

Clair sneezed, then smeared banana on her nose.

"As long as your sister is here, we'll have two pups to clean up whatever mess they leave on the floor." Scott rinsed his coffee cup and set it in the dishwasher. "I need to head out."

She wiped Clair's face. "I hope you end up with enough business this week to pay the power bill."

"Plenty of people stopped in. To complain about the PR firm. Not to shop."

"Who can blame them? I mean, what is the town getting for the money?"

"Nothing that will make a difference. A few thousand doesn't buy much." He kissed Emily's cheek, then Jane's and Clair's. "I'll see my girls tonight."

"Will you bring me some lemon drops?"

"You need a sugar rush?"

"Something like that."

"I'll bring you a bagful." He grabbed his keys off the counter and headed to the garage.

"You girls have the best daddy in the whole world." She placed two sippy cups on their trays, then settled at the table and opened her laptop to her novel. "Time to make some more changes."

Rachel, dressed in pajamas, her hair in a mass of curls, wandered in with her phone in hand and headed straight to the coffeemaker. "Morning."

"Did you just wake up?"

"How can you tell? Oh yeah, I look like a flock of geese tried to build a nest on my head."

"You know today's the deadline for your father's decision."

"Trust me, I didn't forget." Rachel fixed her coffee and took a sip. "I stayed up past midnight putting a proposal together."

"That explains why you slept in. Did you send it to him?"

She carried her cup and phone to the table and sat across from Emily. "It'd be more effective to present it in person." She took a sip. "Charlie said he'd go with me."

"What time's your meeting?"

"I haven't called him."

"Seriously?" Emily looked up from her laptop. "You need to quit stalling, reach out to him, and schedule lunch."

"I will."

"When? After the deadline is over?"

"I needed a minute to wake up."

"You look plenty alert to me."

"Just what I need, a pushy twin."

"That's exactly what you need."

Rachel sighed and set her cup on the counter. "What would I do without a sister giving me orders?" she mumbled. Then she picked up her phone and pressed a number. "Hey, Dad ... yeah, me too. I have the information you need about Willow Falls. Can you squeeze me into your calendar today?" She paused. "I understand ... okay." She pocketed her phone and strolled to the patio door. "It looks like another hot day."

Emily stepped beside her. "Well, what did he say?"

"We're meeting at noon at the Sun Dial Restaurant."

"Where you and Charlie had your first date."

"And the last place I had a meal with my father." A wasp landed on the door in front of Rachel's face. She snapped her finger on the glass, sending the pesky insect flying away.

"Why didn't you tell him Charlie's joining you?"

"I didn't want to give him a reason to turn me down."

"Are you sure that's a smart move?"

"Right now, I'm not sure about anything." She called Charlie and gave him the news. "I'll be ready." She tucked her phone in her pocket. "He's picking me up in an hour."

"How do you think Greer will react when you both show up?"

"He won't be thrilled, but he's too professional to make a scene." Rachel opened the patio door to let in Brownie and Cody. "Yesterday I received a text from Alicia Adams—"

"Your reporter friend, the one who writes a theater blog?"

Rachel nodded. "I haven't seen her in months. She wants to meet and catch up. Maybe we can meet her for dinner."

"Hmm." The germ of an idea popped up and blossomed into a full-blown plan. "Her timing is perfect."

"To share a meal?"

"No. To invite her to come up to Willow Falls and review our play."

"You're kidding, right?"

"I'm dead serious."

"Help me understand. We haven't started with the script, and you're already thinking about publicity?"

"We have to plan ahead."

Rachel pushed her fingers through her tangled curls. "You know it'd be a huge risk."

"Seriously?" Emily chortled. "The entire project is one gigantic gamble, so what do we have to lose."

"Oh, nothing much ... except our reputations."

"Alicia's your friend, right?"

"And your point is?"

"She wouldn't do us wrong." Emily tapped her finger on Rachel's arm. "So, quit hesitating and respond to her text."

"You're in a mood." Rachel shook her head as she pulled her phone from her pocket and tapped the keypad.

"A text to Alicia?"

"No, a plea to the Queen of England. Of course, a text to Alicia."

Her phone pinged.

"From the queen or Alicia?"

"You're hilarious. She's meeting Charlie and me for dinner."

"Good, we have a plan." Emily returned to the table.

Rachel followed. "Not exactly."

Emily raised her brows. "What do you mean?"

"I'll only consider your idea if she offers first."

"Fair enough."

Rachel clutched her coffee cup. "I have to print my proposal, then shower and dress."

"A lot is riding on your trip to Atlanta."

"Tell me about it."

Chapter 25

Thick, dark clouds hovered over downtown Atlanta, adding to Rachel's anxiety. More than once during the drive from Willow Falls, she'd been tempted to call her father and tell him she wouldn't show up at lunch alone. Each time her finger stopped inches above her phone.

The valet held the passenger door open. She stepped out, clutching her purse and a folder. Charlie rounded the front of the truck, pressed his hand to her back, and escorted her to the glass elevator. The doors opened. They stepped inside. As it climbed the outside of the tube-shaped Peachtree Plaza Hotel, she closed her eyes and clung to his arm.

He placed his hand over hers. "The first time we rode to the top, you wore a blue-green dress and silver dangle earrings."

"The color is called teal, and I'm impressed you remembered."

"How could I forget? I couldn't take my eyes off you."

"Today you'll be staring across the table at my father." She paused. "There's something I need to tell you."

"Your father's gonna lecture me about dating his daughter?"

"Not exactly." She swiped away the layer of sweat resting on her upper lip. "The thing is … he doesn't know you're coming."

Charlie's brows raised. "You're kidding. Right?"

"I'm serious."

He snatched his hand away.

"Uh-oh, you're angry."

"More like shocked. If he doesn't pull out a pistol and shoot me, I guess I'll survive."

"No need to worry. He only carries it for protection."

"I'm dating his daughter. He might consider me a threat."

Rachel hesitated. "He doesn't know … we're a couple."

"Today's full of surprises."

Atop the seventy-three-story building, a hostess escorted them to the restaurant's revolving surface and a table covered with a white cloth, beside the floor-to-ceiling windows.

Greer stood.

"Hello, Dad."

"Rachel." He sat.

Charlie pulled a chair out for Rachel, then settled beside her, across from her father.

She set her purse on the floor, the folder on the table. "I hope it's okay if Charlie joins us." *Tell him the truth.* "We started seeing each other before I resigned."

He glared at Charlie.

"I'll pick up the check, payment for showing up unannounced."

"Fair enough."

Rachel clasped her hands in her lap and smiled at her father. "I like your new look. Distinguished."

He fingered his neatly trimmed beard. "I needed a change." The waiter arrived with a glass. "Double martini, extra dry for you, sir. What may I bring you, miss?"

"A glass of Chardonnay."

Charlie held up two fingers.

Greer eyed Charlie. "What's your old man up been up to since he bought that property?"

"He's staying in Willow Falls, waiting for the local construction crew to finish the hotel and start building the winery."

"Interesting." He plucked the olive from his drink and shifted his gaze to Rachel. "What news do you have about the town?"

The waiter arrived with two glasses of wine, then took their lunch order. The moment he left, she opened the folder, removed a three-page document, and handed it to her father. "This explains everything."

Greer propped his elbows on the table, rested his head on his fingertips, and began to read.

She twisted her mother's tennis bracelet as she watched his indifferent facial expression. What made her think a few ideas and an artist's attempt to bring culture to a tiny town in north Georgia would make an ounce of difference to a man accustomed to making multi-million-dollar deals?

Her palms turned clammy when he turned to the second page. If he discovered an ex-con functioned as the hotel's manager, he'd bail for sure. She should have spent more time on the update or at least added more detail. Except there wasn't anything to add.

He turned to the third page.

Rachel held her breath when he flipped the first page up, then lifted his elbows off the table. "I expanded Streetman Enterprise from a small Southern company to a giant in real estate development by making wise risk-reward decisions. In my opinion, Willow Falls has at best a fifty-fifty chance of becoming a profitable tourist town."

Her pulse pounded in her ears. How could she go back and tell Emily, Sadie, and everyone else her father let them down? She had to do something. "Look, I know it's not what you're accustomed to—"

"You didn't let me finish. I refuse to be the reason it fails."

She scrunched her brow. "Are you telling us you're not pulling the funding?"

"That's what I'm saying."

She released a sigh and fought back tears. "Thank you."

"Maybe the hotel will manage to turn a profit." He leaned back and eyed Charlie. "How long have you been dating my daughter?"

"Better part of a year."

"She could do worse." Greer sipped his martini and shifted the conversation to business. During lunch, he expounded on his latest acquisition and listened to Charlie describe the Willow Oak plans. Minutes after taking his last bite, he glanced at his watch. "I have an appointment at two." He stood and held his hand out to Rachel. "Good job on the report, Strawberry Girl."

"I enjoyed spending time with you, Dad."

He nodded to Charlie. "Thanks for picking up the check."

"My pleasure."

He turned and walked away.

Charlie laid his arm across the back of Rachel's chair. "Your father is one interesting character."

"You mean stern and unemotional?"

"How would you describe your father's old man?"

"Cold as ice. He never talked about anything except work." She stared into space. "I don't remember him ever hugging me or anyone else."

"That explains a lot."

"He suffered a fatal heart attack a year before my mother died."

"Your dad obviously didn't have a good role model. Whatever happens, you should continue reaching out to him."

"You know he warned me not to date you; he called you a playboy."

"Guess he's not as smart as he thinks he is."

The waiter delivered the check. Charlie slipped his credit card in the holder. "We have four hours before we meet your friend. What do you want to do?"

"Go to my townhouse and pick up more clothes. The last time I packed, I didn't expect to be gone longer than a week."

"Alone in your townhouse." He grinned. "I wonder what else we can do."

"Hmm. Let me think." She snapped her fingers. "The kitchen needs painting."

"Not enough time."

"Vacuum the floors?"

"Too much work." He signed the receipt.

"We can sit on the deck and talk to my hawk friend."

He stood and pulled her chair out. "I have a better idea."

"Something fun?"

"Oh, yeah."

At six, Rachel and Charlie walked into the Buckhead Diner and found Alicia waiting. The pretty young woman, with flawless skin the color of milk chocolate, greeted Rachel with a hug. "Hey, girl, you're looking good."

"So are you. I'd like you to meet Charlie Bricker."

"The pleasure's all mine." He offered his hand.

"To heck with a handshake. Any friend of Rachel's is a friend of mine." She hugged him, then nudged Rachel. "I have the feeling he's a lot more than your friend."

Charlie grinned. "I'm working on it."

While the hostess led them to their table, Alicia leaned close to Rachel. "He's a real cutie."

"Are you playing Cupid?"

"I'm just saying you should hang on to him."

Moments after they slipped into a booth, their waiter arrived. When they finished ordering drinks, Rachel spread a napkin across her lap. "I'm sorry, I haven't been to your improv group in a while. What's going on with everyone."

"Do you remember the guy with the Greek-theater-mask tattoo?"

"Uh-huh."

"He quit his job and moved to New York City. Last I heard, he landed a small part in a Broadway show."

"He's living the dream."

"Oh, and one of our newest members landed a role in a play written by a director who recently left the Big Apple."

"Are you talking about Gordon Wells?"

"You know him?"

"We had less than a pleasant encounter."

"What a shame some directors are hard to deal with." Alicia crossed her forearms on the table. "I'm dying to hear what's going on with your career."

"For the time being, it's taking an interesting detour." Rachel filled her in on the theater plans.

"Your talent obviously goes way beyond acting."

"I have no idea how to recruit or direct a cast of amateurs."

"You'll figure it out."

The waiter returned with two glasses of white wine and one of red. After he took their orders, Alicia tapped her glass to Rachel's then Charlie's. "Here's to my old and new friend." She took a sip, then set her glass on the table "When did you say the play premiers?"

"Mid-October," Rachel said. "Same weekend the hotel opens."

"And you're counting on it to attract tourists?"

"Along with other improvements the town's making."

"Tell you what. I'll write a review and encourage theater lovers to attend if you schedule a pre-premier for the town's residents four weeks earlier—"

"Ten weeks from now?" How could they possibly finish the entire project in such a short time? "I don't know …"

Alicia tilted her head to the side. "Too soon? What if I treat it as a dress rehearsal?"

"You know it could still need a ton of work."

"Not a problem. I have a good sense about potential."

Charlie nudged Rachel. "The publicity could make a big difference."

"I know." She released a heavy sigh. "Okay, I'm in. Now all I have to do is figure out how to tell Emily and our construction crew to shave twenty-eight days off their timeline."

Chapter 26

Rachel wandered into the kitchen and found Emily carrying Jane from her high chair to the newly expanded playpen. "Good morning, everybody."

"Hey, sis. I can't wait to hear what happened with your father yesterday."

"He didn't shoot Charlie."

Scott looked up from refilling Cody and Brownie's water bowls. "Say what?"

"He kind of showed up unannounced."

"Back to your father," Emily said.

"He's still on board with the hotel."

"That's a huge relief." She wiped the high-chair trays with a damp cloth. "What about Alicia?"

"We need to talk."

"Uh-oh, she's not interested in reviewing our play."

"To the contrary."

Her head tilted. "Then what do we need to talk about?"

Rachel prepared a cup of coffee, then sat at the table, across from Scott. "Timing."

"Of what?" Emily sat beside her.

"Our premiere." She took a sip then relayed Alicia's request.

"What'd you tell her?"

"We could do it."

Emily stared at her as if she'd grown a third eye. "Are you telling me you agreed to cut four weeks off our timeline?"

"If we pull it off—"

"There's the problem, one gigantic if."

"Trust me. Alicia's endorsement is worth the risk."

Scott propped his forearms on the table. "Did you stop to think about Dennis and his crew? You know they added Naomi's garage conversion to their list."

"Which is why Emily and I need to head out."

Emily's eyes widened. "Where?"

"To motivate the crew. Scott, can you watch the twins for an hour?"

"Might as well. It won't matter much if the store opens late."

"Thanks, you're an awesome brother-in-law." She fished her keys from her purse.

Emily followed Rachel to her car and slid into the passenger seat. "You're about to test your power of persuasion."

"We need to stop at Patsy's on the way."

"To do what?"

"Buy some bait."

Rachel parked in Naomi's driveway behind the red Caddie and vintage Rolls Royce. "Someone needs to find a better place to store those beauties."

Emily climbed out, carrying a small white bag with the "Patsy's Pastries and Pretties" logo. "I hope this works."

"It will."

They hustled past the house and found the crew inside the freestanding garage nailing Sheetrock to vertical wall studs. Jack hummed along with a country-pop tune playing on a radio. A newly installed ceiling fan cooled the space and sent swirls of dust floating through the air.

Rachel stepped into the space and took in the view. "How's it going, guys?"

"It's going." Dennis climbed down from a ladder. "What can we do for you, ladies?"

"We figured you could use a break, so we brought you a snack." Emily opened the bag, releasing the scents of brown sugar and vanilla. She set it on a stack of Sheetrock lying across a pair of sawhorses.

Jack reached into the sack. "Oatmeal raisin. My favorite." He withdrew two and handed one to J. T.

"Beware of pretty ladies bringing cookies." He leaned on his crutch and grinned, then took a bite. "Is this a thank-you or some kind of bribe?"

"A little of each." Rachel flicked a fly away from her face. "What else needs to be done to finish this job?"

Dennis set his hammer beside the cookie bag. "Remove those doors, build a wall with a display window and an entry."

"Plus add shelving, build display cabinets, and paint the place inside and out." Jack reached for another cookie. "What's the bribe part?"

Rachel shared Alicia's proposal for a local premiere.

"Didn't see that coming." Dennis removed his cap and swept his hand through his hair. "That's a tall order."

"I know we're asking a lot. The question is, can you finish the theater in time?"

"That depends." J. T. hobbled over. "How many cookies did you bring?"

"A dozen."

"That's a half-decent bribe." He reached in the bag and pulled out two. "Tell you what, you keep bringing us cookies and darn right we'll get it done. Only next time make 'em chocolate chip."

Rachel laughed. "Any flavor you want."

"You guys are real troopers," Emily said. "We owe you big time."

"You don't owe us nothing."

"J. T.'s right." Jack wiped his hands on his pants. "You gave us a chance to work. That's payment enough."

"I hope you all stick around awhile," Emily said.

"Depends on me and Jack finding jobs after we finish Miss Naomi's projects."

"If … I mean when Willow Falls starts attracting tourists, there'll be more work."

"We'll let you guys go back to work." Rachel nudged Emily as they left the garage. "Are you feeling better about the new deadline?"

"Not even a smidgen."

"Maybe you will after we start writing."

"Don't count on it." Emily glanced at her watch. "Gertie's due in fifteen minutes."

"Time to get this project underway."

Chapter 27

Emily set her water on the dining room table. "Miss Gertie's fee for babysitting is a year's worth of lavender soap and first crack as Scott's soda-fountain lady."

"That's what I call positive thinking." Rachel sat beside her sister and pulled back the cover on the frayed leather binder.

"She's not exactly a spring chicken. I hope she can handle the twins."

"You're one room away, so relax."

Emily popped off her chair the second one of her babies cried.

Rachel grabbed her arm. "If you let every little noise distract you, we'll never start, much less finish."

The crying stopped.

Emily dropped back down.

"I read through the script last night. Naomi's grandfather finished writing Percy and Peaches' love story and started act two, the Newport scene."

"Which means we have to finish the second act and write the entire portion about Everett and Lillian."

"That's not all." Rachel paused. "Naomi wants a play that tickles the funny bone and tugs at the heartstrings, right?"

"She thinks it'll have broader appeal."

"There's the problem. There isn't a stitch of comedy in this script. Which means we have to work on all three acts."

Emily slumped back in her chair. "Where do we begin?"

"Right here." Rachel tapped her copy of the Penelope script. "After we finish reading this, I'll pull up the script for another comedy-drama, *Born Yesterday*. It'll give us ideas about writing humorous dialogue."

"Recruiting you was a smart move."

"And I thought you acted out of desperation."

Emily grinned. "A desperately wise maneuver."

After reading, discussing, and taking notes, Rachel logged off the internet and pushed the Penelope script aside. She laced her fingers behind her head and pressed forward. "What do you think?"

"At least I have a better idea than I did two hours ago."

"So do I. Now the real work begins."

"Once we start, we'll need to keep going." Emily stood and stretched her arms over her head. "First, I need a mental break and something to eat."

"Since Jane and Clair are down for a nap, how about I treat you to lunch."

"At Pepper's?"

"Did another restaurant I don't know about open overnight?"

"You're a riot."

Five minutes later, Emily and Rachel stood on the sidewalk, eyeing the chalkboard outside Pepper's Café. "Daily special, Southern-style meatloaf and mashed potatoes. That brings back memories."

"About what?"

She patted her tummy. "The day I learned I carried twin baby girls."

Inside, Mirabelle sat on a stool at the counter beside Sadie's British guest, listening to him complain about Kat Williams' smoking habit. Customers filled the four booths hugging the partially exposed brick wall on the left. The sisters opted for one of the five vacant Formica-topped tables lined up in the center.

Emily pointed to the white vinyl sign hanging on the back wall with the words, "Welcome to Willow Falls" printed in gold, sandwiched between detailed drawings of wine bottles. "At this point, that's the only hint the town's open to visitors."

"At least there's one."

The waitress approached and set two one-page menus on their table. "The special is real good today."

"Works for me."

Rachel nodded. "Make it two."

Mirabelle spun her stool around. "Everyone's talking about the play."

Emily snickered. "Imagine that."

"I've a mind to try out for a role. Did you know my friend Winston wrote a play back in England? You should ask him to help you."

Rachel rolled her eyes.

Emily fingered her rolled-up napkin while trying to conjure up a good reason to reject the offer. "Thanks for your suggestion, it's ..."

"I appreciate the offer." Winston swiveled toward them.

Emily gave Rachel a now-what-do-we-do look.

He fingered his light-blue ascot. "I write murder mysteries, so I wouldn't be much help. Plus, I'm too busy with my book to take on another project." He eyed Emily. "You're a writer. You understand."

She stifled a sigh. "Of course I do."

"In fact, it's time to work on my book." He slid off his stool, nodded as he passed, then walked out of the café.

"He's such a charming man." Mirabelle pulled a chair away from their table and plopped down. "Some of the single ladies around here want him to stay in town longer than five months."

Rachel set her napkin on her lap. "His accent is hard for some people to resist."

"So is his money. Everyone thinks he's as rich as a movie star. I hear Naomi's painting the scenery for the play."

"She is."

"When word leaks out, you'll sell a ton of tickets. How's the writing going?"

"We're just getting started."

"My great-grandpa moved his family down from South Carolina to work for Percy. He helped Scott's grandfather build Hayes General Store. You should include him in your script."

"I wish we could." Emily unwrapped her utensils. "Unfortunately, we're limited to the number of main characters we can include."

"Then I hope you wrote about him in your book." She glanced at her watch. "I need to return to my route. I'll catch up with you two later."

When the café door closed behind Mirabelle, Rachel leaned forward. "We dodged a bullet with Winston."

"No kidding." Emily paused. "Although, we could ask his opinion if we run into a snag."

"Perhaps."

Two elderly ladies scooted from their booth and stopped at their table. The taller woman glanced at Emily, then Rachel. "We've been trying to figure out how people tell you two apart."

"Freckle count," they said in unison.

"Emily spent more time in the sun than me."

The woman stared at Rachel. "Not *much* more."

The shorter lady eyed Emily. "We hear Scott's going to hire Gertie as his soda lady."

"At this point, a soda fountain is simply an idea."

"He's a smart young man. He'll jump on it. Don't you love Winston Hamilton? He's so polite and handsome."

"Yes, he is," Emily said.

"We're heading over to Scott's store. I'm hankering for some of those gourmet jellybeans."

"You eat too much sugar," said the short woman as they headed toward the door.

"At least I don't have a hankering for afternoon toddies."

Emily waited for the door to close. "There are no secrets around here."

"One more fact is clear," Rachel said. "Jumping to conclusions is a favorite pastime."

"You mean Gertie's soda fountain gig?"

"Plus, the so-called new millionaire in town. Imagine the rumors that'll fly when tourists start showing up."

"The stuff good novels are made of."

Thirty minutes after the waitress delivered their daily specials, Emily and Rachel returned home. By five they'd finished outlining the second and third act.

"The way I figure it, we'll need six set changes." Rachel uncapped a bottle of water. "Plus, a decent-sized stage crew."

"It will take a lot of people to pull this off." Emily closed her laptop. "None of them with a lick of experience except you and Naomi."

Gertie stepped in the dining room. "Your sweet babies are in their playpen."

"I hope they didn't wear you out."

"I napped right along with them. Will you ask your husband to bring me a bag of lemon drops? They're my favorite."

"Mine too, and yes, I will."

"Are you going to the big meeting tonight?"

"Wouldn't miss it."

"Good. I'll see you there." She tucked her purse under her arm and walked out.

Emily stood and stretched her arms behind her back. "We can work on the script tomorrow after church."

"Good idea. Charlie's picking me up in a few minutes. We're going to grab a bite to eat before we head over."

"Save me a seat if you arrive first." Her phone pinged. "A text from Scott. They're expecting a huge crowd again tonight."

"We might end up standing along the back wall again."

"Not a problem, as long as you don't try to rope me into another crazy project."

Chapter 28

The nursery's pale pink color, the Cinderella castle painted on the wall, and the iridescent stars on the ceiling failed to calm Emily's anxiety. Scuttlebutt hinted that residents not on board with the town's tourist plan would show up to disrupt tonight's town hall meeting. She breathed in the baby-powder scent and shifted her focus to the twins in their cribs. "Nathan's daughter is coming to stay with you sweet girls while Mommy attends a big ole ruckus."

The doorbell rang.

"She's here."

Cody and Brownie jumped from the oak floor and followed her to the front door. After escorting the sitter to the nursery and giving instructions, Emily drove to town. She parked behind Scott's store, rushed up the alley, and turned toward the church. Inside, she made her way through the crowd and squeezed into the last row beside Rachel and Charlie. "Thanks for saving me a seat."

"Lucky we found one." Rachel set her purse on the floor. "If Nathan keeps calling these meetings, the town will have to build a bigger church."

"Or a courtroom that holds more than a judge and two dozen observers."

"Willow Falls has a judge?"

"We share one with a couple of other small towns."

"I'm surprised you have a mayor and a town council."

Emily knuckle-thumped her. "Hey, we're small, not backward."

Charlie shook his head. "Rachel seems to think a town with fewer than three thousand residents is nothing more than an oversized subdivision."

"You have to admit it isn't a thriving metropolis."

Emily pointed to the front. "Nathan ... our *mayor* ... is about to kick off this meeting."

"Point taken."

Nathan rapped his gavel until the crowd fell silent. "Thanks for coming out tonight. A lot has happened in the past week, beginning with Connor, our seventeen-year-old computer expert. He worked with the council to set up a Willow Falls website."

"This town needs to wise up and enter the twenty-first century," yelled a teenager.

"The best of the new and old," said Nathan. "I found a good deal on an antique player piano up in Greenville. If it's in decent shape, my brother Jacob and I will donate it to the town."

"What about the soda fountain?" shouted Gertie.

Scott stepped beside Nathan. "I'm working on it."

Rachel nudged Emily. "Is he really?"

"Guess he figures Gertie won't quit bugging him until he makes it happen."

Nathan invited Patsy to the front.

The tiny woman, her white hat adorned with three peacock feathers, adjusted the mic. "I grew up and married my Tommy here in Willow Falls. After he died all those years ago, I stayed in town because I love the people who live here." She pressed her palms together and touched her fingertips to her chin. "I'm pleased to announce that every hotel room has been adopted. Sixty families are turning Redding Arms into the most unique small hotel in the South, maybe the whole country."

A woman two rows up from Emily stood. "Who's gonna make sure the rooms don't look ... you know ... cheap and tacky?"

"Kat and Sadie will approve every plan. Now about sprucing up downtown. The storefronts need some paint and repairs. We're also thinking flower boxes, new awnings, and flags with the town's name hanging on light poles."

Gertie dashed to the podium. "Excuse me for interrupting. I have something important to say. Y'all know about Naomi's plan for the play. Well, someone should buy Percy's old mansion and turn it into a fancy tourist attraction."

"That old house has been on the market for more years than I can remember," yelled a woman across the aisle. "Don't you think if anyone around here could afford the place, they'd have already bought it?"

A man wearing overalls stood. "After blowing our money on a lousy PR firm, the council can't contribute a dime."

Scott returned to the front. "Maybe we could all chip in a little money—"

"Easy for you to say," shouted the town's crankiest curmudgeon. "You have money."

Emily crossed her arms. *If he only knew.*

"Fact is, most of us around here are broker than a rusty truck engine."

"He's right about that," said Overalls. "Maybe we'd best forget the whole tourist idea."

"That's backwards thinking," Gertie said.

"Horse feathers. I'm being realistic." He turned and faced the crowd. "How many of you agree with me?"

Half the residents responded.

"We're the smart ones. Everyone else is barking up the wrong willow oak."

"Hold on." Patsy leaned close to the mic. "A lot of people have already stepped up—"

"Yeah, with junk to fancy up a bunch of hotel rooms."

Mirabelle stood and shook her finger at the man. "You mean treasure."

"Hah."

Nathan's gavel rap failed to stop the chaos that erupted between residents who wanted to move forward and those ready to call it quits.

Emily's chest tightened as she listened to friends and neighbors exchange accusations and insults. She cringed. Town council members volunteered their time, and Nathan hadn't earned a dime for his service as mayor. Maybe asking struggling families to dig into their pockets was unreasonable. She tried to imagine what her parents would do. They wouldn't give up ... or would they? At some point reality had to dictate action. Had the town she loved reached that point?

"We need a miracle," Emily mumbled.

A four-year-old boy, dressed in blue shorts, a striped T-shirt half tucked in, and tennis shoes—one untied—stepped into the aisle. He marched to the front and tugged on Nathan's shirt.

The mayor leaned down and listened. He nodded, then lifted the microphone from its stand. The pair moved in front of the podium. Nathan's two-finger whistle quieted the crowd. "Our friend Billy has something to say."

The tot clutched the mic in both hands. "My mommy gives me fifty cents a week to do chores. I like sweeping floors best. I've been saving up." He reached into his pocket, pulled out a handful of change, and looked up at Nathan. "I wanna give you two dollars to buy that old house for Willow Falls."

Nathan held his palm out.

Billy dropped the coins in his hand.

"I think our town has a new motto. 'We are for Willow Falls.'"

A preschool blonde girl wearing a pink dress ran up the side and grabbed the microphone from Billy. "I've got four dollars saved." She looked up at Nathan. "You can have it, Mr. Mayor … to make our town all better."

A twelve-year-old boy sitting on the end of a row stood. "I've been saving for a new guitar, but my old one's fine. I have twenty-seven dollars to donate."

Emily dabbed her eyes. "Sometimes children have more sense than adults."

Rachel sniffed and nodded. "Too bad they don't have a boatload of money."

Charlie pointed to the front. "It's Dad."

Brick stepped up to the twelve-year-old and shook his hand. Then he moved to the front, squatted, and hugged the two miniature donors.

The girl held the mic close to her mouth. "Mr. Bricker wants to talk now."

He patted her head and accepted the mic. "Thank you, sweetheart." He faced the crowd. "Some of you know I'm a bit superstitious. Call it a personality flaw. The fact is I don't need a rainbow or a lucky rabbit's foot to know this town has heart." He paused and glanced around.

Rachel leaned close to Charlie. "What's he going to do?"

"Something big."

Brick smiled at the youngsters. "Your donation is a mighty fine down payment. I've saved some money too. In fact, I think I have enough to add to your contribution and buy that old house."

Stunned silence.

Billy looped his thumbs in his pockets and grinned.

"That's right young man, we're going to turn it into the best tourist attraction in Georgia."

Cheers erupted.

Emily squeezed her sister's hand. "I think we have our miracle."

Chapter 29

Rachel opened the door and followed Brownie out to Charlie's backyard. She sat on the grass, wrapped her arms around her shins, and rested her chin on her knees. Watching her puppy romp with Sarge did little to ease the apprehension churning her stomach. Less than a week before their self-ascribed script-finishing deadline, the play needed a ton more work, and Emily struggled with guilt over spending too much time away from her babies.

Charlie stepped out. He sat beside her and handed over a bottle of light beer. "Time to fess up."

"About what?"

"Whatever's put you in a mood."

"You noticed."

"How could I miss it?"

She stared at the golden liquid shimmering in the bottle. "I don't know what made Emily and me think we could write, cast, and direct a top-notch performance by October, much less by mid-September."

"Sounds like you have a pity party going on in your pretty head."

"More like a big dose of Rachel-rama."

"That word wouldn't qualify in a game of Scrabble."

"I didn't know you played."

"Used to. With my dad and brother."

"It accurately describes the upheaval messing with my brain." She flicked a bug off a blade of grass. "I suppose we could add double-talk to our script."

"Confusing the heck out of your audience is an interesting approach."

"Maybe that's what we need to keep them distracted from a lackluster performance." Brownie raced across the yard and plopped beside her. "What if I'm more suited for the corporate world than the entertainment business?"

"Did you forget how miserable you were at Streetman Enterprise?"

Her mind drifted back to the years she longed to escape her father's control and follow her dream. "At least I earned a good living." Rachel stroked Brownie's back. "There's a good chance our play will end in colossal failure."

"That's an arrogant statement."

She turned and glared at him. "How is fact arrogant?"

"You're dismissing all the people who volunteered to help you and Emily. Like Pepper and her costume committee and the high-school art teacher and his set-building crew. What about Naomi paying you and Emily and her commitment to paint the scenery? Don't forget Dennis and the guys working their tails off to finish your stage on time."

"I see your point. Problem is, none of that will matter if we don't recruit a decent cast and direct them with at least some expertise."

"You really are in a mood."

"For good reason." She sighed. "The whole town is counting on us to pull off a miracle."

"You were a corporate vice president. Don't tell me you can't figure out how to produce one little play."

"There's a lot more to it than you might think."

"I'm not underestimating the challenge." He took a swig of beer. "There is one big upside to this whole play project. It's keeping you from hightailing it back to Atlanta."

"There is that." She gazed at the clouds' pink hue and darkening sky as the sun began its descent below the six-foot cedar fence that kept the dogs in and the critters out. Sarge bounded over and nudged Brownie with her nose. The pup sprang to her feet and chased after her canine friend.

Rachel stretched her legs out. "I'm curious. Is something going on between your dad and Mama Sadie?"

His head jerked toward her. "What in the heck are you talking about?"

"They were together July Fourth and at both town hall meetings."

"What's your point?"

"I guess I don't have one."

He remained silent for a long moment. "My mother broke his heart when she ran off with a younger man."

"That happened a long time ago."

"I don't think he ever recovered." Charlie plucked a weed from the lawn. "I doubt he'll ever trust another woman."

"I hope you're wrong." A gentle breeze rustled the leaves and cooled Rachel's cheeks. Charlie scooted closer to her. His thigh touched hers. His arm encircled her waist. She rested her head against his shoulder and let his strength flow through her. "I'm glad you're here for me, Charlie."

"I wouldn't have it any other way."

Chapter 30

Rachel yawned and carried a cup of coffee to the dining room. "Last night I dreamed J. T. swore a blue streak at church. Residents kicked him out of town. Jack and Dennis were so angry they bailed, leaving us with a half-finished theater."

"Anxiety over the script?" Emily opened her laptop.

"I'm blaming it on the sugar rush from eating a second piece of cherry pie."

"That's easier to swallow."

"You're full of good lines."

Scott stepped in from the kitchen. "Gertie's finally here."

"Thanks for sticking around to help us out."

He moved behind her and massaged her shoulders. "How's it going?"

"We've been working on the script for weeks, and … I don't know … something's missing."

"You two will figure it out."

"We'd better. Auditions are three days away."

He kissed the top of her head. "I'm off to help paint the hotel dining room."

"See you tonight, honey." Emily rolled her head from side to side. "I don't understand why nothing's clicking."

"Something's missing." Rachel moved to the window and watched Brownie goad Cody into a chase. She shifted her thoughts to the dozens of plays she'd attended. "What did all my favorites have in common?"

"Pardon me?"

"The missing ingredient." She spun around. "It's pizazz. People on vacation want fun-filled, feel-good entertainment. Right?"

"That's a no-brainer."

"The best plays blend great story with humor … and music."

Emily eyed her with suspicion. "What are you saying?"

"We have to add music—"

"Are you suggesting we turn the play into a musical?"

"Not exactly. I'm thinking interludes and emphasis for specific scenes. Like in a movie."

"If I didn't know better, I'd swear you were delirious."

"I'm dead serious."

Emily crossed her arms and glared. "Are you telling me you want to find a songwriter willing to work for peanuts and convince him or her to write music in a matter of days?"

"Precisely."

"How is that possible?"

"I haven't figured that part out yet." Rachel paced, then halted. "Maybe someone living around here is a closet composer."

"About as likely as Martians invading Willow Falls."

She rounded the table and grabbed Emily's hand. "Come with me."

"Where are we going this time?"

"To pick the brain of the one person who knows more about this town than you."

"You're kidding."

"Do you want this play to succeed or not?"

"Lead the way, crazy lady."

Five minutes later, they dashed into Pepper's Café as Winston headed out the door. He nodded. "Afternoon, ladies."

They found Mirabelle sitting at the counter eating a piece of chocolate cake. Rachel sat on her left, Emily on her right.

She looked from one to the other. "What? Did I deliver the wrong mail? Or are you two planning to kidnap a U.S. postal employee?"

"Hmm, that would definitely put our town on the map." Emily grinned. "Except we're aiming for publicity, not notoriety."

"Actually, my sister and I need information. So, we came to the most knowledgeable person in town."

Mirabelle's chest puffed. "What do you want to know?"

Rachel propped her elbow on the counter and rested her cheek on her knuckles. "Do any residents have song-writing experience?"

"Why? Are you turning your play into a musical? I like shows with music and dancing. *West Side Story* is one of my all-time favorite movies. It's both funny and sad. Too bad no one around here writes songs."

Emily's shoulders slumped. She swiveled and gazed at the lakeside park across the street, convinced her sister's idea was dead as disco.

"Hold on." Mirabelle wiped her mouth with a napkin. "A few years back, Wayne Peterson mailed a package to a recording studio. A couple of months later, they sent a response. As far as I know, no one sent him any more correspondence."

Rachel peered around Mirabelle. "Who's she talking about?"

"Our retired high-school music teacher. The kids all loved him. Rheumatoid arthritis forced him to leave the job he loved."

"Maybe he's our closet composer."

"That's a stretch."

"There's only one way to find out." Rachel slid off the stool.

"Thanks for the tip, Mirabelle."

"Any time, ladies."

They left the café and headed to Rachel's car. Emily slid into the passenger seat. "You know we're chasing a fantasy."

"Just give me directions to his house."

"Turn on Fall Street."

Following a short drive, Rachel parked at the curb. "What a charming cottage."

"The Petersons have lived here their entire married life."

Emily climbed out, crossed the sidewalk, and opened the picket-fence gate. They followed the winding stone walkway lined with pink begonias. A double swing hung on the front porch. The leaves on a potted lemon tree stood in contrast to white wood siding.

Emily rang the bell.

A short, white-haired woman with a glowing smile opened the door. "My goodness, what a delightful surprise. Please come in."

"Thank you, Miss Agnes. Rachel, meet one of the sweetest ladies in town."

She extended her hand. "It's a pleasure, ma'am."

"Around here, we don't shake hands with friends, we hug." She embraced Rachel. "My husband counted your sister as one of his favorite students."

Emily grinned. "I suspect he considered every student his favorite."

"He did love all his kids. What brings you lovely ladies to our home?"

"An idea Rachel wants to run by Mr. Peterson."

"Sweetie, you can call him Wayne. He's on the back porch."

The wide-plank, wood floors creaked as their hostess led them through the kitchen. The aroma of bacon, cinnamon, and apples made Emily's stomach rumble.

Agnes pulled the screen door open. "We have company, dear."

He eased off a rocking chair and hobbled toward his guests.

"Hello, Mr. … Wayne."

"One of my favorite students." He held Emily's hand in his gnarled fingers and smiled at her sister. "You're obviously Rachel."

"Yes sir. I hear you were Willow Falls' favorite high-school music teacher."

"I was the only one for forty years, so I guess that made me the favorite. Come on and sit a spell. How's your playwriting coming along?"

Agnes stepped out from the kitchen carrying a tray with four glasses of lemonade and a plate of cookies.

"The dialogue is finished." Rachel explained her new idea.

"Interesting concept. Who's writing the music for you?"

"We're hoping you know someone with composing experience."

He ran his fingers through his thick white hair. "I'm sorry to disappoint you, but I don't—"

"My goodness, Wayne. You always were too modest for your own good. I have something to show you ladies." Agnes disappeared and returned moments later, carrying a cardboard box.

"Sweetheart, we don't want to bore our guests with those."

"Nonsense. You've kept your work hidden away long enough." She laid the box in Rachel's lap. "Go ahead, open it."

She lifted the lid and stared at a stack of song sheets. "Did you write all these?"

"A useless hobby."

"It might not have been if you hadn't given up so easily." Agnes shook her finger at him. "After one turn down from a recording studio, he gave up."

Emily nodded. "Believe me, I understand. When I received my first rejection from a publisher, I came close to doing the same thing."

Wayne shrugged. "I figured if the good Lord wanted me to write music for other folks, He'd find a way to let me know."

Rachel plucked a song sheet from the stack. "I noticed a piano in the front room. Would you mind playing this for us?"

He held his hand up. "These fingers can no longer handle the keys."

"He's right." Agnes stood. "But mine can. Ladies, please follow me. And bring that box." She led them back inside and settled at the upright piano. "I know I'm prejudiced, but I'm telling you, Wayne's work is more than a hobby. It's his passion. Will you hand me that first piece?"

Emily closed her eyes and listened to her play a medley of original tunes. When Agnes finished, Rachel leaned close to her sister. "Now, what do you think of my wacky idea?"

"It just moved to the possible category."

Wayne wandered in and sat on the bench beside his wife. "Are you going to make our friends sit through the entire repertoire?"

"Mr. Peterson—"

"Please, call me Wayne."

Rachel scooted to the edge of her seat. "Your work is quite good."

Agnes elbowed his ribs. "That's what I've been telling him for thirty-five years."

"She has a good ear." Emily caught Wayne's eye. "Would you be willing to work with us to add some musical highlights to our play?"

"Of course he will."

Wayne stared at his wife.

She patted his cheek. "I believe the Lord is sending you a message, dear."

A grin deepened the wrinkles around his eyes. "How can I refuse three beautiful women and the Lord."

"Then it's settled." Rachel tapped Emily's arm. "You need to call Scott."

"And tell him what?"

"To create those trophies, because *Percy's Legacy* is going to be a big hit."

Chapter 31

Emily pushed her chair away from the dining-room table. "I want to spend time with my babies before our composer shows up."

"We're at a good stopping point." Rachel stood and pressed her fingers against her lower back, then followed Emily to the den.

"How are my girls doing?"

Gertie scooted to the edge of the sofa. "Why, they're fine and dandy."

"Like wine and candy?" She chuckled and sat on the floor beside the twins. Clair crawled onto her lap. "Did Scott tell you this sweet girl said her first word last night?"

"Uh-huh, dada. Your husband couldn't stop talking about it."

"This morning, he strutted around like a peacock." Emily tapped her baby's nose. "How long before you learn to say Mama?"

Clair pressed her fingers to her mother's lips. "Mama."

"Oh, my gosh." Tears filled Emily's eyes as she held Clair close and kissed her cheek. "You are one smart girl."

Rachel sat beside her sister. "No matter what happens, at this moment, all is right with the world."

Emily wiped one cheek, then the other. "I'm glad you were here to share it with me."

"So am I." She gathered Jane in her arms. "How about you, sweet girl. Can you say Mama for your mommy?"

The baby crinkled her nose, then reached for a toy.

"She'll follow her sister's example soon."

The sisters played and giggled with the twins until the doorbell rang.

"I'll let them in." Rachel pushed off the floor.

"Mama has to go back to work now. Miss Gertie will take good care of you." She kissed Clair then Jane and walked back to the dining room

Wayne set a keyboard on the dining room table. "My grandson's."

"It's almost as good as our piano." Agnes laid down a folder. "Wayne stayed up to the wee hours matching his music to your script."

"I'm impressed," Rachel said.

"I've figured most of it out." He pulled a chair out for his wife. "That is, if you and your sister agree."

"We're eager to hear it."

For the better part of two hours, the elderly couple worked as a team, playing and explaining each number.

Although she didn't know anything about live theater, Emily knew the music added pizazz and punctuated key scenes. Her shoulders relaxed as the idea of delivering a play with original music and scenery painted by a famous artist played in her mind. Maybe the time and effort they were pouring into Naomi's project would pay off after all.

"I'm lovin' it," Rachel said. "Especially that number you're suggesting for the Percy and Peaches love scene."

Agnes pressed her hands together. "Finally, everyone will know how talented this wonderful man is."

"Yes, they will."

Wayne's face beamed. "I'm glad to help. There's one more number I want you to hear."

Gertie slipped into the room and tapped Emily's shoulder. "I'm sorry for bothering you. Mirabelle's at the door. She insists on speaking to you."

"This can't be good."

"Do you want me to send her away?"

"No, she'll keep bugging you until you give in."

Wayne moved a song sheet aside. "Our self-appointed town crier is persistent."

The woman clumped in. A scowl distorted her features. She tossed a letter on the table. "How do you explain this?"

"What is it?"

"A letter to Kat. Read the return address."

"I don't understand."

"I looked the guy up. He's a probation officer." Mirabelle crossed her arms over her chest. "Why didn't you tell me she's a criminal, and what about Missy? Is she a lawbreaker too?"

Memories of Mirabelle's harsh reaction to Sadie's return from prison tensed Emily's jaw. "You storm into my house all fired up, and you have the audacity to ask why?"

"It's my right to know."

"It's wrong to use residents' mail to spy on them."

"Somebody has to pay attention to what's going on around here."

Wayne leaned forward. "You know, my friend, snooping in someone's mail is against the law."

"Don't you think I know that? See for yourself. The envelope is still sealed. I simply noticed who sent it."

"It would be a shame if my sister and mother are forced to change the Mirabelle suite's name."

She glared at Rachel. "Are you threatening me?"

"I'm trying to say that Willow Inn's honorees are people who had the town's best interest at heart."

"You don't think I care about my town?"

"What my twin's trying to say," Emily said, "is we're a few months away from launching Willow Falls as a tourist attraction. The last thing we need is an uproar over two women who are helping make the transition possible."

"And you want me to keep my mouth shut."

Emily breathed deep to keep her composure. "Look, I'm simply asking you to extend the same grace to Kat and Missy that you gave Sadie."

Mirabelle hesitated. "All right. I'll stay quiet unless either one of them causes trouble."

"Fair enough."

She grabbed the letter and stomped from the room. When the front door slammed, Gertie returned. "I couldn't help overhearing." She zipped her fingers across her lips. "Don't worry. I won't say a word to anyone. Like Sadie, those ladies deserve a second chance."

"You're a good woman, Miss Gertie."

"I'm an old lady who wants Willow Falls to succeed so young folks like you and Scott will stick around." She smiled at Rachel. "And maybe you and Charlie will decide to make a home here. Now, if you'll excuse me, I have to put two beautiful girls down for their nap."

Wayne locked eyes with Emily. "You don't have to worry about Agnes and me."

"He's right. We learned a long time ago not to judge anyone."

"You two are a credit to our community."

Rachel scooted close to the table. "With any luck, enough good things will happen to keep residents from caring about Kat and Missy's backgrounds."

"We can hope." Emily forced a smile. "For now, let's hear that last number."

Chapter 32

A suffocating heat wave descended on Willow Falls the day of the auditions. Rachel laid a box of scripts on a table in the high school cafetorium. "How many do you think will show up?"

"Your guess is as good as mine. It's hot as a fried egg in here." Emily set a cooler on the floor, then lifted her hair and wiped the back of her neck.

"Did you call someone about the air conditioning?"

"It's on."

"If it doesn't start cooling down soon, we'll all melt into one giant puddle." Rachel removed a stack of scripts from the box. "I'm counting on you to help me figure out who's coachable."

"What about talent?"

"Chances are, that'll be in short supply. Which means I have to rely on coachability."

"Naomi's walking in."

"At least one experienced player showed up."

"Two, if we count you." Emily leafed through a script. "Maybe there's some hidden talent lurking out there."

"You mean like Wayne." Rachel sighed. "That's probably too much to ask."

Ten minutes before start time, the air had cooled to a tolerable level. Several dozen residents sat at tables, chatting.

Emily leaned close to Rachel. "Mirabelle's here."

"Do you suppose she wants to audition?"

"If she does, I hope to goodness she can act. Otherwise, we'll never hear the end of her grumbling. Well, I'll be." She nudged Rachel. "Look who walked in."

She turned and spotted Missy and Dennis followed by Kat and Sadie.

"Did you know they planned to show up?"

"Didn't have a clue."

Rachel glanced at her watch. "It's nine, straight up. Are you ready to start this task?"

"Might as well." Emily moved closer to the crowd. "Hey, everyone. Thanks for coming in. As y'all know, my sister and I finished writing a play started by Naomi's great grandfather. We hope … correction, we believe *Percy's Legacy* will attract tourists to Willow Falls. How many of you came to audition?"

Nearly everyone raised a hand. "Okay, then. Our director will take over from here."

Rachel stepped beside Emily and glanced at the faces staring at her. "Before we begin, I want you to know that during the past year and a half I sat in my share of theaters with my heart pounding, waiting for my turn to audition. Sometimes the director offered me the part. More often not."

She paused. "I'm telling you this because my role as director is to identify candidates who best reflect each character's personality. Sometimes subtleties make the difference. Although the play has only seven key parts, we'll also need minor players and a good size backstage crew. Each one of those roles is critical to the play's success."

She paused. "Today, I'll ask you to audition two at a time."

Mirabelle raised her hand. "Why with someone else?"

"It's easier to slip in character when you interact with another person. When you come up, Emily will hand you a script. I'll give you a few minutes to review your lines. At some point, I'll give you some direction. And maybe ask you to read from a different scene. Any questions?"

"When will we find out who gets the parts?" asked Mirabelle.

"In two days, at the theater." She paused. "Okay, everyone, who wants to go first?"

The enthusiasm displayed by the initial candidates failed to compensate for their lack of talent. By noon, only two people had exhibited even a modicum of acting skills—Mary, Emily's reporter, and Chuck, the church youth minister. The moment Rachel announced a lunch break, she closed her eyes and massaged her temples.

"Lots of folks are talking about your play." Sadie's voice broke through the fog in her head.

"Emily and I saw you two come in. Do you and Kat want to audition?"

"Heavens, no," Kat said. "We're here for Missy. You know she's struggling to find her place in Willow Falls. So, we encouraged her to try out."

Emily laced her arms behind her neck and pressed her head forward. "Does she have any acting experience?"

"She played the lead in a high-school play." Kat plucked a script off the table. "She claimed it as the one happy memory from her youth."

Rachel eyed the young girl standing by the exit. "Sounds familiar. For her sake, and ours, I hope she has talent. What about Dennis?"

"She begged him to read with her. He gave her a hard time, but finally agreed."

"Good for him." Emily lowered her arms and rolled her head from side to side.

"The four of us are going to Pepper's," Sadie said. "Why don't you and Emily join us?"

"Thanks, but we brought lunch."

When the last person left, Rachel collapsed onto a chair. "It's not looking good."

"We still have a few more folks who haven't stepped up." Emily removed two sandwiches from the cooler.

"What'd you think?"

"You should call Alicia and cancel." She gave Rachel a sandwich.

"That bad?"

"Other than Mary and Chuck, no one came close."

"Then we better pray someone with a smidgen of talent or coachability shows up after lunch."

By the time the candidates returned, Rachel's chest muscles rivaled a rubber band stretched around a foot-high stack of newspaper. Relief washed over her when Naomi volunteered to audition and, despite her partner's poor showing, delivered the day's best performance.

Rachel waited for the artist to return to her seat. "Okay, who's next?"

"Me." Mirabelle moved to the front. "I'm trying out for the Newport maven role."

"You need a partner." Rachel scanned the crowd. No one moved a muscle. "I guess it's you and me." Two minutes into the audition, she knew the town's head gossip needed to stick to delivering mail. Rachel thanked her.

Following a mediocre delivery from two more candidates, Missy and Dennis shuffled to the front.

Rachel smiled at the young woman. "I hear you did some acting in high school."

"Yes ma'am."

"So did I." She tilted her head. "I want you two to read a scene playing Peaches and Percy."

Missy's eyes widened. "The leads?"

"They're about your age at the beginning of the play."

She bit her lower lip.

"I'll give you an easy part."

Missy lowered her chin. "Okay."

Rachel moved close and whispered. "I'm always nervous when I audition."

"Really?"

"Uh-huh. You'll do fine."

After studying their lines, they read a short scene. When they finished, Rachel approached the couple. "I want you to try that again. This time, Missy, pretend you're Peaches and you're in love with Percy."

Her cheeks flushed. "I'll try."

Although their acting stepped up a notch, it fell far from adequate.

When no one else volunteered to audition, Rachel expressed her gratitude and dismissed the crowd.

Mirabelle cornered Rachel. "Don't you think I'd make the perfect maven? I mean she's sophisticated, a natural leader."

"I appreciate your confidence. Emily and I will reveal our decision at the theater."

"I'll be there." She took a step, then stopped and turned back toward Rachel. "I haven't said a word about … you know."

"Thank you."

When Mirabelle stepped out of earshot, Rachel pulled Emily aside. "Did she threaten me?"

"Trust me, we have more leverage than she has."

"We better, because one decision's certain. Naomi's playing the Newport maven."

Chapter 33

Rachel slipped her shoes off and massaged her feet. "Doesn't matter how many times we talk about it. The facts won't change. Despite her mediocre acting, Missy is the only half-decent Peaches candidate."

Emily collected toys from the living room floor and dropped them in a basket. "Why don't you take the role?"

"Missy's better suited for it."

"You know Kat pushed her to audition. We don't know if she'll agree to take the part."

"Which is why Charlie's bringing her over, so we can convince her."

"Who are you casting as Percy?"

"I haven't figured that out yet."

Emily stashed the toy basket behind a plush, overstuffed chair. "What about the last guy who auditioned?"

She shook her head. "If I had the luxury of time maybe. But there's no way I can bring him up to speed in six weeks. Besides, I'm not convinced he'd respond well to coaching."

"That doesn't leave us many choices."

"Tell me about it."

Scott wandered in carrying a dish of ice cream. "The twins are down for the night."

"Thanks, honey. You're a great dad."

"I'm also auditioning for the husband-of-the-year award." Headlights illuminated the living room. "A car's pulling into our driveway. Are you two expecting company?"

"Hopefully our newest cast member." Rachel hopped up and opened the front door. "Come on in and have a seat."

Missy sat on the couch between Dennis and Charlie. She folded her hands in her lap.

Rachel settled in the chair beside Emily.

"If you folks don't need me, I'll go watch the Braves game," Scott said. "If they win tonight, they'll move into the lead in our division."

"They're up by two runs." Charlie propped his ankle on his knee. "We were listening on the way over."

"Thanks for trekking over at this late hour. I've reviewed our audition notes and come to a conclusion." Rachel scooted to the edge of her seat. "Missy, you are the best person to play Peaches."

"I don't understand. I know I didn't do good."

"What matters is your potential and my coaching ability."

"She's right," Dennis said. "You should take it."

"I don't think I can act in front of a bunch of strangers."

"Believe me, I know how you feel." Rachel folded her hands. "I'll help you."

Missy chewed her thumbnail for a long moment. "I'll do it if Dennis plays Percy."

"Hold your horses. I'm no actor. I agreed to audition with you, nothing more. Besides, people around here wouldn't take kindly to newcomers landing the two lead roles."

Emily nudged Rachel and whispered. "We need to talk."

"Now?"

"In the kitchen." She walked out of the room.

"You guys think it over." Rachel followed her. "I know what you're going to say."

"You mean about Dennis being a lousy actor?"

"Plus, the fact that he's right about us taking all kinds of heat if we cast them both." She gripped Rachel's arm. "You have to take the role of Peaches."

"You don't understand. I can't." She moved to the patio doors and watched the last light of day disappear. "Truth is … confidence in my directing ability is teetering between nonexistent and barely middling."

"Are you serious?"

"As Hershey's is to a chocoholic. Which is why I can't split my focus until I find my bearings and figure out how to pull this whole thing off. Besides, she won't do it without him."

"You want to cast two reluctant, untalented newcomers to the leads in a play we expect to put Willow Falls on the map?"

"Maybe they'll inspire each other to heights we can't imagine."

"And England's royal family may book a reservation at Willow Inn."

"Well, there you go." She elbowed Emily. "Sadie already has one of the Queen's subjects staying there."

Emily locked eyes with her sister. "You're going through with it, aren't you?"

"My only choice, unless you want to cancel the whole shindig."

"What if Dennis refuses?"

"We can't let that happen." Rachel returned to the living room.

Emily followed.

Rachel settled across from her targets. "We've been talking … and believe you two would make a good team."

"No way." Dennis crossed his arms. "Look, I appreciate everything you've done for me and my guys, but my hands are full with the construction project."

"Everyone's busy, which is why we'll rehearse at night."

"Missy doesn't need me."

Her eyes pleaded. "Yes, I do."

An endearing look passed between them.

Minutes passed.

Rachel gripped the chair's arms and fought the urge to beg.

Dennis unfolded his arms. "I'll give it a shot."

She released her grip. "Well now, it seems we have our first cast members. I think this calls for hot fudge sundaes." She turned toward Emily. "Don't you agree?"

"Sure." She motioned to her guests. "Come on in the kitchen."

Missy and Dennis followed her.

Charlie leaned back and crossed his ankle over his knee. "Slick move."

"What?"

"How you and Missy conned him into taking that part."

"Oh yeah? What if I manage to turn Dennis into an award-winning actor?"

"The chance of that happening? Zero to one."

"Why the negative attitude?"

"He's a regular guy."

"Oh, I get it." She glared at him. "Regular guys couldn't possibly be attracted to my profession."

"That's not what I'm saying. Look, I just don't understand your profession."

"Maybe it's time you found out."

His brow scrunched. "What are you suggesting?"

"Read a scene with me."

"Not gonna happen."

"Why? Are you afraid you won't measure up?"

"Not on your life. Where's the script."

"Right there on the coffee table." She flipped it open.

He set both feet on the floor and grabbed the script. "What's my role?"

"Everett. I'm Lillian."

Emily, Missy, and Dennis returned with hot fudge sundaes. "What's going on?"

"Charlie's introduction to acting."

Emily dipped her spoon in the ice cream. "This should be interesting."

He read through the dialogue. "It's a love scene."

"Are you intimidated?"

"Heck no. Let's get this show on the road."

He launched into the role with over-the-top animation. Five minutes later, he read the last line, swept Rachel in his arms, and kissed her with passion. When he released her, the audience of three applauded and whistled.

Her heart raced. "At least the kiss deserves a sundae."

"Now, you're talking." He pressed his hand to her back as they moved to the kitchen. "I'll take extra chocolate and a fat cherry on top."

"Coming right up." Rachel removed a carton of ice cream from the freezer. "You were better than I expected. I'm thinking maybe—"

"Stop right there. If you have some insane idea in your head about recruiting me, forget it."

"I'm playing Lillian, which means the guy who plays Everett gets to kiss me with abandon during every performance. Twice."

She scooped ice cream and smothered it with chocolate. "The truth is, no one I auditioned comes close to qualifying." She handed him the bowl. "There's another reason you should take the part."

"You're desperate?"

"Besides that. You'd find out why acting is my passion."

"I'll take your word for it. Besides, I'm not a pushover like Dennis." He dipped his spoon into the ice cream.

"Will you think about it?"

He didn't respond.

"Please?" She held her breath and his gaze.

"I'll promise you that much, but nothing more."

"Fair enough." She turned away, fearing the chance he'd say yes was slimmer than a collapsed soda straw.

Chapter 34

Rachel filled her lungs, then slowly released the air to ease her anxiety. She lifted a box from the passenger seat and carried it into the lobby, where she found Dennis and his crew on their knees installing gold and white floor tiles. "Good color combination. Love the checkerboard pattern."

Jack sat back on his heels. "Miss Naomi has style. By the time we're done, this'll be the fanciest theater in Georgia."

"Indeed, it will." She set the box on the framed-in concession stand. "I brought a thank you for finishing the stage."

J. T. pushed up with his crutch.

She removed a bag from Patsy's and handed it to him. "Double chocolate chip."

He opened it and sniffed. "That's what I call a mighty fine bonus."

She removed a second bag and gave it to Jack. "Oatmeal raisin for you."

"Thank you, ma'am."

"Dennis says you're casting him in your play." J. T. bit into a cookie. "He claims he can't act a lick."

"What matters is his potential. Besides, I'm a good director." She grabbed the box, squared her shoulders, and escaped to the theater before her anxiety became noticeable.

Inside, she set the box on the stage and climbed up the steps. She knew the guys had pulled a couple of all-nighters to meet the deadline. According to Charlie, Naomi gave them way more than cookies to compensate them. They'd insisted on using their earnings to pay him rent.

"The guys have done an amazing job." Emily moved toward the stage. "Have you heard from Charlie?"

"Not a peep." Rachel cringed, presuming his silence meant he didn't know how to turn her down. The prospect of identifying another suitable Everett churned in her stomach. She sat on the stage steps and removed her phone from the box. Should she call and beg Charlie to reconsider? She pulled up her Favorites list and stared at his name until chatter at the back of the theater caught her attention. She dropped her phone in the box, then climbed down and stood beside Emily.

"Are you ready?"

"Not even close."

Mirabelle dashed down the aisle, grinning. "I've been thinking about how the maven should look."

Someone called the woman's name, compelling her to step back. "We'll talk later."

When she moved out of earshot, Rachel leaned close to Emily. "She'll throw a tantrum when she learns she's not getting the part."

"Which is why you have to give her a minor role."

She removed the cast list and a pen from the box, then scratched out a name and added Mirabelle's. "This better satisfy her."

"It will if you make her Naomi's understudy."

Rachel stared at her sister. "Are you nuts?"

"The question is, do you want her as an enemy or an ally?"

Rachel released a deep sigh as she watched the remaining candidates begin to drift in. She had no idea how to turn a ragtag team of amateurs—minus one male character—into a cast of top-notch performers capable of captivating an audience.

Emily's nudge startled her. "What?"

"It's time."

Rachel sighed and glanced at the faces staring at her. For the moment, she empathized with every director who had denied her a role. Disappointing people was painful, especially in a close-knit community. She hoped people wouldn't find fault with Emily. She moved close to the front row. "Don't you love what the guys have done to this old cinema?"

Nods and positive comments.

"We owe them a huge debt of gratitude." She paused. "Before I announce the cast, I want you to know that while Emily helped me observe the auditions, the final decisions were mine alone. As I mentioned in the cafetorium, my job is to select cast members I believe best represent each character."

She held the list in her hand. "When I call your name, please join me up front. Playing the roles of Percy's parents are Mary and Chuck."

They stepped forward.

Rachel glanced at her list. "We're fortunate to have a woman with acting experience to fill the Newport maven role. Naomi Jasper, please join us up here."

She caught Mirabelle's shocked expression as Naomi moved to the front. "Before I announce the remaining leads, I'll call up everyone with a supporting role. Beginning with Mirabelle Paine, who is also Naomi's understudy."

She stood and crossed her arms. "What's that mean?"

"If for any reason Naomi can't make it to a performance, you'll fill in for her."

"Hmph. Does my other part have any lines?"

"As a matter of fact, it does."

"Okay, then." Mirabelle uncrossed her arms and stepped forward.

Rachel exchanged glances with Emily, then continued, "Selecting the two leads wasn't easy." She paused. "Missy Gibson and Dennis Locke, please come up."

Muted grumbles surfaced as the two newest cast members made their way to the front.

"Everyone else is assigned as an extra or a member of the all-important backstage crew."

A woman stood. "Who's playing the other leads?"

"I'm getting to that." She hesitated. "I … because I also have experience, I'll play Lillian." How could she possibly explain Everett's uncast role? She'd have to schedule another audition and hope someone with an ounce of talent showed up.

"I, uh …" Movement in the back of the theater caught her eye. She held her breath. Charlie walked up the aisle. He stopped beside the first row, lifted his palms, and shrugged.

She choked back tears. "Playing Everett Hayes is the guy who fell in love with your town and chose to call it his home—your very own vintner, Charlie Bricker."

She motioned him to the front. "Now I want everyone to join us up here." When everyone stood behind her, she turned to face her team. She clasped her hands to stop the trembling, forced a smile, and assumed the role as their director. "You are now the cast and crew of an original play. Together, we're going to make something magical happen."

After she answered questions and shared rehearsal instructions, Rachel pulled Charlie aside. "When I didn't hear from you, I assumed you'd turned me down."

He held his thumb a half inch from his index finger. "I came this close to saying no."

"What changed your mind?"

"The possibility this play will fulfill your dreams—at least for a while—and keep you here with me. Plus, like you said, maybe I'll find out firsthand what's so exciting about this acting business." He slipped his arm around her shoulders and leaned close. "You'll have to spend a lot of extra time getting this country boy up to speed."

"Is that another reason you agreed?"

"I'm a novice, not a dummy."

Emily joined them. "At least for the moment, Mirabelle seems satisfied."

Rachel dropped her list in the box. "No telling how long that will last."

"Another thing, based on comments I'm guessing the team isn't thrilled about Missy and Dennis getting the leads."

"That's not my problem. Directing this cast to deliver a decent performance by mid-September is my big challenge."

"You mean, ours," Emily said. "I recruited you, so I'm sticking with you until the premiere."

"What about rewriting your novel?"

"It'll have to wait."

Rachel embraced her sister. "Thank you."

"Regardless of the outcome, you and I are a team."

Chapter 35

Rachel held Clair in her arms and sank onto Sadie's love seat. "Your grandma is eager to hug you and your sister."

Emily hoisted Jane on her hip and leaned on the doorframe between Sadie's bedroom and the main room. "Did I ever tell you about Mom's plan to spend a romantic weekend up here with Dad before they opened the inn to the public?"

"How did it work out?"

"It didn't happen. At least their bed's here."

"That gorgeous four-poster belonged to your parents?"

"A wedding gift from Grandma and Grandpa Redding." Emily moved away from the door and placed Jane on the floor beside a basket of toys. "Those slipper chairs are also from Mom and Dad's bedroom."

"Funny how things sometimes work out." Clair climbed off Rachel's lap and crawled to her sister. "Any idea why Mama Sadie invited us for breakfast?"

"Probably because we've been too busy with the play to spend any time with her."

"Or anyone else."

"We needed a break."

Footsteps sounded on the stairs. Sadie breezed in. The aroma of honey and roasted pecans mingled with the coffee scent. "Thanks for coming over. I brought a plate of sticky buns, compliments of Patsy."

Rachel licked her lips. "One of my favorite morning indulgences."

Sadie set the buns on the coffee table beside a stack of small plates, forks, and napkins, then poured three cups of coffee. "How's Naomi's project coming along?" She carried them to the table and sat on a slipper chair.

"Rehearsals begin tonight." Emily moved a bun onto a plate. "What's the buzz around town about Missy and Dennis cast as the leads?"

"Some folks are grumbling. They'll move on, especially if those two do a good job."

Rachel dug her fork into a bun. "I hear Kat's going gangbusters in her new job."

"She knows her stuff." Sadie held her cup in both hands. "Did I ever tell you about the boy I dated when Mama and I first moved to Willow Falls? He played on the football team. Tall and handsome." She paused. "I expected him to invite me to the prom. He shocked the dickens out of me and Pepper when he invited a pretty majorette. After that I didn't date much. I mostly hung out with a group of kids."

She stared at her cup as if seeking wisdom from the dark, steaming liquid. "The thing is, I never learned how to tell when a man is … interested."

Rachel and Emily eyed each other.

"Brick's being real nice to me. We like to talk … and take long walks." Her cheeks flushed. "I'm being silly. We're nothing more than friends." She set her cup on the table and moved to the floor beside the twins.

Rachel wiped her fingers with a napkin. "Don't underestimate your charm."

"What could an educated, successful businessman possibly find charming about an ex-con with a high-school diploma and a couple of on-line management courses under her belt."

"Rachel's right about not selling yourself short." Emily leaned forward and laid her plate down. "You're an intelligent, beautiful woman with a kind heart. Whether it's Charlie's dad or another man, he'll be fortunate to win you over."

"You know Brick's a lot older than me."

"Twelve years isn't that a big of a difference." Emily moved beside her mother and touched her arm. "Has he kissed you?"

"Heavens to Betsy's uncle, no."

"Held your hand?"

Sadie shrugged. "Couple of times."

"There you go, at least you know he likes you."

"As an innkeeper and a good breakfast fixer."

"Believe me," Rachel joined them on the floor. "Men don't hold hands with their landlords or cooks."

"It's all so confusing." Clair climbed onto Sadie's lap and fingered her loop earring. She uncurled the baby's finger. "Sorry, baby girl, that pretty bauble is attached to Grandma's ear." She glanced at Rachel. "I don't want to make a fool of myself."

"You won't."

"She's right." Emily locked eyes with her mother. "I suggest you relax, enjoy his company, and see where the relationship goes."

"How will I know if … he is interested?"

"Your heart will tell you."

Sadie shifted her focus to Rachel. "You've known Brick longer than me. What do you think?"

Charlie's comment about his dad never trusting another woman popped into her head. She didn't want to give her mother false hope, and yet Charlie could be wrong. "Brick would be one smart man to fall for you."

Emily cupped Sadie's face in her hands and gazed into her eyes, the color of the eye on a peacock feather. "And the luckiest guy in the world if you fell for him."

Sadie stared at her for a long moment. Then her lips curved into a grin, and her eyes twinkled with mischief. "I declare, a relationship between a jailbird and a superstitious millionaire would for doggone sure set the Willow Falls rumor mill on fire."

Emily burst into laughter. "Mama Sadie, you are by far the most fascinating woman I ever met."

Chapter 36

Rachel, carrying a stack of scripts, opened the theater's rear entrance and flipped on the lights. She paused and eyed the ten-foot-long table set center stage. "Tonight it begins."

"With a bang, I hope." Emily pulled a cooler beside the table.

"We need to set a script and a bottle of water in front of each chair."

"Where do you want me to sit, Ms. Director?"

"At the other end of the table opposite me."

"Nervous?"

Rachel uncapped a water bottle. "What do you think?"

"That you'll to do an amazing job."

"Is that your version of a pep talk?"

"Uh-huh. How am I doing?"

"Not too bad." Rachel took a drink. "I'm counting on you to be my second set of eyes."

"To do what?"

"Figure out how to direct the cast from ground zero to someplace higher."

"What should I look for?"

"Reactions. Attitude."

Emily's head tilted. "You mean like some kind of psychologist?"

"More like a newspaper reporter sniffing out a story." Movement caught Rachel's eye. "Guess who just arrived?"

"Our overeager mail lady?"

"None other."

Mirabelle rushed down the aisle and climbed onto the stage, her head held high. "I'm ready to learn my part and Naomi's. You know, she's no spring chicken."

Rachel nearly choked on her water.

Emily shook her head.

"Where do you want me to sit?"

"The choice is yours," Rachel said as she recapped her water bottle.

Mirabelle pulled out a center chair, set her purse on the floor, and opened the script.

Within minutes, every cast member had arrived and selected a seat.

Rachel stood at her end of the table, gripped the back of her chair, and scanned the faces staring at her. Should she project confidence or admit anxiety? Maybe a little of each. "Welcome to the magic world of live theater. During the next few weeks, we'll work hard, laugh at ourselves, and experience heartwarming breakthroughs. Right now, I suspect a butterfly or two are fluttering in your chests."

"It's more intense than working for the Willow Post." Mary patted her chest. "A whole swarm of butterflies has taken up residence in here."

"I know what you mean. Mine have two-inch wingspans."

Chuckles confirmed she'd nailed the feeling.

Dennis raised his hand. "What if we can't remember all our lines?"

"The first time I landed a role in a play, I had the same question. I soon discovered that with each rehearsal, the dialogue became more familiar. Then one day"—she snapped her fingers—"it all clicked. I'm confident the same will happen with each of you."

She caught sight of Missy chewing her fingernail. She had to ease her anxiety. "Preparing for opening night is a process. Tonight, we'll begin by reading the script out loud. Then we'll spend several days rehearsing lines and finding the right inflection and rhythm."

Mirabelle snapped her script shut. "I only found four short lines for my character."

That didn't take long. Rachel tapped her script. "True, however she is important to the story."

"Then how come I don't have more lines?"

"Not to worry," Emily said. "Much of your acting is nonverbal, which takes as much, if not more skill."

Rachel flashed her sister a thumbs-up.

Mirabelle's chest puffed. "When do we start acting?"

"In a couple of days. Any more questions?" Rachel glanced around. "Okay, then let's begin."

As the cast read through the script, Rachel observed facial expressions and body language. Mary and Chuck seemed fully engaged. Naomi displayed the most enthusiasm. Mirabelle fidgeted until time to read her part. In between reading lines, Missy chewed her fingernail. Dennis never took his eyes off the script and read his lines without a hint of emotion. Charlie sat back in his chair, his arms crossed, his expression landing somewhere between boredom and annoyance.

By the time they read the last line, Rachel's shoulders and neck muscles ached. She closed her script. "I trust you all have a feel for the play's plot and flow."

Naomi leaned forward. "I'm impressed by the incredible job you and Emily did with the dialogue. You created the perfect balance between drama and humor. The audience will love it."

If we manage to pull off a satisfactory performance. "Thank you for the vote of confidence. It's time to call it a night. Take your scripts home and meet us back here same time tomorrow."

The moment the last cast member left the theater, Rachel collapsed onto her chair. "That counts as the worst read-through I've ever experienced."

"I think they did fine." Emily settled in the chair to her sister's right. "It's not fair to compare our amateurs to the pros you're accustomed to working with."

"If I'm going to have them ready in time, I can't lower my expectations. Tell me what you observed."

"About everyone?"

"Just the leads."

"Three seemed confident." Emily ran her finger along a scratch on the table. "One looked scared to death. Two would rather be any place other than here."

"I know. Dennis and Charlie." Rachel pressed her fingers to the back of her neck. "If we don't find a way to build Missy's confidence and motivate those two guys, we won't have a shot at making this work."

"Looks like we're in for some long hours."

"That's the most accurate statement I've heard all day."

Chapter 37

Emily tapped her fingers on the steering wheel and stared at Rachel. "Did you happen to notice that every business is closed?"

"This town takes Labor Day seriously."

"Which is why cast members are grumbling about an all-day rehearsal."

Rachel's nostrils flared. "Willow Falls' opening night and Alicia's review are thirteen days away. Half the cast can't remember their lines or their positions on stage. Mirabelle is overacting, and Missy's and Dennis's performances have barely reached mediocre. You tell me what other choice we have?"

"Maybe change our names and go into witness protection?"

"Now there's a smart idea. Or do a Thelma and Louise."

"Who?"

"The movie, from the nineties."

"We were too young to talk, much less watch a movie."

"I saw it a couple of years ago. Two women run away and end up fugitives from the law."

"Does that mean we'd have to commit an honest-to-goodness crime?"

"Trust me. Premiering *Percy's Legacy* in its current shape would qualify as a felony."

"We have a second option."

"Get this cast up to speed?"

"Yep."

Rachel snapped her fingers. "Which is why we're rehearsing on a holiday."

"And we come full circle." Emily climbed out, then removed a large white box from the back seat, along with a bag of napkins, paper plates, and plastic forks. "I hope Patsy's double-fudge chocolate cake will make working on a holiday less undesirable."

"Can't hurt." Rachel passed the ticket booth and opened the lobby door. "Couple more days and the guys will have this finished." Inside the theater, she turned on the overhead lights.

"At least the venue is impressive." Emily carried the cake to the front and set it on the stage.

Rachel climbed the steps, then disappeared behind the new royal-blue curtain. Seconds later, the stage lights illuminated, revealing the set for act one, scene one. "Thanks to Naomi's artistic talent, this looks incredible."

"Don't forget the set-building crew and Nathan donating all the furniture."

"I know. The play is one big community project." Her tone hinted annoyance.

Emily pressed her lips together to avoid a snide retort. She settled in the front row and silently prayed for a small breakthrough.

Rachel stood on the stage, facing the set, her arms crossed. Her foot tapped the floor.

As usual, Mirabelle arrived first. "I've been thinking," she said as she rounded the first row and approached the stage.

Rachel stopped tapping and faced the front. "About what?"

"A line you can add for my character."

"Like I told you yesterday … we're not changing the script."

"You don't have to snap at me." She climbed the steps. "I'm trying to help."

"I know you mean well." Rachel uncrossed her arms, left the stage, and sat beside Emily. "That woman is driving me crazy," her voice barely above a whisper.

"At least she's enthusiastic."

"Which is more than I can say for Charlie."

"He's coming around."

"Not fast enough."

As the remaining crew drifted in, Emily mentally questioned if casting Charlie had strained his relationship with Rachel. As far as she knew, other than rehearsals, they hadn't spent time together since the first script reading. Perhaps they were a couple who couldn't work together.

Mirabelle stepped down from the stage and slid into the third row beside Naomi.

Rachel stood and faced her crew. "Emily and I appreciate you giving up your holiday." She smiled. "Pepper's bringing a catered lunch at one. Let's begin from the top."

The cast took their places on stage.

Rachel gave direction, then returned to her seat. Halfway into the scene, she nudged Emily. "I can't figure out what's going on with Missy. One minute she seems relaxed, the next she's stiff as an uncooked spaghetti noodle. Worse, Dennis reacts to her. Either they're both doing okay, or they're a two-team disaster."

"Something's causing the shift."

"We better figure it out fast."

Emily fixed her gaze on the stage.

Five minutes passed.

Rachel snapped her fingers. "I think it's the lights."

"What are you talking about?"

"Watch what happens when Missy turns to the front."

Emily focused on the young woman. Face to face with other cast members, she repeated her lines with relative ease. When she turned toward the audience, her limbs stiffened. Her voice faltered. Dennis responded as if he had a direct link to her emotions.

"You might be on to something."

"We can hope."

When the scene ended, Rachel climbed onto the stage. "Okay, everyone. It's time to become accustomed to the live performance environment. Stage lights up, house lights down. You'll hear the audience when they laugh or applaud, but you won't see them."

She stepped behind the curtain.

The house lights dimmed.

Rachel returned. "Missy, I want you and Dennis to repeat the scene. This time think of this stage as your own private world. The only thing that matters is how you interact with each other and the cast members. Do you understand?"

"Yes ma'am."

"Good. Okay, guys, let's try this again." She returned to the front row and leaned close to Emily. "This better work."

The scene began.

Rachel sat on the edge of her seat.

Emily rubbed the back of her hand. Seconds before Missy's cue to face the front, she held her breath.

The girl turned. She froze, then botched her next line.

"So much for that theory," Rachel mumbled as she collapsed against her seat back. When the scene ended, she moved to the stage. "Time for a break. Lunch is due any minute."

Pepper Cushman strolled down the aisle pulling a wagon. She lifted three boxes and placed them on the stage beside the stack of paper plates and napkins Rachel had set out. "I brought chicken-salad and ham-and-cheese sandwiches."

Emily removed the cake from its box. "For dessert, one of Patsy's most popular items."

"How are rehearsals coming along?" asked Pepper.

"They're coming," Emily said as she cut the cake.

"Everyone's excited about this old theater providing our town with first-class entertainment." Pepper turned away from the stage. "How many seats?"

"Two hundred on the floor, forty in the balcony. Tickets go on sale Friday morning."

"Folks will start lining up an hour ahead, maybe sooner."

"At twenty bucks a pop?"

"The play is a big deal."

Emily sighed. "I hope the performance lives up to their expectations."

"Honey, the only plays most of the folks around here have seen were school productions. Trust me, they'll be impressed."

"I suppose you're right." Emily cut the last piece of cake.

Following lunch, the cast rehearsed all three acts, with little improvement. During the drive home from the theater, Rachel faced the passenger window, without uttering a word. When they arrived, she headed straight to the guest room.

Emily tossed her purse on the kitchen table. "I think Rachel's close to a breaking point."

"She agreed to the shorter timeframe." Scott twisted the cap off a beer.

"I got her into this. I have to help her to find a way to make it work."

He pulled her into his arms and held her tight.

She pressed her face against his neck and breathed in his scent. "Thank you."

"For what?"

"Being here for me."

Chapter 38

Rachel's hands fisted as she struggled to remain calm. "We need to run through that scene again."

Charlie threw his script across the stage. "I don't know what you want. I repeated the lines exactly like you told me."

"What I'm talking about is how you say them." She sighed. "This is a love scene. You have to get inside the character's head. Everett is a passionate man—"

"What is that supposed to sound like? Heavy breathing?"

She lowered her voice. "You know that's not what I meant."

Charlie glared at her. "And there's the problem. Nothing you're saying makes any sense. I didn't want … forget it." He stormed off the stage and dashed out of the theater.

Rachel brushed her fingers through her hair and fought the urge to scream. "Okay, everybody, time to call it a night."

Cast members exchanged glances, then gathered their belongings and headed to the exit.

Emily joined her sister on stage. "Have you ever seen Charlie that angry?"

"The night I rejected his grandmother's necklace." Rachel sat on the edge of the stage. "Do you have any idea what set him off?"

"I think he's frustrated."

"It's obvious he doesn't want anything to do with this play. I should never have convinced him to take the role."

"Too late to second-guess yourself now. You have to go after him."

"I doubt he'll even talk to me. Besides, I don't have a clue what to say." She wiped her moist palms on her jeans. "Will you turn the lights off?"

Emily followed her. "What are you going to do?"

"Try to cool down. Don't wait around for me. I'll walk back to your house."

Rachel climbed down from the stage, grabbed her purse and sweater, and headed up the aisle. Outside, autumn's first cold front raised a layer of goose bumps on her bare skin. She slipped into the sweater and massaged her arms.

What made Charlie so stubborn? Even though she pushed him into taking the role, you'd think he'd at least give it his best shot. She walked past Pearl's salon, rounded the corner, and crossed Main Street. At the edge of the park, she stopped and spotted a figure at the lake's edge, beside the retaining wall. She moved closer. The red-and-white plaid shirt stood out in the dim light.

Charlie.

Walk away and let him stew in his anger. She took one step and halted. *You can't run from this. You won't find a moment's peace until you confront him.*

She stepped off the sidewalk and closed the distance.

He faced the water, his left foot propped on the wall, his forearm resting on his knee. Rachel dropped her purse on the ground and sat facing the street. "The first time I came to this town, you were by my side." She breathed deep to control the quiver in her voice. "I didn't mean to upset you."

He remained silent for a long moment. "In high school, my buddies and I started a rock band. My guitar playing was so pitiful they made me the lead singer. The first time we performed for a group of kids, I forgot half the words." He plucked a pebble off the wall and tossed it in the water. "I don't know if I can deliver what you need."

"Did I ever tell you about my first performance? Ten minutes before the opening scene, I upchucked everything in my stomach." She paused. "The director gave me cup of ginger tea and a pep talk to settle me down."

"Stage fright?"

"Through the roof."

"How'd you get over it?"

"I didn't. I learned to control it. On opening night, I don't eat anything past noon, and I keep a cup of tea close at hand. Even the best actors often question their ability. Keeps them sharp and motivates them to continue perfecting their skills."

"I know it's your job to demand the best from the cast."

"Do you want me to go easy on you?"

"No."

She hesitated, afraid to ask. "Do … you want to quit?"

"You bet I do."

She cringed.

"But I won't." He planted both feet on the ground and cast another pebble in the water, sending it skipping across the surface. "Wouldn't be fair to the rest of the cast."

"What do we do now?"

"Try to put tonight behind us and move on."

"That works." She rested her thigh on the wall as the breeze rustled the leaves and sent miniature ripples cascading across the lake's surface. Charlie agreed to take the role to please her. She had to treat him with respect. "Thank you."

"For what?"

"Sticking with it."

He shrugged. "I'm not a quitter."

"I know. Where's your truck?"

"Behind the theater. Why?"

"I … sort of need a ride home."

"Did your sister abandon you?"

"The other way around."

"Are you ready now?"

"I suppose." She stood.

They walked in silence. When they arrived at his truck, he opened the passenger door.

She climbed in.

He drove the short distance and pulled to the curb.

"Thanks for the ride." She gripped the door handle.

"Wait." He leaned across the console and turned her face toward his. "I'll do my best to nail the role … for you."

Tears welled and spilled down her cheek.

He brushed them away with his fingers. "Everything's going to be okay."

Rachel waited for Charlie to drive away, then opened the front door. She found Emily and Scott in the kitchen. Their sagging postures and blank stares sent a shiver up her spine. She tossed her purse on the table. "What's wrong?"

Emily handed Rachel her phone. "See for yourself."

"What am I looking at?"

"Connor's social media post."

"Who?"

"The high-school wannabe FBI agent."

"How many people know about this?"

"By now, half the town."

Scott glanced at his phone. "Nathan sent a text inviting everyone to another town hall meeting, tomorrow at noon. He'll try to nip this before it gets out of hand."

"Too late." Rachel stared at the pair of arrest photos. "Kat's tough, she'll survive. Missy's self-esteem is already hanging by a thread. This will devastate her." She handed the phone back to Emily. "Why can't this town get a break?"

"Maybe it won't be as bad as we think."

"You're right. It'll be a whole lot worse."

Chapter 39

Rachel glared at the vehicles filling every downtown parking space. "Does everyone in Willow Falls want to get involved?"

"It's a small town. People care." Charlie drove through downtown.

"What's that supposed to mean?"

"Don't take it personally."

He parked his truck in Naomi's driveway.

Rachel climbed down before Charlie reached her door. "People around are too eager to cause a stir."

"Willow Falls is like an old established neighborhood wary of new faces."

"You're telling me that residents don't trust strangers, yet they're trying to turn their private community into a magnet for outsiders?"

"Tourists represent something far more powerful than fear."

"Financial gain?"

"Survival."

They hastened up Main, rounded the corner, and headed to the church. Shouts and angry voices accosted them as they moved through the building's foyer. Like the other Willow Falls town hall meetings Rachel had attended, residents squeezed into every seat and stood along the walls. She nudged Charlie and pointed. They made their way to Emily and Scott, standing behind the last row. "Have you seen Mama Sadie?"

Emily tilted her head left. "One row up on the end with Brick. She's hopping mad."

"Who can blame her."

Nathan stepped up to a podium and pounded his gavel until the din silenced. "Ladies and gentlemen, I called this meeting in response to one overzealous teenager's social media post."

A man in the second row stood. "How is it Connor could find out Kat and Missy are criminals and our sheriff couldn't?"

Shouts erupted.

Mitch made his way to the front and gripped the microphone.

A hush fell over the room.

"First off, being a parolee isn't against the law."

"What about Connor suggesting we run them out of town, Sheriff?"

He fingered his neatly trimmed beard. "His comments are unfortunate but not illegal, either."

The boy's father stood. "His mother and I apologize for the uproar he caused. We took his computer and phone away and grounded him for a month."

"In my opinion, he did us a favor." A woman wearing a bright-orange T-shirt shook her finger at Mitch. "We don't want a thief and a drug dealer we know nothing about living in our town. Besides, Winston Hamilton called that Kat woman a fire hazard, what with her smoking and all."

Her comment unleashed a tirade.

"Yeah," a woman in the last row shouted. "And what about Dennis and those two guys—the one missing a leg and the other one with a messed-up face? For all we know, they're dangerous criminals."

"Is it true they were homeless back in Atlanta?"

Rachel nudged Emily. "Who is that woman, and how does she know?"

"She's a cashier at the grocery store, and I don't have a clue."

Gertie made her way to the podium, her face pinched. "I've lived here all my life, and this is the first time I've been ashamed of my town. Everyone throwing stones needs to toss them aside and give our newcomers a break."

Mirabelle stood and faced the crowd. "Gertie's right. Y'all are overreacting."

Rachel's mouth fell open. "Talk about a shocker."

"No kidding," said Emily. "If I didn't know better, I'd swear that lady was our mail carrier's secret twin."

"What is it with you, Mirabelle?" another woman shouted. "You get a part in Naomi's play and all of a sudden you're Miss Goody Two-shoes?"

Mirabelle propped one hand on her hip and shook her finger at the woman. "I don't like what you're insinuating, Mabel."

"Yeah, well, I'm not crazy about you buckling under to a bunch of outsiders. We're all law-abiding citizens, not criminals and street bums."

Sadie stepped into the aisle.

"This will be interesting," Charlie said.

She moved to the podium. Gertie stepped aside. Sadie gripped the mic. "If you want to blame someone, blame me. I brought Kat to Willow Falls because we needed a qualified person to manage the hotel. And she's doing a great job."

"She's a criminal," shouted Orange Shirt.

"So am I. The thing is, I learned a lot about Kat while we served time together. You need to understand how she ended up here. She was a kid who grew up with a single mother forced to work two, sometimes three jobs to put food on the table for her five children. After Kat graduated high school, she worked her way through college and earned a master's degree in business. A big company hired her, and she rose to a vice president."

Sadie paused. "She stayed single a long time. Then she fell in love with a sweet-talking man and landed him a job at her company. He embezzled a lot of money from their employer and planted evidence pointing to her as the culprit. Like a coward, he disappeared and left her to take the fall."

"Sounds like a big pile of horse manure, to me," shouted Orange Shirt.

Kat walked up the side aisle and stood beside Sadie. "That's the same thing the jury assumed."

She held the mic close. "I don't care what you think of me because I know Sadie told you the truth. What matters is what you think about Missy. She's an innocent young girl who was tossed aside at the age of seven by a drug-addicted mother. For the next ten years the state tossed her from one foster home to another. When she turned seventeen, she escaped an abusive foster parent and found acceptance from a gang of thugs. Unfortunately, she ended up in the wrong place at the wrong time and found herself caught up in a drug sting. Worse, she ended up with a public defender who'd been on the job fewer than three months. She never sold or used any illegal substances."

Naomi slipped from the second aisle and moved to the front. Kat handed her the mic. "I also have something to say. Those men you referred to as bums are injured veterans who served our country with honors. The entire time they've been working for me, they've been perfect gentlemen. I'm telling you, they're good guys."

"You don't know if they're mentally unstable and might one day go all crazy on us," shouted a man standing ten feet from Rachel.

"This has to stop," Charlie said.

Rachel grabbed his arm. "What are you going to do?"

"Set everyone straight." He hastened up the aisle.

Gertie and Mirabelle returned to their seats. Naomi stepped beside Kat.

Charlie faced the crowd. "The three guys who are working their tails off to help this town are living with me. Naomi's right. They're good guys who ended up with lousy breaks."

"Are you gonna tell us another bunch of sob stories?"

"Sit down and listen, Mabel," Mirabelle said. "You might learn something."

Charlie continued. "My new friend, Dennis, worked construction until he and his dad had a falling out. That's when he enlisted. Two weeks after his deployment to the Middle East, his father fell off scaffolding. Crushed his skull. Dennis never had a chance to say goodbye. Two months later he climbed into a jeep with his best buddies and left base on a surveillance mission. A mile out, he climbed out of the jeep to pet a stray dog."

He paused. "Seconds later the jeep hit a landmine. His friends were blown to bits. The guilt over being the only survivor, on top of losing his dad, messed with his brain, and ate his insides like cancer."

Silence.

"Then there's J. T. He grew up in poverty, without a father. He hung his future on landing a football scholarship until a blown knee destroyed his dream. He enlisted, with the promise of a college education. His new goal? Coach football. A landmine ripped his leg from his body."

Rachel's eyes moistened.

Charlie hesitated. "Jack also grew up in a poor neighborhood. His plan to start a landscape business with his older brother fell apart when a teenager texting and driving smashed head-on into his car. After the funeral, he kissed the girl he loved goodbye and joined the army. She promised to wait for him. An exploding mortar shell burned half his body. When his girlfriend saw him in the hospital, she threw up and ran out of the room. He never saw her again."

Orange Shirt stood. "Are we gonna take the words of a bunch of outsiders? Except for our mayor and sheriff, not a one of 'em standing up there is from around here."

"What about Naomi?" Gertie said. "Her kin are Willow Falls natives."

"She's been gone for more than fifty years. That makes her as much an outsider as the rest of them. And we want 'em all outta here."

"I'm not leaving him standing up there alone," said Rachel.

Emily stared at her. "What are you going to say?"

"I'll figure it out on the way to the front." She walked toward Charlie amid a flurry of comments and breathed deep to slow her pounding heart.

When she reached the podium, Nathan rapped his gavel to silence the crowd. "Emily's sister has something she wants to say."

"She can't tell us nothin'. She's another outsider."

Gertie spun around and waggled her finger at the man. "Shame on you, Henry. She has as much right as you to speak her mind." She turned back to the front. "Go ahead, honey. We're listening."

"Thank you, Miss Gertie. A year ago, I discovered the sister and mother I didn't know existed, in a town I'd never heard of. Since then, I've grown to care about Willow Falls and the people who live here." She scanned the faces staring at her, searching for words to sway the naysayers.

"Believe me, I understand why you're upset. You care about your community and want what's best—"

"Darn right, we do," a man in the third row shouted.

"Please, sir. Let me finish. I suspect every person in here has something in their background they're not proud of. If it ever leaked out, you'd want people to see who you are, not the mistakes you'd made. What I'm trying to say is, it's wrong to define people by their pasts. Instead, we owe it to them to look at who they are now." Her voice cracked. "Five individuals working hard to fit in and turn their lives around by helping make Willow Falls successful. That's all I have to say."

She stepped away from the podium.

Nathan returned to the microphone. "An ancient proverb claims the eyes are the window to the soul. Tonight, it applies to our community. I urge you all to go home, think about what you've heard, then make the right choice for Willow Falls. One that will make us all proud." He tapped his gavel. "This meeting is adjourned."

Nathan switched the microphone off and turned toward the five outsiders. "Thank you for risking ridicule and stepping up." He made eye contact with each. "You are all a credit to Willow Falls, and I'm honored to call you all my friends."

"Do you think we helped?" asked Naomi.

"There'll be a few stubborn cases, but I believe most everyone will come around."

Sadie shrugged. "I suppose it's good this all came out before the town fills up with tourists."

Nathan touched Kat's arm. "Are you okay?"

"Are you kidding? I spent four years in prison watching my back every waking minute. This is a piece of cake."

"She's right," Sadie said. "The old saying 'a cat has nine lives' also works for ex-cons and small towns."

Nathan chuckled. "It'd be a blessing if we could stop testing that theory."

Chapter 40

"Will the catastrophes never end?" Emily tossed her phone on the kitchen table.

Scott sighed. "What is it this time?"

"Missy's coming unglued. Says she's quitting the play and leaving town."

Rachel rushed in. "You saw Sadie's message, didn't you?

"Yeah."

"We have enough drama around here to qualify for a Broadway production. I have to go to the inn and try to rescue our play."

"I'm going with you. The babies"—Emily fixed her gaze on Scott. "Can you stay home a while longer?"

"You two go."

"Thanks, hon—"

They rushed to Rachel's car and drove to the inn where they found Missy in the upstairs common area. She sat on the couch between Sadie and Kat, dressed in pajamas, her hair disheveled, her feet bare, her cheeks tearstained.

Emily sat on the coffee table. "What's going on?"

"Some heartless soul snuck in last night and slipped notes under our doors. Missy found this on her floor." Kat handed it over.

She unfolded the sheet of paper and silently read it. *Go back to jail where you belong. We don't want you in our town.* "I can't believe anyone living in Willow Falls is mean enough to do this." She gave the note to Rachel.

"Sadie and I have been trying to convince Missy not to overreact to one heartless coward."

"You don't understand." Missy wiped her cheeks. "It's like being back in one of those terrible foster homes."

Sadie reached for her hand. "My goodness, honey … Kat, me, Emily, Rachel, we all love you."

"Everyone else in town hates me." She jumped up, ran to her suite, and slammed the door.

Emily eyed Kat. "You have to go after her."

"Let her cool down a while."

Rachel dropped onto an overstuffed chair. "It seems someone is determined to sabotage our play."

"You mean the whole town." Emily moved to the chair beside her sister and locked eyes with Sadie. "Who else knows about this?"

"Besides the creep who wrote the note, Pepper and Mitch."

"Maybe Dennis should talk to her," Rachel said.

Kat shook her head. "Missy begged us not to call him."

"Too much is at stake to sit here and do nothing."

Emily stared at her sister. "There's always your Thelma-and-Louise plan."

"Three jailbirds around here is more than enough," Kat said. "Besides, neither one of you has a '66 Thunderbird."

Rachel crossed her leg over her knee. "You've obviously seen the movie."

"Twice. Look, Missy's been rejected her entire life by people who were supposed to care about her. It won't be easy to convince her folks around here are any different."

Emily fingered her mother's diamond engagement ring. How many more roadblocks could she battle before calling it quits? "We need to head home, so Scott can work at the hotel." Emily stood. "Although at this point, I'm not convinced his efforts will make a difference."

Kat's head tilted. "You can't lose faith."

"I'm trying not to."

Voices drifted up from the foyer.

Sadie held her hand up. "Don't leave yet."

"Why? What's going on?"

"You'll see."

The stairs creaked under the weight of multiple footsteps. The voices grew louder. Pepper appeared first. Followed by more than a dozen residents. "Where is she?"

"I'll bring her out." Kat hastened to the Mirabelle Suite, knocked, then stepped inside and closed the door behind her.

Shuffling feet punctuated whispers and quiet chatter as the seconds turned to minutes.

Emily glanced at her watch, then touched Sadie's arm. "I don't think she's coming out."

"Give her a few more minutes."

Emily kept her eyes glued to the door. It opened a crack. She held her breath, then released the air as the door eased open.

Missy, dressed in white shorts and a pink shirt, her hair combed, clung to Kat's arm. As they walked into the common area, Kat patted her hand. "These folks have something they want to say to us."

Pepper grinned. "Whoever left those notes is one rotten apple in a barrel full of good fruit. We're all here to apologize on behalf of the town and tell you that we want you to stay."

"She's right," Gertie said as she stepped up. "You, Kat, and those three boys are doing lots of good here in Willow Falls. You're all part of our family now."

Affirmations followed.

"I knew about you being on parole a while back." Mirabelle touched Missy's arm. "I kept it quiet. Anyway, like our director said, your past doesn't matter. We know you're both good people. We need you to stick around and help make *Percy's Legacy* a big hit."

Another woman moved from the back.

Rachel held her hand in front of her mouth and leaned close to Emily. "Isn't she that orange-shirt woman from the town hall meeting?"

Emily nodded.

The woman faced Missy. "I'm sorry for all the mean things I said last night. Truth is, me and my old man had a couple too many swigs of whiskey before we showed up. So, I wasn't thinking real straight." She shuffled her feet. "Now I am, and I think you should stick around."

Missy pulled her bottom lip between her teeth and stared at the women. The crowd seemed to hold their collective breath.

Missy blinked, then shrugged. "Okay."

"Glory be," Sadie said. "I think you've finally found where you belong."

Kat grinned. "We both have."

Missy's eyes widened. "Wait a minute. What about Dennis?"

"We're heading over to Naomi's next." Pepper touched her arm. "After all, those three guys need to know they're family too."

The crowd gathered around Kat and Missy and showered them with praise.

Emily choked back tears. "This is why Scott and I will never leave Willow Falls. The moment it looks like the town has lost its soul, the good people come through."

Rachel nodded. "I'm beginning to understand why Charlie decided to call it home."

"Maybe one day you'll do the same."

Chapter 41

Rachel moved in front of the first row and faced the cast and crew. "In case you haven't heard, tickets for next week's hometown premiere sold out in ten minutes."

Mirabelle popped up. "Lots of folks who showed up to buy one were disappointed. We should sell tickets for next Saturday, too."

"One step at a time." She glanced at her watch. "Okay, team, it's noon. Let's take it from the top."

As the crew rushed to reset the stage for act one, Rachel settled beside Emily.

"Naomi also suggested two more performances before the big one."

"If rehearsals go well between now and Saturday, we'll consider it."

"What time's your dinner with Charlie?"

"Six. Brick and Mama Sadie are joining us."

"Do you suppose he's kissed her yet?"

"Move that chair a few inches to the right," Rachel shouted to the stage crew, then signaled a thumbs-up. She glanced at Emily. "You're assuming they're more than friends."

'Aren't you?"

Charlie's comment about his dad bubbled up. "I'm trying to remain objective."

"I want a full report tonight when you get home."

"I'll take copious notes." The players moved into position. "Looks like we're ready to start."

When the first scene ended, Emily nudged her sister. "First time no one missed any lines."

"We're making progress. Time to step it up a notch." Rachel climbed onto the stage and pulled Missy and Dennis aside. "Kudos for your best performance yet."

"Me and Dennis thought we did good."

"You're both right." She paused. "In fact, you're ready to make the love scene something extra special. I want you to do it again, and, this time, forget about everyone else in the theater. Focus completely on each other. Missy, when you look at Dennis, I want you to see Percy, the man who makes your heart jump out of your chest. The man you want to spend the rest of your life with."

She lowered her chin. "Yes ma'am."

"Dennis, against all odds, you've fallen desperately in love with Peaches. Think only of her and how you want to lasso the moon for her."

"Okay."

"Good. When I give you the signal, pour your hearts into the scene." Rachel returned to the front row and touched Emily's arm. "We're about to find out if I'm cut out to be a director."

She gave them the go-ahead.

They began. They spoke their lines with all the appropriate nuances, their body language spot on. Then, two minutes into the scene, goosebumps popped out on Rachel's flesh. Something magical happened. The chemistry between the two young people became palpable. They were no longer Missy and Dennis. For the moment, they'd become Percy and Peaches.

Emily gasped.

"You felt it too, didn't you?" whispered Rachel.

"It's like no one else exists except … them. Looks like you're a pretty good director, after all, Ms. Streetman."

When the scene ended with a passionate kiss, the entire team erupted in applause. Rachel jumped to her feet. "That, ladies and gentlemen, is how to deliver a proper love scene."

By five thirty, they'd rehearsed every scene, some more than once. Rachel called her team off the stage. "Give yourself a great big round of applause. You delivered your best rehearsal."

The entire team cheered.

"In fact, you did so well you deserve tomorrow off. We'll begin again Monday night."

"Good call," Emily said. "I'm thinking you won't need me hanging around as much."

"Just one more week. Besides, you're my understudy."

"You already have one."

"For Lillian, not for the director."

"All I have to say is, you'd better eat your veggies and stay away from anyone with a cold. Because there's no way I can stand in for you."

"It's just a precaution, in the event I'm hit by a bus or something."

"Buses haven't passed through Willow Falls in ages."

"Then I guess you're safe."

Charlie wandered over. "What's this about buses?"

"We're talking backup plans."

"I have two beautiful babies waiting for me." Emily shouldered her purse and moved toward the aisle. "You two have fun and say hi to Mama Sadie and Brick for me."

Charlie plucked a stray strand of hair from Rachel's shoulder. "Missy and Dennis delivered a good love scene."

"More like spectacular."

"I don't know how he pulled it off."

"You mean for a regular guy?"

"For anyone."

"It's called acting." She patted his cheek. "I hope you took notes."

"Notes won't help."

After Rachel turned off the lights, they headed to the lobby.

"The guys are coming over after they finish up at Naomi's to finish painting," Charlie said."

"As hard as they work, it's difficult to believe they were ever on the street."

"Makes me think different about the homeless."

They left the theater, strolled across Main Street, and walked around the hotel to the back veranda. The sun casting shimmers of color on the water created a canvas-worthy view. "This is a perfect spot to relax before dinner."

Charlie sat beside her and slid his arm around her waist.

Rachel pressed her hand over his and leaned her head against his shoulder until shouts behind the inn caught her attention. "It looks like Kat ... and Winston. What do you suppose is going on?"

"A debate? An argument? Who knows?"

Sadie and Brick stepped from the kitchen and joined Kat and Winston. Moments later, Winston walked between the inn and hotel. Kat leaned against the garage door. Sadie and Brick headed in their direction.

"We're about to find out." When they arrived, Charlie grinned. "Rachel wants to know what Kat and the Brit are up to."

She knuckle-thumped his arm. "He's curious too."

"No big deal. Winston's carrying on about Kat's smoking." Brick patted his stomach. "I'm starving. What say we head over to Pepper's?"

"Sounds good to me." Charlie stood and grasped Rachel's hand.

They fell in step behind Brick and Sadie. She noticed Brick didn't hold Sadie's hand.

They walked through the park, crossed Main Street, and entered the café. As usual, half the tables were empty. Winston sat alone at the bar, holding a menu.

Brick tilted his head toward the left. "Is next to the window okay?"

Rachel nodded. "Works for us."

Moments after they settled in the booth, the waitress approached. "Evening, folks." She placed four menus on the table. "Pepper's cooked up a delicious special for tonight."

"Works for me," Charlie said.

The others followed his lead.

Brick selected a bottle of wine.

Sadie unwrapped her utensils. "Have you heard the latest? Pepper agreed to take on the hotel's executive chef job. She'll keep on managing the café and train someone to take over in the kitchen."

"Two restaurants in Willow Falls." Rachel spread her napkin on her lap. "What will the locals think?"

"By this time next year, we'll have three," Brick said. "One at the winery."

His tone made it clear he considered the town his. Rachel fingered her fork, wondering if she could one day do the same.

The waitress returned carrying four glasses, a corkscrew, and a bottle of Chardonnay. She opened it and poured. "I hope you like it. The café has only had a liquor license for a couple of months."

Brick took a sip. "It's mighty fine, ma'am."

"I'll let Pepper know." She returned to the kitchen.

"Before dinner arrives, I have an announcement," Brick said. "You know that house next door to Naomi's?"

Rachel nodded. "I noticed a For Sale sign in the front yard the day Charlie and I came to town the first time."

"Tomorrow it's coming down." A smile lit Brick's face. "I now own two old houses on Main Street."

Rachel's eyes widened. "You bought it?"

"Lock, stock, and barrel. I'm keeping my place in Atlanta, at least for a while. But I'll spend most of my time here. The house sat empty for a couple of years, so it needs some work."

Charlie tilted his glass toward his dad. "Dennis and the guys could do it."

"Gonna ask them tomorrow." Brick paused. "Sadie agreed to help me decorate it."

Rachel's gaze shifted from Brick to her mother. What motivated him to ask for her assistance? Free labor, or something more meaningful?

They spent the following hour enjoying dinner and one another's company. Rachel carefully watched her mother and Brick, looking for hints that their relationship had moved beyond friendship. Nothing stood out. Maybe Charlie had been right about his dad.

When they finished their entrée, Brick lifted his glass and smiled at Sadie. "Here's to our project."

The door swung open.

Jack stormed in. He made a beeline to their booth. "Charlie, you and Rachel need to come with me."

"What's wrong?"

"Big problem at the theater."

Chapter 42

Rachel stood on the wet sidewalk beside Sadie and Brick. She pressed her hand to her chest as Dennis pushed water out of the theater lobby with a broom. "What on earth happened?"

"Busted water pipe upstairs in the ladies' room." Jack massaged his scarred cheek. "Miss Naomi's on her way over. So's Jacob, with equipment to dry the place out."

"How much damage?" asked Charlie.

"I'll show you." He pointed to their feet. "You might want to ditch your shoes and roll up your pants."

Rachel slipped out of her sandals. Charlie pulled his loafers off and rolled his pant legs halfway up his shins.

Jack led them to the entrance. Inside, an inch of water covered the newly installed marble floor. A floating paintbrush bumped Rachel's foot. He pointed to a section of dangling ceiling. "It all started up there."

J. T. removed chunks of insulation and chalky material from the concession stand and tossed them in a trash barrel. "Good thing we knew where to turn the water off."

"Today, we finally had a performance breakthrough"—Rachel swept her arm in a wide arc—"and this happens. What do we have to do to avoid disaster around here?"

"Could've been a whole lot worse." Jack nodded toward the heavy curtain covering the theater entrance. "At least it's dry in there. That step saved our butts. Looks like the ramps we built are toast."

"My goodness, what a mess." Naomi gripped her shoes in her right hand and stepped into the lobby. "You never know what lurks in these old buildings. How's the theater?"

"Dry as a bone, ma'am." J. T. leaned on his crutch. "So's the balcony. All the water's down here."

"We can thank our lucky stars the pipe broke before the premiere." She turned in a slow circle. "Can you imagine the fiasco if it let loose with a theater full of people?"

Dennis stopped sweeping. "We should've had someone check those pipes out."

A truck pulled up out front. Jacob and Nathan bolted from the cab and hauled equipment from the bed.

"Looks like our rescue squad has arrived," Naomi said.

Dennis motioned toward the door. "The guys brought a wet-dry vac and dehumidifier."

They exited the lobby and moved to a section of the sidewalk where Sadie and Brick kept the handful of gawkers at bay. "How bad is it?"

"The lobby's a flood zone." Rachel clung to Charlie's arm and ran her hand over the bottom of her foot."

Brick handed her a handkerchief. "This will help some."

"Thanks."

Naomi faced Dennis. "What do my guys need to finish repairs by next Saturday?"

"For starters, a good plumber." He pulled off his sneakers, turned them upside down, and drained the water.

"Does Willow Falls have any?"

Sadie nodded. "One. Emily hired him a few months back to fix a leak at the inn."

"Good. I'll call him first thing in the morning." She turned back toward Jack. "What else do you need?"

"Sheetrock. A lot of it. We can't match that old ceiling. We have to replace the whole thing."

"Tomorrow," Charlie said. "I'll find the nearest building supply store and pick up everything you need."

"Good. We have a plan."

Rachel stared at Naomi. "Did you hear what Jack said? They have to tear down the old ceiling and put up a new one in six days. How is that possible?"

"Don't you worry, honey, my boys will come through."

"She's right." Jack wrung water from his socks, then stuffed them in his sneakers.

Naomi touched his arm. "By the way, I'm paying y'all double overtime."

"No need, ma'am."

"This is why I love you guys. You pitch in, work your buns off, and do whatever's needed, without expecting anything extra. I'm still paying you a fat bonus." She slipped her shoes back on. "Right now, I'm heading home. It's close to my bedtime."

Charlie stepped into his loafers. "After I take Rachel home, I'll come back and give you guys a ride. No need for you to walk both ways."

"Give us a couple of hours," said Dennis.

"Whatever you need."

Sadie and Brick headed back to the inn as onlookers began to leave. Rachel held on to Charlie's bicep, dropped her sandals on the pavement, and stepped into them. "Is it okay if we sit in the park a while?"

"Sure." He covered her hand with his as they walked past Pearl's, crossed Main, and settled on a wrought-iron bench. The streetlight cast a soft yellow glow on the lawn. A distant coyote howl punctuated the night air.

"Thanks for offering to help."

"Buying material is the least I can do."

"I still don't understand how those guys can finish everything in time."

"They'll pull some long hours." Charlie's arm encircled her shoulders. "How are you holding up?"

She leaned close and breathed in the woody scent of his aftershave. "Okay, I guess." An image of his father and her mother sitting across the booth mingled with Sadie's question about Brick's intentions. "What do you think about your dad buying that old house?"

"It's a good investment."

"Is that all it is?"

"He needs someplace other than the inn to stay when he's in town. Maybe he wants to keep an eye on his properties."

"I suppose that makes sense." She massaged the back of her hand with her thumb. "Why do you think he asked Mama Sadie to help him decorate?"

"Why not?" Charlie turned his head and stared at her. "Wait a minute. Are you still thinking something's going on between them?"

"It is possible."

"Why do women think two adults spending time together always leads to romance?"

"She is a beautiful woman."

"And he's old enough to be her ... I don't know ... older brother."

"If he's not interested in her, he needs to quit giving her mixed signals." She brushed his hand off her shoulder, jumped up, and hastened toward the lake.

Charlie caught up with her, grasped her shoulders, and turned her toward him. "Does Sadie think he has feelings for her?"

She gazed into his eyes. "She doesn't know."

He released her shoulders. "I guess it's possible."

"Emily and I ... we don't want him to break her heart."

"Do you want me to talk to him?"

"No." She sighed. "If she is nothing more than a friend ... it would make her look foolish."

"She's too much of a lady to let that happen."

"You care a lot about her."

"Of course, I do. She's your mother." He pulled her into his arms and kissed her.

When their lips parted, she cupped his face in her hands. "You definitely delivered an award-winning kiss."

A grin lit his face. "Falling in love with an actress is one crazy adventure."

Chapter 43

The day before the play's first public performance Emily left *Willow Post* headquarters, walked up Main Street, and turned onto Falls Street. Following weeks of hard work and long hours, she and Rachel were one day away from seeing their efforts come to life. Warmth radiated through her as she gazed at the marquee. Percy's Legacy, An Original Play. A welcome change from the For Rent sign with a missing *n*. The *Jurassic Park III* poster had disappeared from the ticket booth window. The glass sparkled. In the lobby, the guys stood on scaffolding, adding iridescent stars to the new ceiling.

Naomi finished transferring bottles of soda and champagne to a beverage cooler behind the concession stand, then straightened her back. "Tomorrow night, all drinks are on the house." She removed a sheet of paper from her pocket, unfolded it, and gave it to Emily. "Tell me what you think."

"T-shirts featuring a Naomi Jasper original drawing? They'll fly off the shelf."

"I ordered a hundred yesterday. All sizes. When we premiere next month, we'll also sell a fancy souvenir booklet featuring lots of stories related to the play."

"You have a good head for business."

"Years ago, I learned it takes more than talent to make a good living in the arts and entertainment world. I'll be happy to give you some pointers when your book is published."

"Really? I mean, what an awesome offer. Are you and Dennis ready to rehearse?"

Dennis climbed off the scaffolding and wiped his hands on a rag. "Lead the way."

Naomi moved around the end of the stand.

They entered the theater and joined the cast and crew sitting in the first three rows. Rachel faced her team. "Today, we'll run through the performance as if it were opening night; from start to finish."

Missy raised her hand. "Do you think we're ready?"

"We've made a lot of progress during the last few days. After today's rehearsal, we'll be ready."

"Is this with costumes and everything?"

"With everything," Rachel said. "Okay, team, opening act in thirty minutes."

Emily moved to her sister's side. "You look as tense as a tightrope walker's wire."

"We have no idea how a team of amateurs will react to a live audience. It could inspire them to new heights or scare them enough to cause all kinds of problems. Tonight, you are my audience of one. I need to know what vulnerabilities remain."

"You want me to give my honest opinion?"

"Painfully honest."

"I'll do my best." Emily moved to the fourth row and scooted to the center. She laced her fingers, tapped her thumbs, and let her mind drift back two months to the day Naomi first showed her the script. For the first time, she and the sister she'd longed for as far back as she could remember worked to create something special. Together they'd find a way to make it spectacular. Her eyes misted.

Rachel sat beside her. "Are you okay?"

She sniffed. "Better than okay."

"I'll watch from here until the end of act two." She nodded at the high-school music teacher. He positioned his fingers on the piano keys and began the overture. The curtains parted. Dennis spoke the first line.

Two hours later, Emily cheered and applauded as the cast members and crew took their bows.

"Well done," Rachel said as she faced her team. "Tomorrow night we're going to wow the audience right out of their shoes. Crew, go ahead and set the stage for act one. Everyone, rest well tonight. I'll see you back here tomorrow an hour before curtains up."

After Rachel changed, she found Emily sitting on the edge of the stage. "Tell me what you think."

"It wasn't perfect—"

"No kidding—"

"I was about to say they delivered the best performance so far."

"Sorry I jumped to conclusions. It's just … Alicia's due here tomorrow at noon. Everything depends on her take."

"What's your plan?"

"I'll start by taking her to lunch—"

"Didn't you tell me you don't eat before the first performance?"

"I'll risk it. Anyway, then I'll treat her like royalty and show her around town. Maybe she'll go easy on us."

"Or here's another possibility. She might love *Percy's Legacy*."

"At least the theater will impress her." Rachel remained silent for a long moment. "Charlie did a good job playing Everett, don't you think?"

"He's come a long way."

"He still says I need to make sure his understudy is up to par."

"Remember, he only agreed to take the role because we were in a pinch."

"I know. The thing is … as long as I'm Lillian, I can't imagine anyone else playing Everett." She pulled her vibrating phone from her pocket. "Huh."

"Who is it?"

"I don't know, some unknown Atlanta number. Probably nothing."

"Good, I'm ready to head home and soak in a hot tub."

"That makes two of us."

Chapter 44

A white sedan pulled onto Willow Inn's driveway. Rachel hastened from the porch to the sidewalk as Alicia stepped from the driver's side. She embraced her friend. "Thanks for driving up."

"If I'd known the town had this much charm, I'd have come up a long time ago."

"How was the drive?"

"Lots of wild twists and turns when I turned onto County Road."

"Locals call one stretch Devil's Curve."

"Sounds ominous." Alicia popped her trunk and removed her suitcase.

"Come on in and meet my mother."

Sadie greeted them at the door with a gold gift bag in her hand. "Welcome to Willow Inn. I've heard you're Atlanta's most talented reporter."

Alicia hugged her. "And I hear you're the best innkeeper in Georgia." She glanced around the foyer. "This is gorgeous."

"Thanks to Mama Sadie and my sister," Rachel said.

"Too bad I'm not a hotel critic. Although, I could mention this place in my blog."

"I'm putting you in the Nora Redding Suite," Sadie said. "It's the prettiest, and the view across the street is lovely."

"How delightful."

Alicia registered, carried her bag upstairs, then returned to the foyer. "I'm eager to see more of this town."

"There's not a lot to see." Rachel caught sight of Sadie's raised brows. "What I mean is it's small enough to cover on foot." *Don't let your big-city bias creep in again.*

On the way to Pepper's Café, Rachel shared the story about Redding Arms' rescue from abandonment. During lunch, they reminisced about their improv experiences. When conversation shifted to Atlanta's live performance scene, anger at Gordon Wells rekindled.

"Tell me about the play," Alicia said as she pushed her plate away.

Rachel shoved images of the director from her mind and relayed details about Naomi's find. She touted Willow Falls' history, hoping the details would help make up for any performance gaffes.

By the time they walked the town and arrived back at Willow Inn, Rachel's emotions teetered between confidence and mind-numbing anxiety. She escorted her friend into the foyer. "Until the hotel opens, the café is the only place to eat."

"After that delicious lunch, I won't need dinner. Besides, I always carry protein bars. A reporter's emergency stash. I also brought a bottle of wine for us to celebrate after the show."

If there's something to celebrate. Rachel nodded toward the door. "I'll meet you in the parlor after the last act."

"Bring your sister and Naomi with you."

"Okay. Until tonight."

After soaking in a hot tub, Rachel spent the rest of the afternoon rehearsing her lines and willing her mind and muscles to relax.

Twenty minutes before the opening act, Rachel raced across the back of the stage and knocked on the men's dressing room.

Charlie opened the door. "What's wrong?"

"Send Dennis out. Missy's in meltdown mode."

Rachel led the young man to the ladies' dressing area. "I asked everyone to leave so we could have privacy."

Inside, Missy curled up on a couch, her head buried in the crook of her arm. "I don't know if I can go through with this."

Dennis sat beside her. "Did I ever tell you about the first day I lined up with all the other recruits at boot camp?"

She shook her head.

"The second the drill sergeant screamed at us, I wanted to bolt like a little kid."

Her brows raised. "Were you scared?"

"Are you kidding? He darn near frightened me out of my skivvies."

She tugged on her costume collar. "What if the people who pushed those nasty notes under my door are in the audience? I couldn't stand them watching me."

Dennis grinned. "No need to worry. Anybody that mean is too cheap to buy a ticket. Besides, they're probably jealous of the prettiest girl in town."

She sniffed. "My makeup is all messed up."

"Easy fix." Rachel led her to the lighted makeup mirror. "All we needed is a swipe here, a dab there. See, you're as gorgeous as ever and almost ready." She set the microwave for one minute, then removed a cup and placed it on the dressing table. "Ginger tea, my all-time favorite cure for performance jitters."

Missy stared at the liquid. "Does it work?"

"One hundred percent of the time."

Dennis left. The other female players returned.

Five minutes before curtains up, Rachel stood in front of her cast and crew. She swallowed. The moment they'd spent weeks preparing for had arrived. "Have I told you how proud I am of you and all you've accomplished? I want you to think of tonight as a dress rehearsal for friends who are cheering for you. Will we make a mistake or two? Maybe. That doesn't matter because no one will know except us."

She smiled at her team. "Let's go out there and show this town what live theater looks like."

As the actors moved into position, Rachel took her position on the left side of the stage. Her palms moistened.

Charlie stepped beside her. "Looks like Missy calmed down. What about you? Did your ginger tea help?"

"I gave it to Missy. She needed it more than me."

The overture began. Rachel pressed her hand to her stomach to ease the nausea.

The curtains opened. The play began. Early in act one, Dennis missed a cue, throwing Missy off. Rachel held her breath until they recovered.

During the first scene change, a crew member dropped a chair. A loud bang and a not-so-quiet expletive followed.

He apologized profusely. "It's okay," Rachel said. "Just be more careful next time."

Halfway into act two, Mirabelle moved out of position. Rachel's muscles tightened. "What is she doing?" she whispered to Charlie. Seconds later, the town's gossip bumped into a table and sent a lamp crashing into another cast member.

Naomi covered the gaffe with an ad-lib. Mirabelle's face turned beet red. The audience roared with laughter.

Charlie bungled a line during a scene with Rachel and mouthed "sorry." At least he delivered a decent kiss to end the final act.

The audience applauded and cheered during the cast's bows. When the curtain closed the final time, they accosted Rachel with questions about their performance. "Hold on," she shouted. "It's customary for the cast members and backstage crew to mingle with the audience after the final act. Go out there and meet your fans."

Missy's eyes widened. "Are you sure?"

"I'm positive. Now, scoot."

While the team followed her instructions, Charlie leaned close. "Backstage crew too?"

"Not in professional theater. This is amateur hour. Come on, Charlie, we have to take the heat with everyone else."

Residents and cast members crowded into the lobby and spilled out onto the sidewalk. The over-the-top accolades confirmed Rachel's suspicion the audience consisted of theater-going novices. At least their enthusiasm showed they loved their town and wanted *Percy's Legacy* to succeed.

"Everyone seems impressed," whispered Charlie.

"Thank goodness they aren't professional theatergoers."

Emily joined them. "One good thing about your friend's suggestion. Performing for locals who'd adore the cast even if they'd fallen flat on their faces, should help boost their confidence."

"The big question is, will Alicia find enough good things to write about in her blog?"

"I talked to her briefly before she left."

"What'd she say?"

"If I hadn't been wearing street clothes, she'd swear I was you."

Rachel's brow furrowed. "Nothing about the play?"

"Fans interrupted us before she had a chance to say more."

"I'm going to change out of this costume. Tell Naomi Alicia wants to meet her."

Ten minutes later, the three women entered the inn's parlor and found the blogger gazing at the painting over the fireplace. An uncorked bottle of wine and four glasses sat on the coffee table. "This is a great piece." She spun around. "I noticed the painting in the dining room is a Naomi Jasper original."

The artist nodded. "The man who once owned this house bought it years ago."

"I suspect it's worth a fortune now." Alicia moved to the coffee table. "Painting the play's scenery was a stroke of genius." She poured wine and handed out the glasses. "A toast to your extraordinary efforts."

"Enough with the small talk. We're big girls," Rachel said. "We can handle the truth."

"Please have a seat and take a load off."

Emily and Naomi sat on the settee. Rachel dropped onto one of the wingback chairs and fixed her eyes on her friend.

"Okay, here's the skinny. The set is top-notch, and the dialogue brilliant. Naomi, your performance and Rachel's were excellent." Alicia paused and took a sip of wine. "The rest of the cast performed above average."

Rachel sighed. "I guess our new publicity line is 'Come to Willow Falls and watch a better-than-average performance from a ragtag cast of amateurs.'"

Alicia shook her head. "Are you going to make snide remarks or let me finish?"

"Sorry."

"I'm willing to go out on a limb and promote the dickens out of your grand opening because tonight I recognized potential and something more important than mere talent." She leaned forward. "Heart and a deep love for this town."

Emily's eyes widened. "You saw all that?"

She nodded.

"No wonder you're a reporter."

"Noticing subtleties is in my genes. Now, I'm counting on you three to inspire your team to dig deep and deliver the performance I believe is days away from exploding into something special."

"I promise we'll make it happen." Rachel tipped her glass toward Alicia. "Thank you for believing in us."

"My pleasure." She took a sip. "Now, tell me all about this lovely inn."

Following more than an hour of conversation and laughter, Naomi stood. "It's been a delightful evening, ladies, but it's way past my bedtime."

Emily glanced at her watch. "Oh my gosh, it's going on midnight. No wonder my eyelids are drooping."

"Guess we need to call it a night." Rachel embraced Alicia. "You're welcome back any time."

The three women left the inn and crossed Main Street. Naomi turned toward her house. The sisters walked a block to Emily's car. When they arrived home, she slipped out of her shoes. "I'm exhausted."

"Maybe my nieces will let you sleep late."

"Not likely. I'll see you in the morning." She took a step, then paused. "Working with you has been an amazing experience."

"One we'll treasure forever."

Emily embraced her sister. "I'm beyond thrilled about us spending the next few months together."

"So am I."

Chapter 45

Cody's whimper and tail thump awakened Emily. She glanced at the clock, slipped on a robe, and tiptoed into the hall. Squinting from light spilling from the open guestroom door, she stepped inside and found Rachel dressed in jeans and a sweatshirt, lifting a suitcase off the bed. "It's five a.m. Why are you awake … and dressed? And what's with the suitcase?"

"I've been waiting for you to wake up. We … need to talk."

Growing up as an only child, she longed to share secrets with a sister. Rachel's failure to make eye contact sent a fluttering sensation ripping through Emily's chest. Cody nudged her hand, then padded down the hall. Brownie scampered behind him. "In the kitchen. We have to let our dogs out."

She opened the patio door, then switched the coffeepot from Auto to On.

Rachel followed her and dropped onto a chair at the table.

Emily settled across from her and planted her forearms on the table. "You're making me nervous. Did something happen to your father? Did you and Charlie have a fight? Are you sick?"

"Nothing like that. Last night after you went to bed, I was too wired to sleep. So I sat out on the patio." She breathed deep and released a long, slow breath. "Remember the call from Atlanta Friday during rehearsal?"

"The one you ignored?"

She nodded. "I listened to the message."

"And?"

"It came from a well-known Atlanta director. He's casting a new play for the Alliance. The crème de la crème of the city's theaters, with lots of prominent guest performers. Actors clamor to land a role there."

"That's good news, right?"

Rachel cast her gaze downward. "The lead character is a fiery redhead. Seems someone recommended me for the part. The director wants me to audition."

"That's awesome. When?"

"Tomorrow morning."

"Oh, my gosh what an honor. I can imagine his disappointment when you turned him down."

Rachel bit her lower lip.

Emily's breath caught in her throat. "You didn't tell him no ... did you?"

"You have to understand. This is an unbelievable opportunity. Who knows when it will come along again, if ever?"

"That's why your suitcase is packed."

"Yes."

"Let me get this straight." She glared at her sister. "You're abandoning everyone who's been working their tails off to make *Percy's Legacy* successful to what ... chase a dream?"

"I assumed you of all people would understand. What would you do if you had a chance to publish your book?"

"I for darn sure wouldn't run out on my family and friends." Emily's tone hardened. "What about the part of Lillian? Do we cut it or abandon the entire third act? Have you considered Charlie? He'll be furious if you leave him hanging."

"Believe me, I've been mulling all those questions."

Emily's nostrils flared. "For what, a whole fifteen minutes? Last night, we promised Alicia we'd deliver a top-notch performance in four weeks."

"Look, if I land the part ... and it is a big if ... Mary can play Lillian. Her understudy can step in and handle her role, and you've been watching me direct for weeks."

"Is that why you asked me to stick around? Because you've been planning to bail from the beginning?"

"How could you even think that?"

"I don't know. Maybe because that's what you're doing." Emily slumped back in her chair. "I can't believe you're walking out on me."

"I know it puts a burden on everyone."

"That's a freaking understatement."

"You're right. I'm selfish and thoughtless to even consider leaving. The truth is, I have to find out if I'm good enough for the big stage or if I'm simply another mediocre actress whose only chance to land a lead role is sleeping with the director." Her eyes pleaded. "Don't you see? I can't let this chance pass me by without trying."

Emily wanted to scream *you can't go.* But deep down, she understood the raw power of dreams. Her heart ached for her sister. "What are you going to tell the cast?"

"There's no need to upset anyone until after the audition. I'll send a text explaining I'm going to Atlanta for business and give them Monday off."

"What if Charlie wants to go with you?"

"I'm leaving this morning before he has a chance to bring it up." Rachel moved beside her sister. "I need you to keep this under wraps until I find out if I land the part."

Emily studied her pained expression. One fact swirled clear as a spring-fed pool. *Percy's Legacy* couldn't compete with the lure of a big-city production. "You know I can't keep Scott in the dark. He'll figure out something's wrong the second he sees my face. As for everyone else, I'll lay low until you figure out what to do."

Rachel hugged her sister's neck. "I'm packed and ready to go. I promise everything will work out."

"Don't make promises you don't have the power to keep," Emily mumbled as Rachel popped up and dashed from the kitchen.

She returned, pulling her suitcase. "Kiss the babies for me. I'll call you after I know something definite."

Moments after she left, Emily poured a cup of coffee and carried it to the patio. The cool morning air sent a shiver through her. She pulled her robe tight. Guilt washed over her as she hoped Rachel would blow the audition.

The door opened behind her. Scott stepped out and pulled a chair over. "What's going on? Where's your sister?"

"You're not going to believe this." As she relayed the events, her disappointment morphed into something that frightened her—gut-wrenching anger. She burst into tears.

Cody bounded over, planted his front paws on her lap, and licked her face.

She pushed him away. His head cocked as he gave her a what-did-I-do-wrong expression. She stroked his muzzle. "It's okay, fella."

His tail wagged. He set all four paws on the patio, then dashed after Brownie.

Scott reached for Emily's hand. "Maybe the audition won't work out."

"If the director knows what he's doing … he'll snatch her away from us in a heartbeat."

They fell silent and watched the sky turn from black to gray. "Time for the twins to wake up."

"I'll help you dress them for church."

She pulled her hand away. "I can't go."

"Afraid you'll let the truth slip out?"

"Or break down and sob. I'll fix us blueberry pancakes."

"Now you're talking." He stood and pulled her to her feet. "Somehow everything will work out."

"Whatever that means."

An hour later, as Emily stabbed the last bite of pancakes, her phone vibrated. "It's Charlie." She dropped her fork. "Maybe I should ignore him."

"Not a good idea."

"You know he'll ask about Rachel. What should I say?"

Scott shrugged. "The first thing that pops into your head."

"You're not much help." She answered the call. "Hey, Charlie."

"Rachel sent me a text. What kind of business lured her back to the city?"

"Umm … monkey business?" She rolled her eyes at the ridiculous response. "You should call and ask her."

"I did. Twice. She didn't answer."

Now what do I say? "You know it's against the law to hold a cell phone while driving."

"She has hands-free."

"Maybe she forgot to turn on her phone." She cringed at her lame attempt to come across as convincing. "I have to run. My babies need me." She ended the call before he could respond.

"Monkey business?" Scott shook his head.

"First thing that popped into my head." She carried her plate to the sink. "At least I answered. Rachel's ignoring him."

After finishing in the kitchen, she spent the day cleaning the house and playing with Jane and Clair. At ten, she collapsed into bed, hoping exhaustion would help her fall asleep and ease her anger at Rachel.

It didn't.

Chapter 46

Rachel stood in the aisle and gazed at the elegant surroundings. Every other time she'd entered the Alliance Theatre, she did so as a lone individual among hundreds of audience members. Today, she'd arrived as an actress competing for a lead role. She swallowed the lump in her throat and pressed her hand to her chest. *This is it. My big break.*

She spotted a woman standing in the third row, waving. She recognized Michelle, from her last audition. She moved down the aisle and scooted past other actors. "I'm surprised to see you here. Didn't you land the *Penelope* role?"

She nodded, then sat. "I couldn't believe Wells didn't pick you, especially after your dynamite onstage kiss."

"I suppose he wanted something … he didn't see in me." *Did Michelle compromise her ethics to land the part, or was her talent good enough to avoid Gordon Wells' disgusting behavior?*

"It's difficult to know what goes on in a director's head. At least he narrowed it to the two of us."

"I'm glad he chose you for the role."

"It's turned into a smash hit that promises to keep me busy for months. I have to admit I felt bad about stealing Penelope from you."

Rachel shrugged. "The nature of the business."

"The good news is you're perfect for the lead in this role, which is why I recommended you."

"You know the director?"

"He's married to a close friend." She leaned close. "He's one of the good guys."

Does she know about my dinner with Gordon? Impossible. His ego is way too inflated to admit he failed to bed an actress.

"Anyway, the play is perfect for you. Unless you have something else going on."

"Not a thing." The fib rolled off her tongue faster than rainwater rushing toward a storm drain and left an acrid taste in Rachel's mouth. "I've spent the last few months up in Willow Falls with my sister and her family." *Correct the lie. Tell her about* Percy's Legacy.

"Good morning, ladies and gentlemen," the director's voice boomed.

Too late.

While he shared details about the plot and characters, Rachel's thoughts drifted. If she performed as well today as she did for the Penelope role, she knew she'd land the lead. Images of Willow Falls' cast and crew working to improve their performances doused her euphoria. She squeezed her eyes shut. They'd all understand what this meant to her. Why she had to leave. Wouldn't they?

"I'll audition for the female lead first." The director's announcement drew her attention.

"If you're a candidate for the character, come up front."

Michelle nudged her. "That's you."

Along with two other women—one blonde, the other brunette—Rachel eased out of her row and stepped forward.

"Hello, ladies. Do you have any questions?"

The blonde nodded. "When will you make a decision?"

"Before you leave today." He handed each a script. "The tab marks the section I want you to read. My assistant will play the role opposite you. I'll give you twenty minutes to familiarize yourself with the scene."

Rachel sat in the front row and silently read the lines. The scene skillfully blended comedy and drama. Everything she loved about the theater. Her chest tingled. She'd found the perfect script.

The minutes seemed to pass in a flash. When the director requested the blonde perform first and the brunette second, Rachel suppressed a smile. By the time he called her to the stage, her confidence soared.

She breathed deep, blocked out every noise, and mentally slipped into the character's skin. She delivered her first line with ease. For the following thirty minutes, she poured every ounce of talent and experience into the performance. When finished, she turned to the front, anticipating feedback.

Seconds passed.

Her pulse escalated.

"Thank you, Ms. Streetman. Excellent interpretation. You may have a seat."

What, no critique? Is that good news or bad? She returned to the third row.

"You were awesome," Michelle whispered. "Unless I totally misread the director, the role is yours." She removed a business card from her wallet. "I can't stay. Text me the results."

"I will." She touched her friend's arm. "Thank you for recommending me."

"Any time." Michelle tucked her purse under her arm and left.

As the auditions continued, Rachel imagined delivering a Tony-worthy performance in front of an audience filled with discerning fans. They'd see her as a rising star, not a woman who ran out on her friends and sister.

At five, the director sat on the edge of the stage, holding a sheet of paper. "I commend everyone for fine performances. It isn't easy to narrow the field." He paused. "I'll begin with the female lead. The actress best suited to play the role is ..."

When he called her name, adrenalin awakened every cell in Rachel's body. Her elation soared to the mountaintop, then plummeted in one swift decline. How could she tell Emily and Charlie she'd abandoned them to follow her own dreams?

Chapter 47

Emily checked her phone for the umpteenth time. "Still not a single call or text from Rachel."

"You'll have a nervous breakdown if you don't calm down." Scott slathered jam on his toast. "The audition took place yesterday—"

"Yeah, and *Percy's Legacy* rehearsals begin in nine hours." She refreshed her coffee and carried it to the table. "What am I supposed to say to the cast? I'm your new director? Never mind that I don't have an ounce of acting experience. Oh, and by the way, two of you have to learn a new part before our premiere in three weeks."

"Maybe your sister doesn't have results yet."

"Or she's too chicken to tell us the director offered her the part."

Jane dropped a piece of melon on the floor and peered over the side of her highchair, erupting in giggles when Cody and Brownie scrambled to scarf it up.

"Okay, baby girl. Time to remove the temptation." Emily opened the sliding glass door. "Come on, you two mutts."

Brownie bounded out. Cody looked up and whimpered.

"It's okay, fella. You didn't do anything wrong." She patted his head. "Good dog."

He wagged his tail, then padded out.

"If Alicia finds out Rachel's leaving, she's likely to change her mind about writing a blog post." Emily returned to the kitchen table. "Maybe we should postpone the play's official premiere until our director decides to return."

"Bad idea."

"Why?"

"Too many people devoted time and effort for you to call it quits."

"Rachel's the glue that holds everything together. Besides, we agreed I could stop shadowing her and begin working on my novel."

"You want to walk out on everyone, too?"

"It's not that I want to …" Her phone rang. "It's Charlie. What should I do?"

"Answer."

"Easy for you to say." She sucked in air, then pressed the Speaker icon. "Hey."

"She's still not answering her phone. If you don't tell me what's going on, I'll call Mitch and declare Rachel a missing person."

"Don't—"

"I'm on my way over, and I want answers." He ended the call.

"Now what do I do? There's no way I can let Charlie involve the sheriff. If I tell him the truth, I'll break my word to Rachel." She cringed. "My sister put me in an impossible situation."

"Level with Charlie and beg her forgiveness later." Scott carried his plate to the sink, rinsed it, and placed it in the dishwasher.

"Witness protection doesn't seem so bad, after all."

"Are you planning to launch a crime spree?"

"It's one of our backup plans if the play doesn't work out." She moved the twins to their play area, then wiped their trays.

The doorbell rang, followed by footsteps. Charlie zoomed in and faced Emily. "Enough stalling."

She swallowed hard. "You have to promise not to get angry."

"What the devil is going on?"

"A couple of days ago, a director contacted Rachel … to audition for the lead in a play."

Dead silence.

"We're assuming she succeeded. Rehearsals begin this week. Please, try to understand."

His eyes narrowed. "What … that she's walking out on you, me, the entire cast without a second thought? Or that she didn't care enough to tell me?"

"She didn't want to upset you or anyone else before knowing the outcome."

"How thoughtful of her." His tone dripped with sarcasm. "If she manages to pick up her phone and call you, tell her not to bother coming back to Willow Falls."

"You don't mean that."

"The heck I don't. The whole cast should walk out on her. Let her know what it feels like."

"Please don't tell me you're quitting the play too."

"I've a good mind to." His jaw clenched. "But I won't. At least not until you find a replacement."

"We'll figure something out." Emily released a long sigh. "Will you meet me at the theater a half hour early and help me figure out how to tell the cast?"

"Yeah."

"Maybe I should bring a box of cookies to soften the blow."

"A pitcher of margaritas would work a lot better." He headed out of the kitchen mumbling.

Emily collapsed onto a chair. "Does Rachel even care about her actions destroying her relationship with Charlie?"

"We'll find out soon enough."

Emily's head throbbed with pain when she entered the stage door and switched on the theater lights. A figure in the front row startled her. "Charlie? How long have you been sitting there?"

"A while."

She exited the stage and sat beside him. "Did you hear from her?"

"No."

"What if …" A dizzy sensation threatened to throw her off balance. She closed her eyes and gripped the seat's arms. "It's been two days. If something happened to her … we'd have heard … right? Maybe we *should* call the sheriff."

"Same thing I'm thinking."

She pulled her phone from her purse and scrolled to Mitch and Pepper's home number. "What if we're overreacting?" Movement in the back drew her attention. "Someone is way too early."

"I knew I'd find you here."

Emily and Charlie stared at each other, then turned toward the sound of Rachel's voice. "We've been going crazy trying to reach you."

"When I arrived in Atlanta, I discovered I'd left my phone at your house." She moved in front of the stage with her back turned toward them.

Emily released the seat's arms. "I never heard it ring."

"It's on silent. I know I should have called."

Emily stared at the back of Rachel's head, afraid to ask.

Charlie glared. His arms tight across his chest.

"Standing on that stage ... was beyond amazing. My goose bumps had goose bumps. The promise of performing in that theater with a cast of accomplished actors, fulfilled every childhood dream, every career ambition I ever dared imagine. I poured everything I knew about acting into the audition." She paused. "Last night, a bunch of the new cast members went to dinner ... to become better acquainted."

Charlie sprang to his feet and turned toward the aisle.

"Wait." Rachel grabbed his arm. "I'm not finished."

He turned toward her.

"This morning something unexpected happened." She released his arm. "I pictured you and Emily and our cast pouring their hearts into *Percy's Legacy*. The sensation that followed shocked me."

"Guilt? Remorse?"

"Something even more powerful." Rachel sniffed. "Deep admiration for my new family ... and a desperate longing to come back home."

Charlie's eyes widened. "What are you trying to say?"

"I called the director ... and turned down the part."

"Are you serious?" Emily popped off her seat. "What did he say?"

"When I explained why, he said it was an honor to know an actress who kept her priorities straight. He also claimed that any play that pulled a talented performer away from a big opportunity had to be something special."

She looked from Emily to Charlie. "I'm so sorry for not calling. I don't blame you for being angry. Truth is, I didn't want either of you to influence my decision."

Charlie pulled her into his arms. "I was afraid something terrible happened to you."

"Instead, something good happened." Rachel kissed his neck, then pulled away. A smile lit her face. "We have ourselves an honest-to-Betsy good play to produce."

Emily stared at her, then laughed. "You have a long way to go to nail Southern terms."

"I'm creating my own. Think I'll call them Rachelisms."

"Another word you can't use in Scrabble," Charlie said.

When their playful banter ended, Emily reached for her sister's hand. "Welcome home." *For however long you're here.*

Chapter 48

A booming thunderclap followed by a heavy weight crushing Rachel's chest jolted her awake. She blinked, pushed Brownie off the bed, and turned on the bedside lamp. "What's the matter, did the big bang scare you?"

Brownie whimpered, then wagged her tail. Rachel stroked her head. "Just a storm, nothing to worry about." She swung her feet to the floor and eyed the clock. Five forty. "At least it's not the middle of the night." She plucked her robe off the end of the bed, slipped it on, and dropped her phone in the pocket.

She stepped into the dark hall and tiptoed toward the kitchen where she found Emily stroking Cody's back. "Another scaredy-cat canine?"

"I don't know what it is about thunder that makes him crazy."

Rachel sat across from her sister. The coffeemaker's hiss commingled with the patter of raindrops pelting the sliding glass door. A lightning flash preceded a muted rumble. "The storm woke me from a strange dream."

"You remember it?"

She nodded. "I was back in Atlanta auditioning at the Alliance. Alicia ran onto the stage and accused me of being a traitor. Said she'd written a blistering blog post about misplaced loyalty."

"Delayed guilt?"

"Are you playing the role of Willow Falls' psychologist?"

"You're the actress, not me." Emily yawned. "It is strange your friend hasn't posted anything about our play. I hope she didn't have a change of heart."

"She's a busy reporter, and she has a family."

"Coffee's ready. Want some?"

"You sit still. I'll pour you a cup." Rachel moved to the counter and lifted two cups from the cabinet. "About my promise to release you from director shadowing—"

"Are you reneging on the deal?"

"On the contrary. Since I'm back on board with the play, I have plenty of free time during the day."

Emily's eyes widened. "Are you offering—"

"To watch my nieces while you pound the keys on your laptop." She carried coffee to the table. "Call it payment for letting me and Brownie invade your home."

"You're my sister, you're always welcome."

"It looks like I'll be here a while."

"Is that good news or bad?

"Good because I'll spend more time with you, Mama Sadie, and Charlie." She focused on the steam curling from her cup. "As far as my career goes, that's another story."

"What you did for all of us ... I don't know how we can possibly repay you."

"Easy. Make *Percy's Legacy* the best small-town play to ever hit the stage." Sounds from the baby monitor drew her attention. "Time to exercise my new role as aunt and nanny."

"Are you sure?"

"Positive." Rachel patted her sister's hand, then dashed to the nursery.

Inside, she turned the overhead light on and moved beside the cribs.

Clair gripped the railing and pulled to her feet.

"Looks like you two pretty girls are ready for breakfast."

Arms wrapped around Rachel's waist. "Morning, gorgeous."

"Back at you, handsome. I trust your wife won't mind her hubby hugging another woman."

Scott jerked his arms away and stepped back. "Rachel?"

She turned toward him and laughed. "In the flesh."

His eyes were the size of saucers. "Is Emily okay? Is she sick? What are you doing in here?"

"Relax, Papa Hayes, she's fine. I'm giving her a break so she can return to writing."

"You and my wife need to start wearing nametags."

"And abandon the pranks we missed growing up without each other? Not a chance."

He brushed his fingers through his disheveled hair. "From now on, I'm not approaching either one of you from the back."

Rachel lifted Clair from her crib. "Your daddy's a party pooper."

Scott reached for Jane. "Your Aunt Rachel has a warped sense of humor."

"Think of all the fun your girls will have growing up."

"Another pair of redheaded twins." He delighted Jane with a raspberry. "Willow Falls doesn't have a clue what it's in for."

They made their way to the kitchen and placed the babies in their highchairs.

"Your sister darn near gave me a heart attack." Scott poured a cup of coffee, then plopped beside Emily.

"Did you kiss the back of her neck, honey?"

"I came close."

"My goodness. What will Charlie say?"

"That he's relieved you're not both living in his house."

The front doorbell rang, followed by footsteps. Mirabelle rounded the corner, leaving wet footprints in her wake.

"Good grief, lady, the sun's not even up." Scott pulled his robe tight. "Didn't I tell you to knock first?"

"I rang the bell. What more do you want?"

"You could wait for us to answer. Or is that asking too much?"

"The door was open."

"My sister and brother-in-law need to do what every other normal person does. Lock the front door." Rachel filled two sippy cups.

Mirabelle huffed. "No one around here bothers with locks."

"I've noticed."

"Anyway, have you seen it?"

Scott glared at her. "What are you talking about?"

"Alicia Adams' blog."

"Are you serious?" Emily's fingers raced across her keyboard. "I found it."

Mirabelle plopped onto a chair and tapped the table. "Are you gonna read it?"

"You are one impatient woman." Emily focused on the screen. "Alicia titled it 'Win for North Georgia.' She says, 'What is the next logical step when a famous artist finds a partially written script about her hometown's colorful history? Hire Emily Hayes, a talented writer and her twin, Rachel Streetman, an accomplished actress, to finish it. The result? *Percy's Legacy*, a delightful production featuring original Naomi Jasper scenery. Although the play isn't a musical, it showcases original background and interval tunes created by a local composer. Rachel, who also performed brilliantly, directed the three-act play and turned local talent into a formidable team. The two leads Missy Gibson and Dennis Locke show potential as up-and-coming young performers.'"

Rachel placed cereal puffs on the babies' trays. "She obviously saw something in those two."

"There's more. 'The other players, including Naomi, poured their hearts into the performance. I found the newly renovated venue reminiscent of a miniature Fox Theater, and the sets impressive. Theater aficionados who thrive on discovering new talent should click on the Willow Falls website and reserve a seat for the play's premiere, scheduled for the second weekend in October.'"

Mirabelle's chest puffed. "She said we were good."

Emily's head jerked toward her. "You're not upset she didn't mention your name?"

"Alicia likes the play. That's what counts."

"Are your sure you're not an imposter?"

"Next time she watches it, she'll mention me." Mirabelle pushed off the chair. "I have to go to the post office and sort today's mail." She took a step, then halted. "Sorry for tracking in water."

"We'll take care of it." Scott headed to the garage and returned with a mop.

"Your friend did an amazing job," Emily said.

"Now the pressure's on to deliver the goods."

"If the rest of the cast reacts as well as Mirabelle, they'll work their buns off to prove Alicia right."

"I need to thank her." Rachel pulled her phone from her pocket and tapped a text message. Moments later, her phone pinged. "She responded. Says something's cooking at the station that could help Willow Falls even more than her blog. She'll call when she has more info."

"What do you think she's talking about?"

Rachel slipped her phone back in her pocket. "I don't have the slightest idea."

Chapter 49

Following Nathan's closing prayer, Emily stood and stretched her arms behind her back. Eager to spend a quiet afternoon working on her novel, she slung her purse over her shoulder. Scott and Charlie stepped into the center aisle and picked up on their discussion about the Atlanta Falcons' win-loss record.

Rachel remained seated.

Emily tapped her shoulder. "Are you glued to your seat?"

"Alicia called twenty minutes ago. She left a message."

"What'd she say?"

She held up her index finger and pressed her phone to her ear. "You're not going to believe this."

"Is she writing another blog post about the play?"

Rachel handed her phone to Emily.

She listened to the message. "I don't believe it." She played it again. "We have to do something ... today."

Scott turned toward her. "Are you ladies coming?"

"I need you to take the twins home, honey. I'll ride with Rachel."

"Did something happen?"

"We'll fill you in when we get home."

Rachel eyed Charlie. "Want to join us at Emily and Scott's?"

"No way I'm gonna miss whatever set you two off."

"Bring your dad and Mama Sadie." She clutched Emily's hand. "We have work to do." They made a beeline to Nathan.

Thirty minutes later, Rachel parked in Emily's driveway. Charlie's truck and Brick's car were parked at the curb. Nathan pulled in behind her, followed by Pepper.

"I hope the council takes this as good news." Rachel opened her door.

Emily stared at her. "Why wouldn't they?"

"Plenty of reasons."

Emily stepped out and rushed to the porch.

Rachel followed close behind.

Scott met them at the door. "Why is the town council showing up?"

Nathan and Jacob approached. "All we know is your wife told us Willow Falls' future is on the line."

"That's a permanent condition." Scott stood to the side.

The newcomers brought the number of people crowded in the den to ten.

Rachel stood in front of the flat-screen television. "Is anyone familiar with *Around Georgia*? It plays on the Friday evening news."

Pepper held a finger up. "I am."

"What's it like?"

"Some of the stories are positive, like the one about a teacher who saved a student's life. More often they're hit jobs. I remember a blistering account of a rural community's failed attempt to attract new businesses. Why are you asking?"

"I received this message from my friend Alicia." Rachel held her phone up and tapped the Play icon. "The station manager read my blog post and asked a lot of questions about Willow Falls. He sees a follow-up story to our competitor's piece about failing Georgia towns. Bottom line, I'm bringing a camera crew up a week from Monday to film a segment for *Around Georgia*. Although I'll control the filming, our program manager has the final say about the three-minute segment. Needless to say, the town needs to put its best foot forward."

"What in blazes does that mean?" Scott crossed his arms and leaned against the wall.

Pepper scooted to the edge of her seat. "I think she's trying to tell us we have one week to put lipstick on our town's mug."

"This could accomplish what the PR firm couldn't," Emily said.

"Or it could turn out way worse than the Travel Titan's publicity." Pepper's head tilted. "Nathan, you're our mayor, what's your take?"

"It's a big risk. Three of you are from Atlanta. What would it take to impress a big-city television crew?"

"First off"—Brick eyed Jacob—"will your guys have the hotel ready for a tour?"

"The guest rooms are done. My crew's a couple of days from finishing the lobby and dining room."

"That's a start. The problem is downtown. It still looks old and run down, and the six empty retail spaces are a big problem. News crews focus on the negative."

Silence punctuated by sighs.

Tension crept down Emily's spine as she pictured a reporter standing in front of a vacant store delivering a scathing review.

"I have an idea." Brick ran his finger along his jaw. "Charlie and I will set up a temporary tasting bar in one of the empty spaces. We'll bring cases of Georgia wine, some shelves, a long table—"

"I have both in my store," Nathan said. "I'll give you a good price."

"Deal. We'll need someone to paint a mural."

Emily touched Nathan's arm. "Your daughter painted the Cinderella castle in our twins' nursery. Do you think she'd be willing?"

"Let her sign it, and she'll paint a picture on the side of a building." He scratched his head. "Something else we can do. Set up the tourist bureau we discussed at our last council meeting."

"I've been noodling on an idea," Pepper said. "Most of the families around here trace back to the town's original inhabitants. Can you imagine the pieces of history they have packed away? We can invite folks to donate some items and create a history museum. Something different from Naomi's house and the mansion Percy built for Peaches."

Brick nodded. "That takes care of half the vacant spaces. You have to find a way to camouflage the remaining three."

"Your ideas are all clever." Rachel sighed. "And they'd work if you had enough money and time to put them in place. The fact is we have seven days, which makes everything you're suggesting impossible."

"Not if we recruit enough people to help."

Rachel stared at Nathan. "Are you suggesting another town hall meeting?"

He shook his head. "We're all town hall weary. We need a different approach. Give me a minute to think." He moved across the room and faced the window overlooking the backyard.

Emily scanned the faces staring at the back of the mayor's head. She recognized the look of hopeful anticipation, and yet she knew Rachel and

Brick were both right. Empty storefronts shouted failure, and one week wasn't enough time to accomplish even a fraction of the ideas the council had thrown out. "Maybe we should contact Alicia and beg off."

"Not yet." Nathan spun around. "I need to jot down some notes."

Scott scampered to the desk and removed a pad of paper and a pen. "Here you go."

"Thanks." He filled the page with notes, then pointed to a printer. "I need a copy for everyone here."

"Done." Scott printed then distributed the copies.

"Here's what we're going to do." Nathan's tone projected optimism as he outlined his plan. When finished, he along with Pepper, Scott, and Jacob grabbed their phones and began contacting residents. Charlie and Brick huddled to expand on their tasting-room idea.

Rachel pulled Emily aside. "Give it to me straight. Does his plan have the slightest chance to work?"

"We have four hours to find out." Emily removed her phone from her pocket and punched in a number. "Hello, Mirabelle. Hold on a sec." She held her hand over the speaker and smiled at Rachel. "Will you check on the twins? This will take a while."

Rachel clung to Charlie's arm and gawked at the crowd gathered in the park. "How did seven people inspire these folks to show up with only a few hours' notice?"

"Good old-fashioned phone chain and a well-crafted call to action."

Emily nodded. "Plus, the chance to see their faces on television. They'd go bananas if a movie crew ever pulled into town."

"Like that will ever happen."

A shrill microphone squeal sent fingers rushing to ears.

"Sorry, folks." Nathan detailed plans, then directed residents to move to one of the empty stores slated for a facelift.

Rachel sighed. "If they pull this off, *Around Georgia* will have one heck of a story to tell."

Chapter 50

Memories bubbled up as Emily peered over the theater balcony railing. Begging her mom for a dozen spotted puppies after watching *101 Dalmatians*. Sneaking into the empty theater with teenage buddies to mix adult beverages with their favorite sodas. Sitting in the last row kissing Scott.

"It's looking good." J. T. hobbled down the steps and stood beside her. "If that crew coming to town tomorrow isn't impressed by all the work everyone's done, I'll have to knock some sense into their heads with my crutches."

"I don't know how you guys found the time to pitch in at the last minute."

"We pulled a couple of all-nighters, along with a lot of people."

"Maybe you and everyone else can finally get some rest."

"Not me. I have to study for tomorrow's gig."

"Nathan made a good decision when he asked you to take it on."

He shrugged. "Glad to help out." He yanked a stapled stack of notebook paper from his back pocket, then dropped onto a seat.

"I'll leave you to your work." She eased up the aisle and down through the lobby. On the sidewalk in front of the theater, she lowered her sunglasses, grateful the forecast called for clear skies and mild temperatures to continue through the weekend. At the corner her heart swelled with pride as she gazed at Main Street's transformation: colorful new awnings, flower baskets alternating with *Welcome to Willow Falls* flags gracing the newly painted streetlights.

She stopped in front of an empty storefront to admire the newly painted window sign—The Old-Fashioned Christmas Shoppe—connected to Patsy's Pastries and Pretties.

The high-school art teacher stepped back. "What do you think?"

"Looks awesome."

"Patsy claims the store will open the same weekend as the hotel."

"Who knew she had enough money stashed away to create a whole new business?"

"The town's full of surprises. Did you see the murals my students painted on the empty stores' windows?"

Emily nodded. "They're a work of art." She moved on and walked into Pepper's Café where she found Patsy and Sadie sitting at the counter, hunched over a laptop.

"Did you ladies discover a hot new computer game?"

"Better." Sadie tapped the screen. "It's Willow Inn's new website. Can you believe every room is booked for the grand opening weekend?"

"Including Kat's and Missy's suites?"

"Uh-huh. Naomi says they can move into her guest rooms until they find a permanent place to live."

"Good for her. I hear hotel reservations are starting to come in."

"Thanks to these fancy sites." Patsy brought up the Willow Falls website. "Watch what happens when I click this little gizmo. Up pops my store. Connor made this so easy, even old ladies like me can figure out how to make it work."

"He's one talented young man. Too bad he's so full of mischief."

"Who is?" Pepper breezed in from the kitchen carrying three bowls.

"The town's wannabe FBI sleuth." Sadie sniffed the air. "Whatever's in those bowls smells yummy."

"Smoked-cheddar chicken mac and cheese." She set them on the counter along with three spoons. "Tell me what you think."

Emily dug her fork in and savored the smoky taste. "Best mac 'n' cheese ever."

"Good. I'm serving it to our TV crew tomorrow for lunch."

"Our town will wow the willies out of those big-city folks, especially after Naomi's big surprise." Patsy's hand flew to her mouth.

Emily peered around Sadie. "What big surprise?"

"Sorry, sweetie. I promised to keep it a secret."

"Is she donating a painting to the town?"

Patsy zipped her thumb and index finger across her lips.

"You know once the cat's out of the bag," Pepper said, "it's impossible to shove it back in."

"That kitty will have to roam around without a home until tomorrow."

"Can I bribe you with a slice of apple pie?"

Patsy shook her head. "These lips are sealed."

The café door swung open. "Afternoon, ladies."

"Hello, Winston." Pepper set utensils rolled in a napkin on the counter.

"Something smells good."

"Tomorrow's special."

He slid onto a stool. "When the hotel opens, the town's likely to be overrun with tourists."

"That's the plan." Emily stepped back. "I need to go home and start working on my book … again."

Patsy turned toward her. "How's it going?"

"It isn't. Too many calamities keep popping up."

"We're due for some disaster-free days."

"Way past due." Emily slipped off her stool. "Winston, ladies, enjoy your afternoon."

Chapter 51

Rachel gazed at the willow trees standing proud against the cloudless morning sky. "It's a gorgeous day."

Emily nodded. "Thank goodness the weather is on our side."

She leaned on Willow Inn's railing and spotted a chipmunk scampering to a hole dug in a patch of dirt between the box hollies and the porch. "Today will either end in disaster or slingshot Willow Falls into a new future."

Emily ran her fingernail along a crack in the wood. "I'm banking on the slingshot."

"Where's Mama Sadie?"

"Fixing a bowl of chicken soup for Winston. Seems he's come down with the flu. She threatened to evict him if he stepped one foot out of his suite."

"The last thing we need is him exposing Alicia and her crew."

A van sporting a television station logo turned the corner from County Road to Main Street. "They're here."

"It's showtime." Rachel smoothed her jacket and moved to the sidewalk.

Emily waited at the top of the steps.

Alicia slid from the van and rushed to meet her. "Who ordered this gorgeous weather?"

"We wouldn't let it rain on our favorite TV reporter," Rachel said.

Two men stepped out and headed their way.

"Meet Kevin, my cameraman."

He removed his ball cap. "Ladies."

"And our equipment guy, Al. They don't talk much, but they're the best in the business." She turned to Kevin. "Grab your gear, guys. We'll film the inn first."

When they headed back to the van, Alicia pushed her sunglasses to the top of her head. "I'm jazzed about today. However, you need to understand I can't guarantee the station will air this story, and if it does, how it will turn out."

"We know." She touched Alicia's arm. "We have a few surprises for you."

"Surprises make a good story."

While Emily escorted Alicia and her crew into the inn, Rachel removed her phone from her pocket and pressed Charlie's number. "Send him over." A half hour later, she led Alicia to the inn's driveway and Naomi's red Cadillac. "Meet one of our town's newest residents, Jack Parker."

He stepped out and tipped his ball cap. "It's a pleasure, ma'am."

"Thank you, sir." Alicia touched his burn-scarred arm. "War injuries?"

"Yes ma'am."

She turned to Kevin. "Get a shot of our handsome young driver."

Jack's lopsided smile beamed as he opened the passenger door. "This is a fine town, Ms. Adams."

"Indeed it is."

Rachel and Emily climbed into the back seat while Kevin and Al headed to the van. Jack backed onto Main and turned on Falls Street.

Emily leaned forward. "If you don't mind, we'll start with the waterfall."

Alicia looked over her shoulder. "Perfect."

Following a trek on the trails, Jack drove back to town and parked across from the Antique and Furniture Emporium. Nathan stood on the curb. He opened the passenger door. "Welcome back, Ms. Adams."

Alicia climbed out. "Thank you, Mayor."

Kevin approached with his shoulder-mounted camera. Al handed Alicia a cordless microphone. She held it close. "Tell us, Mayor Dixon, what prompted residents to invest time and resources into Willow Falls?"

He blinked. "Our colorful history and one couple's vision. God rest their souls. It all begins around the corner. If you will, please follow me."

At the end of the block, the entourage turned left. Chatter rose to a deafening crescendo as hundreds of men, women, and children joined in boisterous applause and cheers. Kevin aimed his camera toward the throng. Alicia held her microphone to capture the moment, then leaned close to Rachel. "Their enthusiasm tops the chart."

"We're just getting started. Meet today's tour guide, another new resident, Officer J. T. Brown."

Wearing his dress blues, J. T. ambled over on his crutches, one pant leg rolled up and pinned. He tipped his cap. "It's a pleasure, ma'am."

Alicia activated her mic. "What brought you to Willow Falls, sir?"

"Necessity. Folks around here needed help, and me and a couple of buddies needed jobs. Call it a mutual back-scratching."

"Sounds interesting. What's the first stop on our tour?"

"Willow Falls' Historic Museum."

Alicia held her mic at her side and nudged Rachel. "Why didn't you show me the museum—"

"A week ago, it didn't exist. Like Emily told you. We have a few surprises."

J. T. led the way to the previously empty space adjacent to the *Willow Post* headquarters. A seventies-something woman, dressed in 1890's attire, guided them through an array of documents, photos, and sundry artifacts while amusing the crew with tales about the town's earliest residents. As they reached the last scene, she pointed to a faded black-and-white photo of a young woman wearing the crimson gown that was displayed on a headless mannequin. "Our winery owner found that dress and picture of the real Peaches in Percy's attic. My late husband's kin helped build that fancy house."

"Thank you for showing us around." J. T. held the door open. "We have another fine tourist attraction next door."

"One more venue that sprang up overnight," whispered Rachel as they made their way to the Willow Oak Museum and Tasting Room.

Brick opened the door. "Welcome."

Charlie, wearing a T-shirt touting the vineyard and winery, directed them to an exhibit illustrating the entire wine production process.

"From Vine to Stem." Alicia touched the image of a half-filled wine glass. "Clever play on words. I assume the tastings aren't from the vineyard we passed on the way into town."

"Correct assumption. Although the samples are all Georgia-produced wines. Eventually, we'll move the tasting room to the winery."

After interviewing Charlie and Brick, Alicia stepped into the crowd gathered in the street and captured comments from dozens of spectators clamoring to step in front of the camera and offer their perspective on Willow Falls' transformation.

Ten minutes into what seemed more like a comedy routine than an interview, Alicia stepped onto the sidewalk.

"Folks around here are proud of their town," J. T. said as he thrust his thumb over his shoulder. "This here is the new tourist bureau. We'll conduct tours twice a day to start."

Alicia pointed to the sign painted on the window. "We Are for Willow Falls. Is that the town's motto?"

"Yes ma'am."

"Clever. Are you the newest tour guide?"

"I'm the only one." He grinned. "Next stop, Hayes General Store."

The crowd followed as they walked the half block. Inside, a player piano resounded with a lively version of "Give My Regards to Broadway." Two residents sat at a barrel table engrossed in a game of checkers. Scott, dressed in a bowler hat and a vintage suit topped with a frock coat, led the crew to an old-fashioned soda fountain.

Gertie, also wearing period garb, greeted them with a hearty handshake. "I fixed you and the boys the best milkshakes in Georgia." She pushed three tall glasses across the counter and pointed to the microphone.

"Turn that on, and I'll give you a blooming good interview."

"Yes ma'am." Alicia aimed the mic at her.

Gertie stared at the camera. "Before Naomi Jasper, she's a famous artist, and Emily Hayes, her husband owns this fine store ... Anyway, before they found that old script and wrote *Percy's Legacy*, nobody around here paid much mind to our founders. Peaches performed as a vaudeville singer until Percy rescued her. Back then, uppity rich people called her occupation shameful. I don't know why. After all, she kept all her clothes on."

Rachel suppressed a laugh.

Alicia pressed her hand to her lips as her eyes crinkled from a smile. "Thank you, Miss Gertie. Your observation is enlightening. I'll take my milkshake with me while the owner shows us around the store."

"You have to wait for your cameraman to finish his drink."

Kevin set his camera down and reached for the milkshake.

"Not too fast, young man, you'll end up with a brain freeze."

By the time they finished their shakes and filmed the store, lunchtime had rolled around. Across the street, residents lined up outside Pepper's Café complaining about the Closed to the Public sign.

Mirabelle stood in front of the door with her arms planted across her chest. "Pepper's not letting anyone in except the TV people, so they can eat in peace."

Emily leaned close to Rachel. "How did you get her to stand guard?"

"Told her we'd show Alicia the hotel room she adopted."

"You're getting the hang of small-town politics."

"This city girl can still learn a thing or two."

Following a peaceful lunch, the entourage visited Patsy's Pastries and Pretties for dessert and a tour of her new Christmas Shoppe, then made their way to the hotel. Kat met them in the lobby with an outstretched hand. "Welcome to Redding Arms."

Alicia lifted the microphone. "I hear this hotel has quite a history."

"Indeed, it does. After sitting idle for thirty years, this beautiful building has been given new life. Our goal is to combine the opulence of a century-old grand hotel with the ambiance of a visit to a loved one's home."

Kat led a tour through the lobby and dining room before stopping at the elevators. "You are about to see why our suites are as inviting as a friend's guest room."

"She's good," Rachel whispered to Emily.

"We're fortunate Mama Sadie recruited her."

The doors opened. They stepped inside. Kat pressed two. "Every guest room in Redding Arms has been lovingly adopted and beautifully decorated by a Willow Falls family."

Alicia's eyes widened. "That's a unique approach."

"This is a unique town."

The doors opened on the second floor.

They moved through the foyer and turned the corner. Mirabelle stood tall and pointed to a brass plaque on the wall beside an open door. "Welcome to the Paine Family Suite. My ancestors helped build this town. My grandma was a fine lady and a master quilt maker. This room is dedicated to her."

Inside, a quilt featuring a Christmas tree created from a patchwork of green-and-white patterned squares hung behind the bed. An array of vintage holiday cards displayed in an antique frame decorated the wall to the right. Another handmade quilt with a Christmas theme lay across the bottom of the bed.

Mirabelle plucked an eight-by-ten framed document from the dresser and read her grandmother's story. When she finished, her eyelids lowered.

"What a heartwarming story," Alicia said.

"She was more like my mother than my grandma."

Alicia turned to Kevin. "Capture this lovely lady standing beside that magnificent quilt."

Mirabelle's face beamed as she ran her fingers along the quilt's edge.

When Alicia moved back to the hall, she turned to Kat. "I'd like to film one more room."

"Excellent." She stepped across the hall and used a master key to open the Cushman Suite. "You met Pepper at her café."

"Her mac and cheese was de-lish-i-ous."

"She's the hotel's new executive chef. Her husband's the sheriff. They incorporated their love for old classic movies into their theme." Kat held the door open. "The posters represent her favorites. She included *The Wizard of Oz* for the kiddies.

Alicia stepped inside. "*Casablanca* and *Singing in the Rain* are on my top-pick list."

"This is the only room with a DVD player," Kat said. "All these films are here for our guests' enjoyment."

Alicia picked up a copy of *My Fair Lady*. "Willow Falls residents are full of creativity."

"Indeed they are."

After Kevin captured the scene, they returned to the lobby. J. T. led them from the hotel, past Willow Inn and up the block to the mansion Percy built for Peaches. An attractive young woman dressed in a nineteenth-century gown guided them through the first-floor rooms and told stories about Peaches' elaborate parties. "The upstairs will be ready for tourists in a couple of weeks."

"It's a beautiful home."

"For a lady who didn't take her clothes off in public," whispered Emily.

"One more stop." J. T. escorted the crew across the street to the Naomi Jasper Museum and Art Gallery.

Alicia stopped while Kevin filmed the home's façade.

Their hostess met them on the porch. She showed them the main floor and shared stories about her family and life as an artist; she then led the way out back to a miniature two-story, gingerbread-style structure painted pale green with pink-and-white accents.

She stood on the porch facing the camera. "My father built this for my sixteenth birthday. It's where my career began before an agent discovered my work. After that, I spent most of my life in Charleston, South Carolina."

She pointed to Alicia. "Please turn off your cameras and microphone."

"Are you sure?"

"Positive."

Alicia signaled Kevin. He lowered his camera.

"Thank you," Naomi said. "Soon after I retired and moved back to my hometown, three young heroes came to Willow Falls to begin their lives anew. They helped me prepare my home for tourists and transformed my garage into a lovely gift shop. Like all veterans, they deserve more than our respect." She paused. "I believe we all have a duty to do everything we can to make their lives whole. Come up here with me, J. T."

He hesitated, then hobbled to Naomi's side, dropped one crutch, and laid his arm across her shoulders.

"I've grown to love this young man and his two friends as the sons I never had." She looked up into J. T.'s eyes. "Which is why Monday morning I'm driving you to Atlanta where you'll be fitted with a state-of-the-art prosthetic leg."

Emily gasped. "That's her secret."

Tears erupted as Rachel watched big, tough J. T. swipe his hand across his eyes and lean down to kiss Naomi's cheek.

"There's more." She pointed to the gift shop. "Every penny our museum visitors spend will be used to cover the cost of the limb and the training he'll need to learn how to walk on it."

"Ms. Jasper ..." Alicia choked up. She dabbed her eyes. "Is your gift shop open for business?"

"Yes."

"Good, because I'd like to buy a souvenir."

Naomi's grin crinkled her eyes. "Follow me. I know the perfect item for a beautiful young professional."

"You have to love this town," Emily said as she swiped her fingers across her cheeks.

Rachel nodded and swallowed the melon-size lump in her throat.

Chapter 52

Emily stood at the patio door with Clair on her hip and gazed at raindrops spilling from a single dark cloud. "I swear half the residents have called to ask what's going on with *Around Georgia*." She faced Rachel. "If Alicia doesn't give us an answer soon, I'll toss my phone in the lake and move to Montana."

"That's a long commute."

"Not long enough. If the story doesn't air in two days, it won't do squat to help us boost reservations for grand-opening weekend."

"Editing hours of film to a three-minute segment takes time."

"Unless they decided not to air it. Or worse, plan to present a negative story. What do you think they'll do?"

Clair curled her fingers and rubbed her eyes, then yawned.

"How would I know?" Rachel reached for her niece. "What I do know is Jane's in her crib for her afternoon nap, and I need to take this little angel to join her sister so their mommy can work on her book."

"Not sure I can concentrate."

Rachel nuzzled Clair's neck as she moved toward the hall. "We have to tell your mommy to quit worrying about something she can't control."

"Easy for you to say, it's not your town," Emily said under her breath.

"I heard that."

Emily carried her laptop to the den and her new writing spot, her recliner. She opened her novel and stared at the screen. Too many images rattled in her head to focus. She plucked her phone from the end table and scrolled through the photos she'd snapped during Alicia's tour. If the story didn't run, the station's mailbox and inbox would overflow with letters and messages from angry residents. After spending hundreds of hours accomplishing what seemed impossible, who could blame them?

She closed her laptop and set it on the end table.

"Are you giving up after ten minutes?" Rachel stood with her arms crossed.

"It's no use. I might as well go work on the newspaper."

"Aren't you postponing this week's edition until we hear from Alicia?"

"I need to figure out what to write if the station doesn't air the story or we get negative coverage." She pushed off the recliner. "Promise to call me if you hear from her."

"Cross my heart."

Emily drove to town, parked in front of the *Willow Post* headquarters, and stared at the empty sidewalks, a stark contrast to Monday's crowds. She climbed from her car and walked to the front door. Not in the mood to write an article any more than working on her book, she hoped a stroll would stimulate her creative juices.

She passed the new museum and tasting room, both closed until the following weekend. At the corner, she paused at the vintage cast-iron mailbox. While the red color had faded over the years, her memories of mailing letters to Santa, begging for a sister, remained fresh. So much had changed since those days. She continued walking until she reached Pepper's Café and glanced inside. Mirabelle sat at the counter beside Winston Hamilton, most likely bending his ear. It seemed the town's British celebrity had kicked the flu in record time.

An elderly gentleman walking his dog approached. "Afternoon, Emily, or are you Rachel?"

"Emily."

"Pleasant day for a walk."

"Yes, it is."

"Any word on that television show?"

She struggled to keep her from rolling her eyes. "Not yet."

"Maybe you'll hear something today." His dog tugged on the leash. "Say hi to Scott."

"Will do." As she watched him move on, she questioned if residents understood the impact a tourist invasion would have on their town.

A calico cat slithered from the curb and stretched around her leg. She stooped to pick it up. "Who do you belong to?"

It meowed, then sprang from her arms and dashed across the street. Emily followed and strolled through the park to the hotel's back lawn, where a mother duck and four ducklings waddled from the sand into the lake.

"Those little ducklings just hatched." Kat sat on the veranda steps with a cigarette balanced between two fingers. "I need to kick this habit."

Emily strolled over and sat beside her. "I tried smoking once. Nearly choked my insides out."

"It's good you never started." She paused. "The inn's booked full. A few more hotel reservations came through this morning, bringing us to forty percent occupancy for opening weekend. If Alicia's story hits the airwaves, and it's positive, we should fill the rest."

"You did an amazing job showcasing the hotel."

She snuffed her cigarette on the ground and pocketed the stub. "Not bad for an ex-con."

"Before long, people around here will forget you and Missy served time."

"Might take a while."

They sat in silence until Emily's ringtone sounded. "It's Rachel." She removed the phone from her purse and pressed the Speaker icon. "Please tell me you have good news."

"Hold on, I'm conferencing you in … Alicia, are you still there?"

"Bright-eyed and full of good news."

"Emily's on the line."

"Hey, girl, I hope your hometown is prepared for some awesome publicity because the most positive story we've ever done on *Around Georgia* is going live Friday."

"Are you serious?"

"In two days, millions of Georgians who never knew Willow Falls existed will discover your town is far more than a dot on the map. That's not all. Our program director's brother lost both legs fighting in Iraq. When I told him about Naomi and J. T.'s new limb, he decided to send us back to Willow Falls to cover Redding Arms' grand opening and the *Percy's Legacy* premiere."

"You're our town's newest champion," Emily said.

"Nonsense. My crew and I simply reported the truth, which in the end always prevails."

Kat leaned close to the phone. "We'll reserve a couple of hotel rooms for you, on the house."

"You're a sweetheart. I have to run. See you a week from Saturday."

Emily's pulse accelerated as she dropped her phone in her purse and bolted to her feet. "I have to run."

"To where?"

"*Willow Post* headquarters. I have a newspaper to print."

Chapter 53

Animated conversation charged the air in the Hayes' den as the Friday afternoon sun dipped toward the horizon. Emily sat on the floor beside her sister, holding a plate of appetizers on her lap. "The last time a television program generated this much excitement the Atlanta Falcons were playing in the Super Bowl."

Kat pulled the tab on a Coke. "At least we know this show's outcome before it airs."

"Thank goodness. Otherwise, I'd be a certified basket case," Emily said. "I don't know how the editors cut hours of film into a three-minute segment."

"With a giant pair of scissors." Sadie bounced Clair on her knee.

Brick sat beside her with baby Jane cuddling in his lap. "Three minutes of free publicity is worth its weight in gold."

Scott dipped a shrimp in cocktail sauce. "I guarantee every resident is glued to a television."

"Dennis called the rehab center to clue J. T. in." Charlie slapped a piece of cheese on a cracker. "I knew a kid in high school who had an artificial leg. One time he took it off and scratched his head with the foot. Freaked the teacher out. He was one funny guy."

"J. T. has no idea what he's in for," Scott said. "As the first Willow Falls resident with a prosthetic leg, he'll become an instant celebrity."

Rachel set her plate on the coffee table. "I heard Nathan hired him as the town's official tour guide."

Scott nodded. "He starts grand-opening weekend." He glanced at his watch. "It's T-minus two." He aimed the remote and increased the volume.

Conversation halted as seven pairs of eyes fixed on the flat-screen television. Twenty minutes into the program, Alicia's face appeared on the screen. A radiant smile lit her face. "If you've ever discovered a gem hidden in your backyard, you'll understand what the *Around Georgia* crew experienced last Saturday in Willow Falls. The experience began with a ride in one of the town's two vintage taxis, a 1953 Cadillac convertible donated by renowned artist Naomi Jasper."

Emily's limbs tingled with excitement as she watched three amazing minutes of footage featuring every tourist attraction and listened to Alicia's interaction with residents.

As the segment wound down, the reporter appeared on-screen. "A visit to Naomi Jasper's exquisite new museum featuring notable antiques, her own paintings, and works from other well-known Southern artists provided far more than a visual delight. It gave us a glimpse into the artist's soul."

A lump formed in Emily's throat as the coverage shifted to Naomi, standing on her workshop porch with J. T. Alicia continued, "Every dollar spent in her gift shop will help fund a young veteran's new leg."

The program ended with a shot of residents cheering on Main Street and Alicia's voiceover. "Willow Falls is far more than a town offering unique attractions and delightful accommodations. It is the essence of a community with a heart, eager to devote time, talent, and resources to create something magical. A precious jewel waiting to be discovered. This is Alicia Adams reporting for *Around Georgia*."

Rachel sprang to her feet amid her family's applause and cheers. "We couldn't have done a better job if we'd written the segment ourselves."

"We shouldn't have wasted money on that PR firm," Scott said.

"I can almost hear the town's collective cheers." Emily's phone rang. She held it up. "Hi, Mirabelle."

Her voice boomed, "Did you see me showing off my grandma's quilt? Is it true TV makes you look heavy? Maybe I should lose a pound or two. Tell your sister I promise not to knock any more lamps over during the play."

Rachel leaned close to the phone. "I know you won't, and by the way, you looked good on TV."

"I did, didn't I? I'll see you tomorrow night for rehearsal."

Scott's phone buzzed. "Hey, Gertie."

"Our soda fountain looked like it's straight out of the past, don't you think?"

"Yes, it did."

"We should add a variety of ice cream flavors to the menu, and some sprinkles. Kids love ice cream cones. Oh, and maybe some homemade fudge."

"I think we'll stick to sodas and milkshakes a while longer."

"You have to start thinking ahead, young man. Your store is on the verge of being famous all over the South."

"Thanks in part to you, Miss Gertie."

"Hold on, everyone. Our hero reporter is on the line." Rachel pressed her phone's Speaker icon. "You did an amazing job. The show turned out far better than anything we could have imagined."

"Would you believe our program director and one of our camera operators booked rooms at the hotel? I hope the town's ready because Willow Falls' tourist industry is about to explode."

As Rachel's conversation with her friend continued, Emily moved to the window and struggled to choke back tears.

Scott stepped beside her and encircled her shoulders. "You're thinking about your parents, aren't you?"

"The inn, Redding Arms, our town's future … it all began with their vision."

Tears won out and spilled down her cheeks. "A hotel and a couple of rooms at the inn bearing their names isn't enough to honor everything they've done."

"What do you have in mind?"

"I don't know … something special."

"I'll bring it up with the council, see what we come up with." He paused. "Maybe our family's financial problems are about to come to an end."

She leaned her head against his shoulder as the vision of a bright future for her family and her hometown dried her tears.

Chapter 54

Sadie admired the new painting adorning the wall in Mitch and Pepper's dining room—their contribution for J. T.'s new leg. The pastel image of a quaint village invoked memories of her early days in Willow Falls before tragedy changed her life forever. The friendship she and Pepper forged as teenagers had given her strength during her darkest days in prison.

Her eyes shifted to Brick, sitting across the table from her. She smiled at his animated gestures as he and Mitch discussed last week's Atlanta Falcons' winning touchdown with three seconds left on the clock.

He caught her eye and winked.

Heat crept up her neck as she lowered her eyelids. She enjoyed every moment they were together and found his quirky superstitions charming. Yet deep down she knew their relationship would never move beyond friendship. After all, a worldly man like Reginald—the name he found too highfalutin to use—could attract any number of sophisticated, educated women.

She spooned the last bite of caramel cheesecake into her mouth, as everything thirty years behind bars had stolen from her whizzed through her mind like a movie on fast-forward. If she couldn't see herself as a desirable woman, how could anyone else?

"I'm considering making this dessert a standard on the hotel's menu." Pepper's voice broke through Sadie's reverie.

"What?"

"The cheesecake—"

"Oh ... great idea. Who wouldn't love it?"

"Reservations came in strong today. According to Kat, the hotel booked nearly full for grand-opening weekend."

"The power of the media and favorable PR." Brick reached for his wine glass. "After the station's follow-up story, both the hotel and the inn are likely to have reservations well into next year. If I hadn't bought that house, I'd have to sleep in my car."

Mitch reached for his wine glass. "That would also land you in jail."

Pepper chuckled. "What he's saying is, it's unlawful to live on the street in Willow Falls."

Sadie glanced at Brick. If Mitch did arrest him, at least they'd have something in common. "Emily and Rachel said the play's premiere sold out."

"From famine to feast in one week." Pepper laid her fork across her dessert plate and caught Sadie's eye. "You've contributed a lot to Willow Falls. Helping Emily finish the inn. Bringing Kat and Missy to town—"

"I didn't do squat compared to everyone else."

"My friend still has a hard time accepting compliments." Pepper snapped her fingers. "You know what I want to do?"

Mitch tapped his glass. "Bribe me and Brick into cleaning up the kitchen?"

"Nope. The four of us need to go to the park and gaze at the moonlight shining on the lake like you and I did when we were teenagers."

"Works for me." Mitch picked up a wine bottle and a corkscrew. "Except this time instead of sneaking cups of Coke and Jack, we'll legally enjoy an adult beverage. What do you say, you two? Are you game?"

Brick leaned back. "Sounds like a winner to me. What about you, Sadie?"

"It's a bit chilly."

"I'll grab a couple of blankets and jackets." Pepper nudged Mitch. "Grab four glasses, honey."

Brick touched Sadie's arm. "Are you okay with this?"

Why is he asking? Does he want to bow out? Stop second-guessing. "Sure … I mean it's not that cold."

He grinned. "I'll keep you warm."

"Okay, folks we're heading to the park to enjoy a glass of wine and friendship." Mitch winked at Pepper. "And maybe a kiss or two."

"Just like old times. Except this time, you're the law."

Five minutes later, they parked on Main Street and strolled across the park. The moon cast a silvery glow on the water. A gentle breeze created a symphony of lapping water and rustling leaves, with the hoot of a distant owl added to the mix.

As the settled on the wall, Mitch uncorked and poured the wine. "To good friends and bright futures."

"And to beautiful ladies who are a hundred times better than rainbows and four-leaf clovers." Brick tapped his glass to Sadie's.

"You've got that right, pal." Mitch took a sip.

Pepper patted his knee. "Do you remember where you proposed to me, honey?"

"How could I forget? We sat on a blanket under that tree behind the hotel. Except it wasn't so big back then." He paused. "Someone's over there now."

Sadie focused on the tiny red glow of a cigarette. "It's most likely Kat. She changed her smoking spot from behind the inn to keep Winston from giving her a hard time. When she moves to Naomi's that problem will be solved."

"Or she could quit smoking." Pepper nudged Sadie. "Do you remember the time we snuck out of your stepfather's house and met our buddies for a secret, late-night swim party? Mitch and I were already an item."

"Do I ever. There were so many of us on the floating platform it doggone near capsized."

"When the parents found out about our spiked punch, they grounded nearly every kid in town." Mitch laughed. "Except you, Sadie. How'd you escape parental wrath?"

"I guess Mama figured me upchucking my guts out was punishment enough."

"She was a smart lady."

"About most things … not the man she married."

"How about we find a grassy spot to spread our blankets," Pepper said as she stood and grasped Mitch's hand. They moved away from the wall and the hotel.

Brick slid his arm around Sadie's shoulders, sending a quiver up her spine. He'd never done that before. It could be the wine, or maybe he wanted to keep her warm. After all, she did make a fuss about the temperature.

They strolled beyond the retaining wall beside Hayes General Store and spread blankets on the grass. For a while they reminisced, laughed, and sipped more wine. During a lull in conversation, Pepper whispered in Mitch's ear, then turned to her friends. "We'll be back in a bit." They stood and walked away.

Brick turned to face Sadie. A smile lit his face. He reached for her hand and stroked her fingers. His thigh touched hers. "You're the most fascinating woman I've ever met."

What did he mean by fascinating?

He moved closer. She breathed in the spicy scent of his cologne. His breath caressed her cheek like a soft feather.

Her heart pounded against her ribs. *Is he going to …?*

He slipped his hand behind her neck, pulled her close, and kissed her tenderly as if sensing her inexperience.

She closed her eyes, wishing the moment would never end.

When their lips parted, he gazed deep into her eyes. "You feel it too, don't you?"

"I …"

"Think maybe we're falling for each other." The way he finished her sentence touched her soul and created the first deeply romantic moment she'd ever experienced.

Until heavy footsteps disrupted the moment. Mitch yanked his phone off his belt, punched a number, and broke into a run. "Sound the emergency siren. The hotel's on fire."

Chapter 55

Sadie sat paralyzed in stunned silence. Were the orange flames curling up a column, lapping at the veranda's roof an illusion? Brick leapt to his feet and raced behind Mitch. The emergency siren screamed, sending an undeniable signal to her brain. The fire was real.

She clasped Pepper's extended hand and sprang to her feet. By the time they sprinted across the park, flames engulfed the rear veranda.

Kat sprayed water from a garden hose in a futile attempt to douse the blaze.

Within minutes, the town's sole fire truck careened around the corner.

Mitch and Brick dashed to the curb.

The volunteer fireman sprang from the driver's seat. The men attached a hose to the hydrant and hauled it behind the hotel. Mitch released the nozzle. A high-powered stream of water slammed into the flames.

Scott's car screeched to a halt behind the truck. He jumped out. Seconds later, Nathan and Jacob's cars braked. The three men attached another hose, ran to the back, and sent another torrent of water into the inferno.

Sadie clasped her hand over her mouth and watched the veranda roof collapse in a sheet of flame. Intense heat seared her cheeks. Scott and Jacob aimed their hose at the brick wall above the destruction.

Neighbors gathered to gawk, shoot videos and pictures, ask questions, and speculate.

"What happened?"

"I think a gas line broke."

"I didn't hear an explosion."

"Do you think someone set it?"

"An arsonist in Willow Falls? Impossible."

"If the hotel burns down, we're in a heap of trouble."

Sadie pressed her fingers to her ears. Her first grown-up romantic moment had been shattered by disaster. Would Brick call it a sign? Her legs buckled. She dropped to the ground, consumed by guilt over selfishly focusing on what she feared had been her first and last romantic kiss.

Ashes floated up and burned out as they drifted skyward.

At some point, the fire disappeared in a cloud of steam and smoke, leaving behind the acrid odor of charred wood.

Kat shut off the garden hose and trudged to Sadie and Pepper.

Mitch followed her. "Do you have any idea what happened?"

She wiped soot from her face. "All I can tell you is the fire was no accident."

"That much I know. Did you see anything suspicious?"

"I think I saw movement on the porch moments before the flames erupted."

"You think?" His tone accusing.

"It's dark. I can't say for sure."

Sadie stared at Mitch. Did he suspect Kat? She landed in prison for embezzlement, not arson. Did it even matter?

Scott rounded the corner. "The hydrant's shut off."

Mitch mopped sweat from his forehead. "I need to check the interior."

Brick approached; his face covered in sweat and soot. He held Sadie's hand as they moved to the front and stepped into the lobby.

The door to the veranda stood wide open. The stench of smoke hung heavy in the air. The wall of windows and half the ceiling were black with soot. Light shining through the soot-darkened chandelier created an eerie brown glow. Dirty water flowed in rivulets across the marble floor.

Mitch moved to the back and walked from one end of the window wall to the other.

Kat dashed in. "What a mess."

Sadie stumbled to the stairs and dropped to the first rung. A conversation she'd had with Emily after her release from prison pushed its way to the surface. "Maybe my daughter had it right. The hotel is cursed. You have to cancel reservations."

Kat sat beside her. "No way. Too many people invested resources and sweat to let a little fire damage destroy the town's future."

Sadie gazed wide-eyed at her friend. "A little damage? The back porch is a stinking pile of charred wood. The lobby is a blackened mess. Who knows how many problems all that water caused?"

"She's right." Jacob swept his arm in a wide arc. "There's no way my crew can clean this mess up and finish the repairs in one week."

"Don't jump the gun, Jacob." Pepper stooped and plucked a wood splinter from a puddle. "You've seen what residents accomplish when they work toward a common goal."

Sadie stared at her. "What idea's rattling around in your head?"

"We'll rally the town one more time." She straightened. "For an old-fashioned barn raising."

"How many times can we go to the well?"

"I think Pepper might be on to something." Nathan flicked an ash off his arm. "Tomorrow morning, instead of a regular church service, I'll make an appeal."

"We have one more giant issue," Kat said. "It'll take weeks for the insurance money to come through, and there's not enough cash in the hotel bank account to cover the cost of materials."

"Charlie and I have as much at stake as everyone else around here." Brick stepped forward. "We'll buy whatever you need. You can pay us back after the insurance comes through."

Jacob grasped his shoulder. "If residents aren't too tapped out, we have ourselves a plan that might work."

Mitch returned and stood beside Pepper. "There's something fishy about that fire."

"What are you trying to say, honey?"

He scratched his beard. "Don't know yet. But I aim to find out."

Kat rose to her feet. "I'm heading back to the inn for a shower. All this soot is making my skin itch like crazy."

"Come on guys," Scott said. "We need to load those hoses back on the fire truck."

Pepper sat beside Sadie. "Can you imagine the damage if we'd stayed at home after dinner?"

She longed to tell her friend about Brick's kiss, but the words refused to form. Somehow, she had to pretend nothing happened. "I'm ready to go home." Sadie stood. "When Brick comes back … tell him I'll see him tomorrow."

"Why don't you wait and tell him yourself?" Pepper grasped her shoulders. "You know he's crazy about you. That's why Mitch and I left you two alone."

"Things aren't always what they seem." She pulled away and headed to the front door. Outside, she caught a glimpse of Brick helping Mitch fold a firehose. She dashed across the grass and down the driveway beside the hotel, then collapsed on the inn's back steps. She trusted Pepper's judgment, and yet …

A figure rounded the corner.

Her breath caught.

Brick dropped beside her. "It's been a wild night."

"Too bad about the hotel."

"I meant what I said back there, before the fire. At least the part about me falling for you." He paused. "Maybe you think twelve years is too big a difference for us to have a romantic relationship."

Is he having second thoughts? Or is he afraid I can't fall for an older man? Without warning, emotion compelled her to do something she never in her wildest imagination thought she'd do. She turned his face toward her and kissed him. He pulled her into his arms and kissed her back.

If their relationship never moved beyond this moment, at least she finally understood the power of passion.

Chapter 56

Emily paced, stopping every few seconds to listen for the garage door. Rachel drummed her fingers on the kitchen table. "You're gonna wear a path in the floor."

"I don't understand how the hotel could catch on fire."

"I know it sounds crazy, but Brick's omen theories might have merit."

Emily glared at her sister. "What's that supposed to mean?"

"Maybe Willow Falls isn't meant to become a tourist attraction."

"You're wrong." She dropped on a chair across the kitchen table from Rachel. "I don't care how many disasters erupt. This town can't give up and cast aside Mom and Dad's vision like a pile of fish heads."

"I suspect folks around here are weary from dealing with catastrophes."

"Which is why someone needs to light a fire under them."

"Interesting choice of words."

At the sound of the garage door, Emily stood. She dashed to the kitchen door, yanked it open, and waited for Scott's truck to pull in.

Her chest tightened at the sight of his soot-covered face. "How bad is it?"

"The back porch is toast. The lobby's a filthy mess. As far as we can tell the fire didn't affect the rest of the hotel. Hard to know about water damage."

"I assume Kat and Mama Sadie are canceling reservations," Rachel said.

He shook his head. "Pepper seems to think the town will rally one more time and fix the damage—"

"Before next weekend. Is she nuts?"

"Probably." Scott opened the fridge and grabbed a bottle of water. "Charlie and his dad offered to pay for materials."

"They should know it takes more than a stack of wood and shingles to rebuild a back porch."

"Everyone knows it's a monumental task. Tomorrow morning, we'll find out if residents have enough fight left to make it happen." He downed the water in one long gulp, then wiped his mouth with his sleeve. "You two can stay up and debate the town's future as long as you want. I'm heading to the shower, then to bed."

Scott's dour tone and pinched expression made Emily cringe. "I've never seen him so discouraged."

"Like every other person on the face of the earth, he can only take so much before calling it quits."

"Is that what you're doing?"

"Not yet, but I'm close."

The frustration in her sister's voice gave Emily pause. "We're both exhausted. I suggest we go to bed and see what happens in the morning."

"Is that Willow Falls' new motto, 'Wait and see what happens'?" She released a long sigh. "Sorry, it's just … every time this town takes a step forward, it gets knocked on its tail."

"I know that's how it seems."

"That's how it is." Rachel stood and rolled her shoulders. "Don't worry. I won't bail on you, even if we go down in a heap of flames."

"Uh-huh. And you called my comment interesting."

Emily sat in the third row between Scott and Rachel. She pressed her thumbs against pressure points in the back of her neck. The discordant voices from residents crowded into the church intensified the throbbing pain.

Rachel crossed her leg and pumped her foot. "One of Willow Falls' biggest drawbacks for tourists, it's a one-hotel town. When something goes wrong, there's no alternative, no backup plan."

"We could pitch tents in the park and call it a canvas hotel," Charlie's tone mocked.

"How about knocking off the sarcasm? I'm just saying small towns have big disadvantages."

"Because they're not big cities?"

Emily nudged her sister. "Shush, you two. Nathan's about to begin."

The crowd quieted as their pastor stepped up to the podium and opened with a prayer. When he finished, he transitioned to his role as mayor. "I won't pretend this is an ordinary Sunday or a typical worship service. Instead, it's a turning point for all of us."

"Rumor is someone set that fire," shouted a man. "Do you know who's to blame?"

Mitch lumbered to the front and stood beside Nathan. "We don't know what happened. Rest assured an investigation is underway."

"I might be able to help, Sheriff." The British accent seemed out of place.

"I've never seen Winston in church before," whispered Emily. "Why do you suppose he showed up today?"

Rachel shrugged. "Your guess is as good as mine."

Mitch's brow furrowed. "I'm listening."

"I'm not suggesting Kat started it, but she smokes behind the hotel. Maybe she flicked a cigarette in a pile of dried-up leaves."

"There's your answer," Rachel said as muted comments rippled through the crowd.

Mitch tapped the mic until silence resumed. "At this point, I'm not in a position to draw any conclusions. I suggest all of you disregard our visitor's comment and let me do my job." He returned to his seat.

Emily leaned close to Rachel. "Mitch looks plenty mad."

"Do you think he suspects Kat?"

"Who knows what's going on in his head."

"Thank you, Sheriff." Nathan scanned the crowd for a long moment. "As your pastor and the town's mayor, my heart is heavy. I know how hard you've worked and how much you've overcome. This morning, I'm asking you to dig deep and find whatever is left to help us create a miracle and repair the hotel in time for Saturday's grand opening.

A woman sitting in the third row raised her hand. "Most of us have already spent more time and resources than we have, Nathan. How can you ask us to do more?"

"She's right," a man shouted. "We're tired of fighting."

Mirabelle turned and faced him. "Are you suggesting we give up and let all our hard work go to waste?"

"I'm saying, enough is enough. From now on, I'm looking out for me and my family."

"So am I," Mirabelle said. "Which is why we need to fix this problem."

"Somebody else better step up because I'm done." He and his family moved into the aisle and headed toward the exit. More than a dozen families followed.

Mumbles abounded.

"Quiet down, everybody." Nathan tapped the mic. "It's not our place to judge."

The crowd fell silent.

"For the next few minutes, I want everyone to clear your minds, listen to a song that touches my soul … and let it reach in and touch yours." He nodded toward the front row. His wife moved to the piano. Their daughter stepped beside her father.

Mary's fingers caressed the keyboard. The melody "On Eagle's Wings" filled the air. Her daughter held the microphone close and sang the first chorus.

Emily closed her eyes and let the song wash over her like the first warm day in spring. As she listened to the words … an image of Willow Falls rising from ashes consumed her. Tears filled her eyes and spilled down her cheeks.

Rachel sniffled, then touched her hand.

At that moment, Emily grasped the power of the town's motto "for Willow Falls."

When the song ended, a hush fell over the room. Nathan's daughter returned to the front row. Mary stood beside her husband.

Gertie pushed up from her seat in the second row. "Tell us what we need to do, Nathan."

By one o'clock, six men, including Charlie and Scott, had driven in their pickup trucks to the nearest building supply store open on Sunday. A number of other residents showed up at the hotel to clear the debris. Women headed home to make sandwiches for the workers. Kids set up a lemonade stand.

Emily pushed the stroller to the retaining wall, then knelt beside her babies. "Do you see all those people working hard to clean up all the mess? They're heroes who make this town special. Mommy's going to take lots of pictures to put in our paper."

Rachel squatted beside her sister. "I've been thinking."

"Something profound?"

"That depends." She flicked an ant off the stroller tire. "This town might not be such a bad place to call home after all."

Emily's mouth gaped. "That's quite a revelation."

"More like an eye-opener."

"Is my city-slicker twin turning into a country girl?"

"I'm closer today than yesterday."

Chapter 57

Five minutes after Sadie called, Emily found a parking spot on Main Street, three doors from Redding Arms. Her heart pounded as she covered the distance to the inn. Sadie's tone had hinted something wasn't right. She rushed into the kitchen and found her mother leaning over a desk in the nook that served as her office. "What's so urgent we couldn't talk on the phone?"

"Not here." She steered Emily outside. Next door the morning crew prepared a foundation for the hotel's rear veranda. Residents working in eight-hour shifts had cleared the debris in less time than anyone believed possible.

She followed Sadie around the cars and trucks and up her apartment stairs. The second they stepped inside, Emily faced her mother. "Did something happen? Are you sick—"

"I'm fine." She broke eye contact. "Yesterday, after everyone left the church, Mitch asked Kat to meet him in Nathan's office. He grilled her for an hour."

"Because of Winston's comment? How does that man know she was anywhere near the hotel when the fire started?"

"We saw her smoking back there."

"What do you mean we?"

"Mitch, Pepper, Brick, and me. We ... went to the park after dinner."

"What kind of questions did Mitch ask Kat? Is she a suspect?"

"I don't know. She said she couldn't talk about it."

"If she did drop a lit cigarette ... could he charge her for accidentally starting a fire? Would that violate her parole and send her back to prison?" Emily moved past the kitchenette and dropped onto the love seat. "I don't want to lose her."

Sadie sighed. "People tend to think once a criminal, always a criminal."

"I don't believe anyone in town sees you as a criminal."

She settled on a slipper chair. "I've been around long enough to win folks over. Kat's still new."

Emily scrunched her brow. "I still don't understand why you called me."

"All I know is Pepper wanted you here while I wait for her to call."

A sense of dread kindled in Emily's chest. Maybe Kat had started the fire. "Do you think Mitch wants me to give you moral support when … he arrests Kat?"

"Won't do us any good to think the worst."

"What are we supposed to do, pretend nothing's wrong?" Emily moved to the dormer window overlooking the back of the inn. A spider web stretched across the glass. An unsuspecting fly struggled to escape. She watched the spider inch toward its victim. "Wait a minute."

A memory edged into her mind and took form. "Kat doesn't litter." She spun around. "I watched her snuff a cigarette in the dirt then put the butt in her pocket. She couldn't possibly have started that fire."

Sadie's phone rang. She held a finger up and listened. When the call ended, she stood. "That was Pepper. Mitch wants us to meet him in the inn."

Emily's heart leaped to her throat as they dashed down the stairs, across the parking space, through the inn's kitchen and dining room.

They found Mitch in the foyer, pacing. He stopped the moment he spotted them and removed a clear plastic bag from his jacket. He handed it to Sadie. "Have you seen this before?"

"No."

Emily stared at the can of lighter fluid, missing a cap. "What is it, I mean, where did you find it?"

"On the ground between the inn and a shrub. Hasn't been there long." He pulled a small scrap of black fabric from his pants pocket. "Does it look familiar?"

Sadie shook her head. "What's going on, Mitch?"

"Do you clean Winston Hamilton's room?"

She nodded. "Every day when he's at the café for lunch. He's there now, isn't he?"

"I need you to go in. Don't touch anything. Just look around for a shirt that matches this fabric."

"Are you thinking he's—"

"No time for questions."

"Okay, I'm on it." Sadie dug the master key from the bottom desk drawer. She rushed to the Carly Suite and unlocked the door.

Mitch paced.

Emily wrung her hands.

When Sadie returned, her face had paled. "In the closet."

"Was the door open or closed?"

"Open."

"Good." Mitch turned to Emily. "I need you to escort me into the room." She led the way.

He headed straight to the closet. "Will you look at that." Tossed on the floor beside a pair of dirty black jeans lay a black cotton shirt, a piece missing from the cuff. "It seems Mr. Hamilton isn't such a fancy dresser after all." He picked it up. "I do believe we have a suspect."

Emily's jaw dropped. "I don't understand. Why would he try to burn the hotel down?"

"I don't know." The sheriff used a pen to remove an empty soda can from the dresser. He dropped it in a plastic bag, then walked out of the suite and set the bag and the shirt on the check-in desk.

Emily followed. "What are you going to do now?"

"Wait for Winston to return from lunch. You two go on in the parlor."

Emily's heart nearly exploded in her chest as she dropped onto one of the wingback chairs. Why would a writer who wanted peace and quiet set a fire and cause turmoil?

Sadie sat in the other wingback chair. Her fingers drummed the arm. "He's full of gumption, coming here and fooling everyone—"

"You're assuming he's guilty."

"Dollars to donuts Mitch will find his fingerprints on that lighter-fluid can."

"How could he have fooled an entire town?"

"The accent, his name—"

"Did anyone ever see him writing? Maybe he's not even British." Emily's mind drifted back to the day he arrived in town. The roll of bills he pulled from the duffle pocket. How his shoulder drooped when he carried the bag to his room ... as if it weighed a ton. "Is it possible his duffle is full of stolen money?"

"At this point anything's possible."

They fell silent.

Mitch hiked his hip on the check-in desk and folded his arms across his chest.

Emily's mind raced with images from television shows. Cops cornering suspects. Throwing them on the ground. Guns blazing. Dramatized for effect. She shook her head to erase the pictures. She locked her eyes on the foyer, waiting for a real-life drama to unfold.

The minutes ticked by. Sweat popped out under her arms and on the back of her neck. Serious crimes didn't happen in Willow Falls. Until now.

The front door opened.

Sadie's fingers stopped drumming.

The man who'd charmed an entire town walked into the foyer. "Afternoon, Sheriff." He glanced in the parlor, then back at Mitch. "Is there a problem?"

Mitch held the black shirt up. "This yours?"

Winston hesitated as if mentally debating how to respond. "I … think maybe my sleep shirt. Why?"

Mitch pushed off the desk and moved between Winston and the door. "Seems it's missing a piece." He removed the fabric scrap from his pocket. "Any idea how this ended up beside the wall facing the hotel? A foot from an empty lighter-fluid can?"

Winston's face paled. "Someone must have stolen it." His accent had vanished.

In one swift movement, Mitch slapped handcuffs on the man's right arm, yanked it behind his back, then cuffed his left. "Winston Hamilton, you're under arrest for arson. You have the right to remain silent …"

Emily tuned Mitch out and closed her eyes. Within hours, the whole town would know what happened. The rumors would run the gamut from their sheriff making a false arrest to capturing a serial killer. She prayed he'd discover the truth before the incident paralyzed residents and made them afraid to welcome strangers to their town.

Chapter 58

Rachel laid a stack of paper plates and plastic bowls on a ten-foot-long table, then fixed her eyes on the freshly painted lobby. No one would ever suspect that four days earlier soot and grimy water marred the space. The whole town acknowledged that residents had performed an honest-to-goodness miracle.

Gertie plugged two Crock-Pots into an extension cord. "It's hard to believe Winston Hamilton, I mean Bernard—that's an odd name for a criminal—was as phony as a seventy-dollar bill. Come to think of it his accent sounded a bit over the top."

Rachel stifled a laugh. Suddenly, half the residents claimed they suspected something had been askew with the man who'd charmed his way into their lives.

Pepper set a large bowl on the table. "Turns out, he's a master of deception and a skilled criminal." She added dressing and tossed the salad. "When Mitch ran his prints, he discovered a warrant for his arrest for a string of Canadian safe-cracking robberies. Each one ended with the banks going up in flames."

Gertie picked up a ladle and lifted the lids to stir, releasing scents of tomatoes, beef, and chili powder. "Smart way to cover up evidence."

"It worked for a while. Until an undamaged surveillance camera captured his image. After his face appeared on Canadian television, he stole a car and smuggled thousands of dollars across the border. He ditched the vehicle in New York, hitchhiked to Virginia, and hired a limo to drive him to Willow Falls."

Gertie's head tilted. "Why did he pick this spot?"

"At the time we were an obscure town way under the radar."

"A good place to hide."

Pepper nodded. "Until we were a week away from becoming a tourist attraction. According to Mitch, Winston—I mean Bernard—figured burning the hotel would slow us down and keep someone who might recognize him from checking in."

"He wasn't such a clever criminal, after all." Rachel opened a package of napkins. "I don't understand why he didn't check out and move on."

"Mitch thinks because he'd paid through November, a sudden change of plans would raise suspicion."

Rachel raised her brows. "More than a fire?"

"At some point, every criminal makes a mistake."

"Something else that doesn't pass the make-sense test. Why did he always wear an ascot and long sleeves?"

"Another cover-up." Pepper peeled plastic wrap off a tray of sandwiches. "He had a distinctive dragon tattoo on his left arm. The tail curled up to his neck. Sadie and Kat swear the next time a guest shows up dressed wrong for the season and carrying a wad of cash, they'll get fingerprints and call Mitch."

Rachel pulled a cooler to one end of the table. "I doubt they'll have to play super-sleuths. With Willow Falls' new role as a tourist town, it won't appeal to crooks looking for a hideout."

"You never know who might check in." Gertie set the lids back on the Crock-Pots and placed the ladle on a napkin. "If Emily pays attention, she could gather enough material for a good whodunit."

"Hmm." Rachel laid a finger on her cheek. "A story about our town's mysterious cash-toting villain. I think you might be on to something, Gertie."

"Honey, at my age, I'm chock-full of good ideas."

"Yes, you are," Pepper said. "What would our town do without you, sweet lady?"

Mirabelle wandered in carrying a tray of brownies. "I hear Mitch is sending Winston, aka Bernard, back to Canada."

"Officials picked him up this morning."

"I could smell something fishy about that guy. Always wearing those neck scarves, even in ninety-degree weather." She laid her tray on the table beside cookies from Patsy's. "We're lucky he didn't burn the whole town down. How's the work out back coming along?"

"The veranda is all framed in," Pepper said. "They're finishing the floor today. Roofing work starts tomorrow."

"Nobody or nothing can stop Willow Falls." Mirabelle plucked a brownie from the tray. "Time to go back to delivering the mail."

"Thanks for bringing dessert."

"I'll bring a couple of cakes tomorrow. Like little Billy said, I'm for Willow Falls." She waved over her shoulder as she headed to the door.

Pepper opened the newly installed doors leading to the veranda. "Come on in, guys, lunch is ready."

Rachel moved away from the table and leaned back against the check-in desk. Charlie, Jack, Dennis, several dozen men, and three women strolled in, peeled off their gloves, and lined up. While Pepper and Gertie served, she turned and eyed three original paintings created by Naomi, untouched by soot or water.

"Her painting of Hayes General Store is my favorite." Charlie set his plate on the desk, then picked up a sandwich.

"I can't decide which I like best—her Willow Inn or Main Street rendition. Is J. T. working with you guys?"

"Not today. He's putting the last coat of paint on Naomi's gift shop."

The door behind the check-in desk swung open. "As of five minutes ago, the hotel is booked full for the entire month." A smile lit Kat's face. "And you guys are doing a bang-up job on the veranda."

"It's better than the original; two feet wider and wired for ceiling fans."

"Good things can rise out of ashes."

Rachel nodded. "Like Atlanta, all those years ago."

"Looks like Pepper and Gertie can use my help," Kat said. "I'll talk to you two later."

Charlie dipped his spoon in the chili. "Dad and Scott are picking up new rocking chairs this afternoon."

"Brick's taken to small-town life better than I expected."

"I'm beginning to think I was wrong about him not falling for another woman."

Her eyes probed his. "Do you know something the rest of us don't?"

"It's the way he looked at your mother when she brought sticky buns to the crew this morning. You know they were in the park the night the fire started."

"Yeah, with Pepper and Mitch." She made a mental note to grill Pepper. "I've learned there's something special about small towns you can't find in big cities."

He swallowed a bite. "I'll be."

"Don't read too much into the comment. Living in Atlanta still has way more advantages."

"I know, if one hotel burns down, you have hundreds more to haul your luggage to."

"Are you making fun of me?"

"Never. Well, maybe a little. I'm still banking on turning you into a country girl."

She broke eye contact. "The play's sold out for Saturday night."

"Slick."

"What?"

"The way you changed subjects without skipping a beat."

"You're a good man, Charlie Bricker."

"And she transitions to flattery to confuse the male. You know what would work even better?"

"A pat on the back?"

"A big, sloppy kiss in front of all these guys."

"How could a girl refuse such an irresistible suggestion?" She kissed his cheek.

"Not big or sloppy, but it'll do." He bit into a brownie. "Want a bite?"

"Another offer I can't turn down." She bit a large chunk and savored the rich chocolate taste.

"I'd call that an oversized bite."

"You didn't specify the size."

He patted her cheek and popped what remained of the decadent dessert into his mouth. "Gotta get back to work."

As she watched him head outside, her mind wandered to the night she refused to accept his grandmother's necklace. If he offered it again, she wouldn't turn it down.

Chapter 59

The sun had yet to creep over the horizon when Emily stood on the sidewalk fronting Redding Arms. She gazed at the refracted light shining through the doors. By evening every hotel room would be filled with guests eager to form their own opinions about the town touted as Georgia's newest jewel. Although all the detail had been planned to perfection, opening-day jitters turned her palms sweaty.

She walked into the lobby and sat on the full-circle high-back seat positioned below the chandelier.

"You couldn't sleep either?" Kat approached carrying two cups of coffee.

"I'm imagining Mom and Dad sitting here waiting to greet the guests." She paused. "They'd be pleased with the way everything turned out."

"It's good we paved the empty lot at the end of Main Street for parking."

"Who's driving guests from the lot to the hotel?"

"Jack. I had to do some fancy talking to convince him." Kat sipped her coffee. "He worried that some people would be put off by his scars."

"Riding in a vintage Rolls Royce driven by a wounded veteran is the perfect way to experience a town with a huge heart."

"That's what I told him, but less eloquently. I hired a couple of teenagers to drive the golf cart and transfer the luggage." She pointed her thumb over her shoulder. "The baby grand is tuned. The town's music teacher is scheduled to show up at eleven, an hour prior to our advertised check-in. Same with Patsy's fresh-baked cookies."

"Live music and chocolate chips." Emily gazed at her coffee shimmering under the light. "If another catastrophe doesn't pop up, you'll have out-of-towners singing our praises before they visit the first attraction."

"You can pack your worries away. The theater flood and hotel fire pre-disastered the town."

"What?"

"It's a term from an old Robin Williams' movie meaning another disaster is astronomically unlikely."

"I guess we've had more than our share of problems."

When the sky turned from inky black to pale blue, Kat glanced at her watch. "The front-desk staff is due any second." She stood and straightened her skirt. "Today begins a new chapter in the Willow Falls story."

"Mom and Dad's dream"—Emily's voice cracked—"lives on."

"You know they're up there, loving their perfect new life."

"Smiling down at the town they gave everything they had."

The first guests arrived forty-five minutes before official check-in time. Emily introduced herself and extended her hand to the mature couple. "Welcome to Willow Falls. Where are you folks from?"

"Gainesville, the Georgia version. I'm Hank. This is my wife, Susan."

"How did you folks hear about our grand opening?"

"Alicia Adams' blog," Susan said. "We attend every play she recommends."

"Plus, the story about Naomi Jasper's sales helping that veteran." Hank nodded toward the door. "The nice young man who drove us from the parking lot said his friend is the town's tour guide."

"If you'd like, our guest relations expert will sign you up for a tour."

"That's what I call first-class service."

Emily escorted the couple to the check-in desk, where Kat extended a warm welcome. "Which room did you folks reserve?"

"The one with the vintage movies," Susan said.

"The Cushman Suite is an excellent choice. Pepper is our hotel's executive chef and her husband Mitch is the town's sheriff."

Hank grinned. "You don't suppose he left a set of handcuffs hidden under the bed, do you?"

"My husband's a retired police detective. Whoever came up with the idea of residents adopting rooms was brilliant."

"The credit belongs to Patsy Peacock. She owns Patsy's Pastries and Pretties and The Old-Fashioned Christmas Shoppe." Kat pointed to the tray of cookies. "A taste of her pastry expertise."

"We'll definitely check her place out." Hank plucked a cookie from the tray.

"If you expect to have enough cookies for arriving guests, keep them away from Kevin and Al." Emily turned at the sound of Alicia's voice.

"Welcome back."

Susan's eyes widened. "You're Alicia Adams, the reporter."

"In the flesh."

She grasped Alicia's hand in hers. "I'm one of your biggest fans. We read every blog post, and we loved your story about this town."

"It's a pleasure to meet you. As soon as my guys set up will you answer a few questions on camera?"

"I'd be delighted."

Two more guests strolled into the lobby, launching a steady stream of new arrivals. At one o'clock, twenty tourists gathered around J. T. The sight of him pulling up his pant leg and explaining how his new limb worked warmed Emily's heart.

Kat stepped beside her. "Every one of his tours is booked solid."

"Who knew a homeless vet would become the town's rock star?"

"Survivors fascinate people."

"Survival is Willow Falls' story." Emily turned to watch Alicia and her crew begin their interview. "I have to tell her about the fire and miraculous recovery. We have plenty of videos and photos of the restoration."

"Small-town hotel veranda rises from ashes like a mythical phoenix soaring into the sun-filled sky."

Emily smiled at Kat. "Who knew our hotel's talented manager had a poetic streak."

"Thank you for taking a chance and hiring me."

"Getting you and Missy is one good outcome from the Travel Titan's rant."

Chapter 60

Emily clung to Scott's arm as they slipped into the balcony's second row. "I wasn't this nervous when I checked into the hospital to deliver the twins. It's like giving birth with more than two hundred people watching to see what pops out."

"At least you aren't screaming with pain."

"No, but I am reeling from anxiety. We have no idea how a room full of strangers will respond. Not to mention that Alicia's expecting a dramatic improvement. What do you think of the program?"

Scott opened to the first page. "*Percy's Legacy*. An original play begun by Eugene Butler, finished by Emily Hayes and Rachel Streetman." He pulled a pen from his jacket pocket. "Excuse me, Ms. Hayes, may I have your autograph?"

"You're hilarious."

He snickered and leaned close. "I think you need a different response when your fans make the same request."

"What fans?"

"Oh, I don't know. Maybe everyone in the theater?"

Emily entwined her fingers with Scott's, filled her lungs, then slowly released the air.

"I call that a first-class sigh."

"For the last year, I've dreamed about signing copies of *Percy's Legacy* the novel, at a fancy book-launch party."

"Succeeding as a playwright is nothing to sneeze at."

"I know. Makes me more eager to fix my book."

Scott squeezed her hand and kissed her cheek. "By this time next year, you'll be known as Willow Falls' first published novelist."

"I wish."

★ ★ ★

Rachel poured ginger tea into two cups and handed one to Missy. "Our pre-premiere cocktail."

"Do all those strangers out there make you nervous?"

"Here's the way I look at it. Those folks are expecting a small-town production. When they see what we deliver, they'll be over the moon."

"You really think so?"

"I can feel it in my bones." She gulped her tea and set the cup on the dressing table. "Come with me, Missy, aka Peaches. Time to inspire the team."

Rachel stepped in front of the cast and crew gathered backstage. "Tonight, I stand here in awe of how far you've come." She bit her lip as she struggled to tamp down her emotions. "Not long ago, you were a team of amateurs, led by an inexperienced director. You worked hard and poured your hearts into this project. As a result, you've become an impressive cast of performers. Each one of you played a vital role in making tonight possible."

Rachel scanned the faces staring at her. "In five minutes, the curtain will open." She paused. "One thing I know for certain, we will surpass the audience's expectations by a mile and delight every person sitting out there with a performance that will establish Willow Falls as a theatrical gem."

Cheers and applause erupted.

Missy raised her hand. "Is it okay if I say something?"

"Of course."

"I want to thank everybody for accepting me and Dennis into your family." She locked eyes with Rachel. "Most of all, thank you for believing in all of us and helping us achieve more than we ever imagined possible."

"I wouldn't trade these past few months for anything." *Including a starring role in Atlanta's premier theater.*

Mirabelle snapped her fingers. "As we showbiz folks say, let's break a leg, kids."

"Well said. Now, let's go out there and wow our audience."

The lights flickered.

Rachel sniffed. "Take your places. It's showtime." She stepped to the side and pressed her hand against her pounding heart

Charlie approached and leaned close. "Good speech, coach. The question is, do you believe everything you said?"

She wiped her eyes. "What's more important is they have to believe it."

"Trust me, they do."

The musical overture began. A flurry of butterfly wings beat against Rachel's chest. She held her breath as the curtains parted.

Dennis delivered the opening line with perfection. Missy rose to the occasion and didn't miss a beat. Rachel mouthed each line along with her actors. To her delight, their delivery exceeded her expectations. When the act ended, the rousing applause made her heart dance. Other than one missed cue, skillfully covered by Naomi, act two remained flawless.

"You've created a top-notch cast, Miss Streetman," Charlie whispered.

"Maybe I'm not so bad at directing after all."

During intermission, she cornered her team backstage. "Did you hear the audience response? They love you."

Mirabelle snapped her fingers. "I didn't knock over a lamp—"

"Or miss a cue." Rachel smiled. "Okay, everyone, let's set the stage for act three and deliver a performance worthy of a standing ovation." She moved to the side.

Charlie stood beside her. She gazed into his eyes. "Hello, Mr. Bricker. Are you ready for your official debut as Everett Hayes?"

He tapped the tip of her nose. "The question is, Miss Lillian, are you prepared for the best kiss this town has ever seen?"

"Why, Everett," she spoke with an exaggerated Southern accent. "You'd do that in front of all these strangers?"

"Like Rhett said to Scarlett, 'You should be kissed by someone who knows how.'"

She tilted her head. "When did you start quoting lines from *Gone with the Wind*?"

"After you roped me into this acting gig and made me watch the movie."

"You don't have a mustache, my dear, but you are every bit as handsome as Mr. Butler."

"And you, lovely lady, are drop-dead gorgeous."

"Why, Everett. You are such a flatterer."

The lights flickered.

Dennis and Missy moved into position as elderly Percy and Peaches.

The act began.

Charlie played Everett's role like a champ. When the play ended with his passionate kiss, she imagined tears of joy and heartfelt emotion rippling through the audience. As the minor players took their bows, a third of the audience stood. With each new cast member's moment of glory, more people rose from their seats. The applause escalated.

The moment Rachel and Charlie stepped center stage, every member of the audience stood.

When Dennis and Missy moved into the spotlight, the cheers, whistles, and applause reached a crescendo with enough power to blow the roof off the theater. As the applause died down and the cast scrambled to make their way to the lobby, Rachel wrapped her arms around Charlie's neck. "I think I've unleashed a closet performer. And that kiss. All I can say is wow, you nailed it."

His lips curved into a smile as he gazed into her eyes. "I'm beginning to understand what's so all-fired exciting about this acting business."

"Does that mean you're not as eager to turn Everett's role over to a newbie?"

"And let another man kiss you like I did? I'll stick around for a while. Right now, we should go meet our fans."

"*Our* fans? Why Charlie Bricker, you really have taken a liking to my world."

"I admit the applause gave me a giant adrenaline rush."

They held hands as they moved toward the steps leading from the stage. A man carrying flowers stepped into the aisle from the last row. He moved against the exiting crowd toward the stage.

Rachel pressed her hand to her chest. Was she hallucinating? She squeezed her eyes shut, then opened them.

He moved closer. *I'm not imagining.* "I don't understand. How …"

Charlie squeezed her hand. "I called him."

They descended the steps.

The man passed the first row and turned toward them. "Hello, Strawberry Girl."

"You came."

"I'm sorry it took me eight years to attend another one of your performances." He presented her with one of two sprays of red roses. "There's no doubt my beautiful daughter has found her calling."

Tears spilled down Rachel's cheeks as she embraced her father. After thirty-one years, she'd found her daddy.

Chapter 61

The lobby teemed with activity as Rachel, Charlie, and her dad joined cast members signing autographs, accepting praise, and posing for photos.

Emily and Scott made their way over. "Mr. Streetman, what a surprise." She touched his arm. "Thank you for the beyond-generous gift you sent to our daughters. You have no idea how much it means to have their education secured."

"It's the least I could do for keeping you and Rachel apart all those years." He gave her the other spray of roses. "For expert writing."

"How sweet."

A woman approached. "Which one of you is Emily Hayes?"

"I am."

She pointed toward Mirabelle. "That cast member said you're writing a book about Percy and Peaches."

"I am."

"When you finish, I'd be happy to pass your business card along to some people I know."

Why hadn't it crossed her mind to have cards printed? "I'm uh—"

"I'll give you one of mine." Scott removed a card from his wallet and wrote Emily's email address on the back.

"Thanks." She glanced at his card. "Hayes General Store. I'll stop by your place tomorrow. This is a charming town. A pleasant break from the city."

Emily smiled. "We're delighted you chose to spend some time with us and hope you come back."

"I might do that." The woman locked eyes with Rachel. "You're not new to acting. I don't suppose you have a card hidden in your costume."

"You're right."

"I also have a lot of contacts in the entertainment world. Do you mind giving me your email?"

Rachel rattled it off.

"Thank you, ladies. I'll be in touch."

Emily grasped Scott's arm. "Do you suppose she really knows people?"

He glanced at her card. "Don't count on her help unless you're willing to pay. She owns a public relations firm."

"The same one the town hired?"

"Nope."

"She a smart marketer," Greer said. "I guarantee you'll end up on her email list. If you'll excuse me, I'd like to meet Naomi Jasper. I'll catch up with you in a few minutes."

Two young ladies rushed up to Charlie. "We loved your performance, and that kiss was the best." The shorter woman handed her phone to Rachel. "Will you take our picture?"

"I'd be delighted."

The women pressed on each side of him. His pained expression resembled a man desperately needing to escape. Rachel grinned as she snapped the photo. When they left, she patted his cheek. "What do you think about your first groupies, honey?"

"The applause is cool. This touchy-feely stuff from strangers … not so much. Think I'll forego future after-the-show lobby appearances."

"And disappoint all the ladies?"

"More like stay clear."

Alicia finished an interview with Naomi and dashed over. She looked from Emily to Rachel. "I don't know how you did it, girlfriends, but you delivered one of the best regional theater performances I've seen in a long time. I'm telling you, the difference from a few weeks ago and tonight is amazing." She pointed to the sprays in their arms. "Gorgeous roses. Who's the fan?"

"My dad. Alicia, meet Greer Streetman."

"It's a pleasure, sir. What do you think of your daughter's performance?"

"She's a natural."

"Indeed she is." Alicia shifted her focus to Charlie. "You delivered a dynamite final scene. I suspect every woman in the audience will go home tonight and demand that her man deliver kisses to make her toes curl. Right now, I need to capture some more footage. I'll see you at the cast party."

Rachel leaned close and whispered in Charlie's ear. "In case you're wondering, you curled my toes."

He stared at her, then burst out laughing.

As the crowd thinned, the players headed to the dressing rooms. Rachel's heart drummed in her chest as she listened to the ladies' exuberant comments and accolades. When Missy rushed from the room, she stood alone and turned in a slow circle, savoring the moment. She'd helped write, then direct and star in a hit play. She slipped her dress onto a hanger and placed it on the garment rack as an image of her upgraded résumé danced in her head.

Although the night had exceeded anything she'd imagined, the desire to perform with a professional cast on a prominent stage in front of hundreds of sophisticated theatergoers remained. At some point, she'd explain it to Charlie and hope he'd understand.

She glanced around one more time, then turned off the lights and joined him for their stroll down Falls Street, across Main, to Willow Falls' first cast party.

Chapter 62

Emily's heart swelled with pride as she and Scott stood beside the grand staircase and watched Sadie and Brick greet Willow Inn guests and shower compliments on the arriving cast, crew, and their families. "A year ago, who would have imagined we'd celebrate live theater in our corner of North Georgia?"

"Willow Falls is no longer an obscure town no one's heard of."

Kat welcomed folks to the dining room, where appetizers and desserts covered the table. Bottles of wine and soft drinks, provided by Brick, filled the antique mahogany buffet.

Alicia strolled in from the porch with Kevin and Al. She sandwiched Emily's hand in hers. "Like I told your sister, the play turned out amazing. I plan to sing its praises on my website. And the story you suggested about the hotel's recovery from that nasty fire will have tourists coming in droves to find out what makes Willow Falls so special."

"How can we thank you for all you've done?"

"Keep feeding me good stories. I smell something delish."

"Compliments of Chef Pepper and Patsy Peacock's pastry talent."

Scott inched his arm around Emily's waist. "We're about to experience big changes around here. I hope enough tourists buy merchandise from Hayes General Store to give us a decent living."

"After all you've done to keep the town alive, you deserve way more than decent." Her phone pinged a text. "It's from the sitter. Jane and Clair are sound asleep. Cody and Brownie are keeping watch."

"Good. We can stay a while and become better acquainted with your sister's father." He nodded toward the door. "He just walked in."

Brick clasped Greer's shoulder. "Well I'll be, the old man shows up on opening night. It took you long enough."

"Your son persuaded me. He's a typical Bricker, minus the insane superstitions."

"If I didn't know better, I'd think the workaholic businessman grew a heart."

"A big one," Rachel said. "Mama Sadie, I want you to meet my dad, Greer Streetman."

Sadie stared at him for a long moment. "I can't tell you how many times over the years I tried to imagine how you looked, what you were like." She touched his arm. "Thank you for raising my daughter."

"My wife fell in love with baby Rachel the first time she held her. I loved her as my own flesh and blood and raised her the best I knew how. That said, the gratitude needs to flow your way." His Adam's apple bobbed. "What you did for your daughters qualifies as an act of love and bravery far beyond anything I've ever done." He leaned down and kissed Sadie's cheek.

"It all turned out good."

Brick punched Greer's arm. "Come on, old friend. I'll pour you a glass of wine and let you spin tall tales about your last round of golf." They strolled to the dining room and disappeared around the corner.

"Will you look at that?" Charlie reached for Rachel's hand. "It took fewer than two minutes for our dads to transition from business associates to good buddies."

"I don't know if you bribed, threatened, or coerced my father. All that matters is you succeeded."

"When it counts, I'm a persuasive guy."

"Yes, you are. This calls for a celebration. I'm starving."

Sadie looked from one daughter to the other. "Patsy sent over lemon cake—"

"With buttercream frosting?" the twins said in unison.

Rachel licked her lips. "I hope it's not gone."

"I cut two pieces and hid them in the buffet. You and your sister find a seat. Scott, Charlie, and I will serve you cake and champagne."

"There's an offer Rachel and I can't refuse."

"Amen to that, sister."

They moved to the parlor and settled on a pair of upholstered chairs in front of the bay window.

Sheriff Mitch poured a cup of coffee and strolled over from the antique sideboard. "Congratulations for hitting a home run tonight."

"I heard Pepper's pre-theater dinner impressed Alicia and the crew," Rachel said.

Mitch's eyes gleamed. "She claimed the steak au poivre rivaled any meal served in a fancy Atlanta restaurant. Somehow my wife managed to keep the café open despite near nonexistent profits. She's earned way more than compliments."

"As the hotel's executive chef, she'll come closer to earning what she's worth." Emily propped her elbow on the chair's arm and rested her chin on her fingertips. "Everyone's talking about our hero sheriff capturing a dangerous criminal."

"Some hero. I should've been more suspicious from the get-go."

"Why would you? I mean, crime isn't exactly an everyday event around here."

"Doesn't matter. It's my job to keep the town safe. Folks need to start locking their doors."

Rachel propped a hand on her hip. "Same thing I've been saying for the past year."

"Small-town habits are hard to break."

"No kidding."

Charlie, Scott, and Sadie returned carrying cake and champagne flutes. "At your service, ladies."

"I could get used to this." Rachel spooned a bite into her mouth and closed her eyes. "As good as ever."

Emily tasted a dab of icing. "A perfect ending to an amazing night."

"It's not over yet." Rachel nodded toward the foyer.

Alicia strolled in, holding a plate and a glass of wine. Guests followed her like a throng of teenage groupies, inundating her with questions.

Sadie shook her head. "Looks like your friend needs rescuing."

Guests continued to squeeze into the parlor, bringing the volume to a near-deafening roar. Within minutes, Alicia moved to the fireplace and turned toward the crowd.

Her cameraman emitted a shrill whistle.

The din died down.

Alicia set her wine glass on the mantel. "I want you to know how much I appreciate everything you folks have done to make us feel welcome. For those of you who are guests in this lovely inn, tomorrow morning you'll experience the best breakfast this side of the Mississippi."

"Uh-oh," Sadie mumbled. "Pressure's on."

Brick stroked her arm. "You're up to the task."

She patted his cheek.

Emily gave her sister a did-you-see-that look.

Rachel nodded.

"Are we gonna be on TV again?" shouted a boy sitting on the floor.

"Good question, young man," Alicia said. "The answer is a definite yes. Maybe as soon as Friday."

Mirabelle raised her hands. "Did you film the play?"

"Yes, we did."

"Act two? The one I'm in?"

Alicia nodded. "Another yes."

"How do you decide what to cut and what to keep?"

"That's a question you'd have to ask the program director."

Mirabelle raised her hand again. "Can you make a suggestion?"

"I'll do my best, but it boils down to which three minutes can present the best story about Willow Falls. The more people who visit your town, the more will know about your suite upstairs and the one honoring your grandmother at the hotel."

"You're right."

"Alicia is one smart cookie," Emily whispered to her sister.

"I think it's time for a rescue." Rachel laid her plate on the floor and joined her friend. "We're fortunate the station sent us a film crew to do a follow-up story on our town. For now, let's give Alicia, Kevin, and Al a round of applause and let them relax and enjoy this party."

Her use of the term *our town* captured Emily's interest. If *Percy's Legacy* attracted enough interest, Rachel would have a good reason to stay in Willow Falls for a long time.

Chapter 63

Emily closed her laptop and set it on the end table. "Seven chapters down, fifty to go." She stood and stretched her arms over her head.

"At this rate, you'll finish by Christmas." Rachel glanced at her phone. "Charlie's on his way over with his dad and Mama Sadie. I'm telling you, something's going on between those two."

Emily sat on the floor beside her sister. Clair crawled onto her lap. "Do you think she'll tell us?"

"Only one way to find out. We'll corner her before the news comes on and point-blank ask her."

"What are you gals up to?" Scott strolled into the den.

"Some investigative work."

He plucked Jane from the floor and nuzzled her neck. "Is your mommy gathering material for a new book?"

"A novel about Willow Falls romances after Percy and Peaches. Great idea, honey."

Rachel nodded. "Perfect theme for a small-town soap opera or a Hallmark movie."

"In my dreams."

"Sometimes dreams come true."

Footsteps sounded on the foyer floor. "We're here." The three new arrivals stepped in.

Emily pushed up and placed Clair in Brick's arms. "You guys entertain the babies while we ladies bring you drinks."

Rachel stood and motioned for Sadie to follow her.

"What are you two up to?"

"Do we look curious?"

She eyed Rachel. "As a week-old kitty."

Emily removed a pitcher of lemonade from the fridge and set it on the counter. "We were wondering what's happening with you and Charlie's dad."

Sadie's cheeks flushed.

Rachel snapped her fingers. "I knew I saw a spark."

"Oh my gosh." Emily grasped her mother's hands. "He kissed you, didn't he?"

"Even better. I kissed him back."

"If Rachel and Charlie ever decide to marry and you and Brick tie the knot, you'll be her mother and her mother-in-law. Right?"

Rachel removed three glasses from the cabinet and set them on the counter. "Talk about an intriguing family tree."

"I declare, you two are getting way ahead of yourselves. I'm still an ex-con, and he's an educated businessman—"

"And blessed to have you in his life," Emily said as she released her mother's hands.

"I suppose he could do worse." Sadie shrugged. "At least now I know how to tell if a man is a little interested."

"That night we had dinner at Pepper's I saw the glint in his eye when he looked at you. Trust me, he's way more than a little interested."

Charlie meandered in. "The news is on in five minutes. Do you ladies need some help?" He glanced from one to the other. "Did I interrupt something important?"

"Just girl talk." Emily handed him the pitcher and grabbed three beers from the fridge.

Rachel plucked the glasses off the counter. "Come on, gang. Time to watch the latest edition of *Around Georgia*."

Scott turned up the volume as the adults gathered around the television. Following twenty minutes of news, footage of the hotel fire appeared on the screen with Alicia's voiceover. "One week before Willow Falls' official launch as a tourist destination, fire consumed Redding Arms' back porch. Did it stop this brave town? Not one bit."

As her monologue continued, the video morphed to footage of residents clearing debris and rebuilding, then ended with a shot of the new structure. "Residents pulled together, cleaned up the mess, and rebuilt the back veranda in time to greet the hotel's first guest." The scene shifted to Alicia's interview with the

Gainesville couple, followed by J. T. showing his new leg to a group of tourists. The segment continued with Alicia walking toward the playhouse marquee and into the lobby. "Our visit continued in this historic theater watching a premiere of *Percy's Legacy*, an original play about the town's fascinating history."

Scenes of the play, including one with Mirabelle in the background, filled the screen while Alicia shared tidbits about the story and its production, followed by interviews in the lobby with enthusiastic audience members. The final shot scanned the façades of the hotel and Willow Inn. "When I first visited this town, I touted it as a hidden gem. Now I know it is far more. Willow Falls represents all that is good and noble in our country. A community of people who care for each other; who pick themselves up and overcome seemingly insurmountable obstacles with grit and determination. A small town with a big heart and a delightful experience to offer guests. This is Alicia Adams, reporting for *Around Georgia*."

Emily's ringing phone disrupted the cheers. "What do you want to bet, that's our favorite mail lady." She grabbed it off the coffee table. "Hi, Mirabelle."

"Alicia did us proud, huh."

"Yes, she did. And once again, you looked good."

"Thanks. My hubby says I look like a movie star. I think he's buttering me up, so I'll fix his favorite dinner. Tell everyone hi."

"Will do." Emily ended the call.

"Well now," Brick said. "Tonight's big publicity win calls for a celebration. I'm treating our family to dinner at Pepper's."

Emily nudged her sister and whispered, "Did you hear how he said *our family?*"

"And the way he looked at Mama Sadie."

"You're right. He's way beyond a little interested."

Emily stood in front of the bedroom window staring at a moth flitting around the gas lamp illuminating their front sidewalk.

Scott moved behind her and wrapped his arms around her waist. "What captured your attention, mama bear?"

"I've been thinking about Willow Falls' future."

"It finally looks like we have one."

"If tourism takes off ... will the town turn into something we don't recognize? Will we lose everything we love about it?"

"Progress always brings risk." He kissed the back of her neck.

"Scott Hayes, are you trying to change the subject?"

"Yeah, how am I doing?"

"Not bad." She turned and melted into his arms. "You remember what Alicia said about curling ladies' toes."

He kissed her forehead. "Uh-huh."

"If mine curl any further, my toenails will tickle my soles."

He grinned, then closed the blinds and shooed Cody out of the room. "Sorry, fella, you're not invited to this party."

Chapter 64

Emily dropped beside Sadie on the settee in Willow Inn's parlor. "I think the entire population showed up this afternoon."

"Folks are pleased we closed the inn to out-of-towners for Christmas and opened it to locals."

"Today reminded me of the old days when Mom decked out our home for the holidays, which didn't officially begin until she invited everyone over for a tour. Continuing the tradition here makes perfect sense."

"I've never seen so many Christmas trees in one place. Nine, plus all the other decorations. I declare, we've turned the inn into an honest-to-goodness Christmas wonderland." Sadie pointed toward the nine-footer poised in front of the bay window. "That's my favorite."

"Mom's peacock tree. Patsy helped her pick out all the ornaments."

"A couple of the inn's guests already booked rooms for next December. Said the decorations put them in the mood." Sadie patted Emily's knee. "We have another reason to celebrate. You finished your book."

"I couldn't have done it without Rachel's help." Emily slipped out of her shoes and wiggled her toes. "Now the toughest job begins—attracting a publisher."

"There's a lot to this writing business."

"Way more than I realized." Emily shifted her gaze to her mother's prized nativity figures holding center stage on the mantel. "In an hour, our celebration continues with family and close friends."

"When is our special guest arriving?"

"Around seven thirty. One of the few secrets ever kept in this town."

"That's because only six of us know what's going on."

"Hello." Pepper's voice drifted in from the foyer. "We're here."

Sadie popped up. "I'll come help."

"You and Emily stay put. Patsy and I will clear everything and reset in a jiffy."

"Are you sure?"

"Positive."

"Thanks, I admit I'm slap worn out." She dropped back onto the settee. "After all the challenges the town faced, it's good the year is coming to an end."

"Folks around here are used to hard times and roadblocks. Which begs the question, can they handle prosperity?"

"If the town doesn't get too big for its britches and lose the qualities that make it special."

"We'll find out soon enough." Emily yawned. "It's almost time for the twins to wake from their nap."

"Why don't you rest before our next round of guests arrives and let me take care of my grandbabies?"

"Didn't you say you're exhausted?"

"Honey, I'm never too tired for grandma duties." Sadie patted her cheek, then walked out of the parlor.

Scott ambled in and sat beside Emily. "Today's like old times."

"With a new cast of characters."

He reached for her hand. "How are you holding up?"

"Better than I expected, except I'm starving." Her stomach grumbled. "I haven't had a bite since breakfast."

"There's a cure for your problem." He stood and pulled her to her feet. "Let's fuel you up for the next round of celebration."

They strolled to the dining room and found Pepper lighting a flame under a chafing dish, releasing the scent of sweet-and-sour meatballs.

"My wife, better known as Willow Falls' soon-to-be-famous author, needs a pick-me-up."

Patsy pointed to her left. "You sit right over there, and I'll fix you up a plate."

Scott escorted her to a chair beside the window facing the front porch. "What do you want to drink?"

"A tall glass of cold water and a glass of wine."

"Coming right up."

As Emily took in the view, she fingered the child-size antique sleigh Scott's great-grandfather crafted. So many memories lived in this old house— some good, others heartbreaking. She brushed the bad aside and focused on the future. A small-town inn and hotel presented a host of potential stories for an aspiring novelist.

"Here you go, sweetie." Patsy handed her a plate holding an assortment of appetizers.

"Thanks, everything looks delish." She scooped crab dip with a cracker and popped it in her mouth. "Tastes even better."

Sadie entered, pushing the twins' stroller. "My grandbabies are fed and ready to party."

"Hey, pretty girls. I suspect your grandma has toys ready for you." Pepper lifted Jane and carried her to the parlor. Patsy followed with Clair.

Emily smiled at her mother. "I hope you don't mind sharing our babies with honorary grandmas."

"Not one bit." She paused. "I'm blessed beyond anything I ever imagined."

"Life is good."

"Yes, it is."

Emily moved to the parlor's entrance and marveled at the scene playing out. Dennis sat on the settee beside Missy. He plucked a piece of cheese from his plate and dropped it into her mouth, then scooted closer until their thighs touched. Her cheeks blushed.

Naomi and her longtime friend Patsy sat in the wingback chairs and exchanged humorous stories about out-of-town visitors. Pepper and Kat discussed adding a Sunday brunch to the hotel menu options. Mitch, Charlie, Scott, J. T., and Jack huddled by the bay window debating which professional football team would make it through the playoffs.

Brick and Sadie sat on the floor with Jane and Clair.

Rachel, holding a glass of wine, moved beside Emily. "This is the most joyful Christmas I've ever experienced."

"Are you admitting you don't miss the big city?"

"Not exactly. Although being here with the people I love most is ... well, it's almost perfect."

"I declare," Sadie's voice boomed. "Look, everyone." Heads turned as Jane took a step and pitched into Brick's outstretched arms.

Cheers erupted.

Moments later, Clair followed in her sister's footsteps.

Tears formed as Emily watched her mother's face glow with joy. "What a perfect time for my babies' first steps."

"A precious first for you and their grandmother."

"And maybe their future grandpa." Emily's heart swelled. Love bloomed in Willow Falls. Tourists touted her hometown as Georgia's newly discovered gem. Theatergoers sang the play's praises. Maybe the new year would bring one more blessing. She closed her eyes and imagined opening a box filled with books titled *Percy's Legacy*, by Emily Hayes.

After snapping dozens of photos, Rachel laid her phone on a cabinet. Watching her extended family delight in the twins' milestone filled her heart with pleasure. *This Christmas couldn't be more perfect, unless …*

"You were fourteen months old the day you took your first step."

Her heart pounded as she spun at the sound of the familiar voice.

"Merry Christmas, Strawberry Girl." Her daddy gathered her in his arms.

"The second time in three months. How did I get so lucky?"

"You invited me for the holidays."

"I didn't know if you'd come."

"Neither did I." He released her.

She gazed into his eyes. "I'm glad you did."

He brushed a stray curl from her cheek. "I think your sister's husband wants our attention."

Scott stood in front of the fireplace, facing those gathered. "Every year, Hollywood and Broadway present their superstars with Oscar and Tony awards. Tonight, we're adding a new honor—one I promised, but quite frankly didn't expect to deliver. Ladies and gentlemen, the nominees for Willow Falls Wonder Woman of the Year are Emily Hayes and Rachel Streetman. The judges' final decision is …"

He removed an envelope from his jacket pocket and opened it with flair. "This is a shocker. It's a tie. Now what do we do?"

Charlie called out from the parlor entrance. "Not a problem. We have twin prizes." He carried a pair of foot-high trophies resembling an Oscar in a miniskirt.

Scott snapped his fingers. "The men in this family are smarter than they look. Come on up, ladies."

Cheers and whistles accompanied the sisters as they made their way to the fireplace.

"Glory be! I didn't expect to win." Rachel laid on a thick Southern accent. "I want to thank all the people who made this possible, especially Mama Sadie's other daughter."

"Aren't you a dear to share this award with little ole me?" Emily copied the Southern slur.

"Honey pie, we shared a teeny, tiny living space for nine months. It's only natural we share this here award."

"Why, yes it is, dahlin'." Emily paused. "If I may be serious for a moment, much of the credit for the play's success goes to Naomi Jasper for her vision."

"Nonsense." The artist dismissed the comment with a hand wave. "I simply found the old script. You ladies did all the work."

"We appreciate you trusting us." Rachel paused. "Working with Emily and an amazing cast of actors has been beyond wonderful. Thank you all for helping me discover why you love this town."

Amid applause, Emily and Scott moved away from the hearth.

Rachel stepped beside her father.

"Hold on, everyone. I have something to say." Charlie paused. "When Rachel asked me to play the role of Everett Hayes, I thought she'd lost her mind. It took me two days to decide what to do. Turns out, I made a wise decision. Not because I'm talented. I couldn't act worth a darn. The truth is, working with her gave me insight into her world and helped me understand the depth of her passion."

He hesitated. "That experience led me to ask her father an important question. Lucky for me, he said yes."

Rachel's heart thumped against her ribs as Charlie moved close.

He reached for her hand and pressed it to her lips. "I love you more than words can express. I want you to know that whether you choose to pursue your dreams here in Willow Falls, in Atlanta, or on Broadway, I want to be with you." He dropped to one knee and removed a small black box from his pocket. "Rachel Streetman, will you do me the honor of marrying me and making my life complete?"

She knelt beside him. Their arms entwined. "Yes, Charlie Bricker, a thousand times, yes."

The room erupted with cheers as they kissed. When their lips parted, she gazed into his eyes and knew that life in Willow Falls with the man she loved rivaled her childhood dream and offered far more than fame.